Beyond
Tula

A Soviet Pastoral

Beyond Tula

A Soviet Pastoral

•

ANDREI EGUNOV-NIKOLEV

Translated by
AINSLEY MORSE

BOSTON
2019

Library of Congress Cataloging-in-Publication Data
Names: Egunov, A. N. (Andrei Nikolaevich), author. | Morse, Ainsley, translator.
Title: Beyond Tula : a Soviet pastoral / Andrei Egunov-Nikolev ; translated by Ainsley Morse.
Other titles: Po tu storonu Tuly. English
Description: Boston : Academic Studies Press, 2019. | Series: Cultural revolutions: Russia in the twentieth and twenty-first centuries | Includes bibliographical references.
Identifiers: LCCN 2018057557 (print) | LCCN 2018059716 (ebook) | ISBN 9781618119742 (ebook) | ISBN 9781618119735 (pbk.)
Classification: LCC PG3476.E48 (ebook) | LCC PG3476.E48 P613 2019 (print) | DDC 891.73/42--dc23
LC record available at https://lccn.loc.gov/2018057557

ISBN 978-1-61811-973-5 (hardback)
ISBN 978-1-61811-974-2 (electronic)

Book design by Lapiz Digital Services

Cover design by Ivan Grave.

Published by Academic Studies Press.
28 Montfern Avenue
Brighton, MA 02135, USA
press@academicstudiespress.com
www.academicstudiespress.com

For Bela and Massimo

ACKNOWLEDGMENTS

Many heartfelt thanks for help and encouragement from my family, Oleh Kotsyuba, Ilja Kukuj, Massimo Maurizio, Sophie Pinkham, Alexander Skidan, Ivan Sokolov, Bela Shayevich, Faith Wilson Stein, Boris Wolfson, Ekaterina Yanduganova, and many others.

The translator and publisher express gratitude to Vadim Somsikov, representative of Egunov's estate, for permission to publish this work.

TABLE OF CONTENTS

A SOVIET PASTORAL

Who thought that peaceful vistas cannot be
A fine arena for catastrophe?[1]

Andrey Egunov published *Beyond Tula: A Soviet Pastoral* in 1931, under the pseudonym Andrey Nikolev.[2] This novel invites the reader to take an outrageously tongue-in-cheek jaunt through the earnestly boring and unintentionally campy world of the Socialist Realist "production novel."[3] It has a transparently insignificant plot: a young writer from the city comes to visit his engineer friend in the country for a couple of days, and everything ends by the grave of Leo Tolstoy. The novel's homoeroticism is obvious, yet unobtrusive enough to have slipped past the censors. The dialogues are snappy and darkly clever, and strange and terrible things happen in between the cheerful rompings and silly flirtations. As one critic put it, the novel is "*gourmandise*—in its hedonism and perfectionism; and it possesses a negative charm—for there is abhorrence and terror hidden behind the clowning and the brilliance of its style."[4] Egunov himself commented elsewhere on the paradoxical capacity of goofy antics to

---

1   "Kto vydumal, chto mirnye peizazhi/Ne mogut byt´ arenoi katastrof?" From Mikhail Kuzmin, "The Trout Breaks the Ice" (1929).

2   Egunov published *Tula* under the pseudonym Andrey Nikolev, which refers to the minor eighteenth-century Russian poet Nikolay Nikolev (1758–1815). With a nod to literary-historical precedent with Russian writers like Alexander Bestuzhev-Marlinsky and Mikhail Saltykov-Shchedrin, I refer to him as Egunov-Nikolev in connection with *Beyond Tula*, but just Egunov elsewhere.

3   Socialist Realism—which strove to "depict reality in its revolutionary development"— was the official artistic policy in the Soviet Union from 1934 to perestroika. The production novel was a popular early genre—its plot reflected early Soviet efforts to rapidly industrialize, modernize, and improve the nation's production of goods and raw materials.

4   Aleksandr Zhitenev, "Antre Liamer & Faiginyu," *Novaia real´nost´* no. 29 (2011).

convey both the "agony of experience" and the metaphysics buried within language itself.[5]

Egunov was born September 26, 1895, in Ashgabat, the present-day capital of Turkmenistan. His family moved to St. Petersburg in 1905. There young Andrey studied at the prestigious Tenishev Gymnasium, alongside other famous-literati-to-be like Osip Mandelstam and Vladimir Nabokov. He graduated from St. Petersburg State University in 1918 with a degree in classics and subsequently embarked on postgraduate studies in Russian literature, but the postrevolutionary reorganization of the university system caused him to be excluded (as the son of an imperial officer) after one year of study. Egunov found work teaching at the new "workers' faculties" (*rabfak*) and as a private tutor. He continued his work in classical philology and was active as a translator; his translation of Plato's *Laws* was published in 1923 and is still read today.[6]

Beginning in the early 1920s, Egunov was also a member of a more informal collective of translators and friends, known as ABDEM (the acronym is made from the first letters of the participants' last names). The group collectively translated and published *The Adventures of Leucippe and Clitophon*, by Achilles Tatius (Gosizdat, 1925) and *Aethiopica* (or *Theagenes and Chariclea*), by Heliodorus of Emesa (Academia, 1932). These works— early romances or "novels"—were considered frivolous and met a lukewarm reception among the contemporary scholarly community. But the latter half of the 1920s also saw the flowering of Egunov's own literary career: between 1928 and 1932 he wrote most of the poems in the cycle "Elysian Joys," the first draft of the long poem "Objectless Youth," and the novel *Beyond Tula*. Another novel, *Vasily Island* (Vasilii Ostrov), was written in 1929 but lost along the way. During this period, Egunov took part in the lively artistic and literary life of 1920s Leningrad; in particular, he was friendly with the OBERIU poets (especially Konstantin Vaginov) and with Mikhail Kuzmin and his circle. Egunov was arrested in 1933 under suspicion of anti-Soviet activity, much as the OBERIU poets Daniil Kharms and

---

5 Andrei Egunov-Nikolev, "Osmyslenie," in *Bespredmetnaia iunost'* (Moscow: Intrada, 2009), 39–40.

6 See the Egunov bibliography at the end of the book for a more complete list of publications.

Alexander Vvedensky had been a few years earlier.[7] He was sentenced to three years' internal exile in Siberia.[8]

* * *

With a nod to his work as a classics scholar, Egunov-Nikolev subtitled his novel "A Soviet Pastoral": one of the many source texts for *Beyond Tula* is a second-century Greek romance written in the form of a travelogue, *The Incredible Wonders beyond Thule* of Antonius Diogenes.[9] As a romance (or adventure novel), Diogenes' work belonged to the "low" genres like comedy or satire. Egunov-Nikolev had a number of motivations for affiliating his *Beyond Tula* with both the pastoral and the classical romance. Aware that nothing about his writing style fell in line with the increasingly rigid cultural politics of the late 1920s and early 1930s—the ever-greater emphasis on the unambiguous heroism and epic historicism that would soon become Socialist Realism—Egunov-Nikolev took a neat sidestep by flaunting the banal and fantastical aspects of his work.

At the same time, the novel also features an exaggeratedly ideal protagonist, the young engineer Fyodor, who acts out a canonical early Soviet plotline: the struggle of the new, technologically advanced Soviet way of life with the prejudices and ignorance of the unenlightened peasants. Serious Fyodor—who at twenty-two claims he "can't remember life before the revolution"—is thus juxtaposed with the utterly irreverent Sergey, who at twenty-six is a jaded vestige of the ancien régime (Fyodor's mother, an opera singer who shows up halfway through the novel, is an even more outrageous vestige). Meanwhile, Fyodor and Sergey's romantic involvement conspicuously undermines the contrast between their worldviews. A similarly ironic and uneasy relationship to the new requirements in life and literature can be observed in other early Soviet experimental fiction such as Yuri Olesha's *Envy* or Konstantin Vaginov's cult classic *Goat Song* (both

---

7   The OBERIU (Union of Real Art), a group of experimental absurdist poets, existed for a few years in the late 1920s and early 1930s.

8   Egunov was arrested under suspicion of involvement with the controversial thinker/ideologue Ivanov-Razumnik; in fact, he was not involved with Ivanov-Razumnik, but was denounced following the arrest of some other members of Octopus, a literary group he occasionally attended.

9   The only existing account of the work comes from Photius (http://www.tertullian.org/fathers/photius_copyright/photius_04bibliotheca.htm), who praises it highly for its vivid narration, its clarity, and the gracefulness of its descriptions.

published in 1927–28). A certain kind of literary homoeroticism was not unusual for this time period—contemporaries of Egunov like Olesha and Isaac Babel incorporated the early Soviet cult of the male body and sexuality into their prose, at times quite provocatively. Even as Egunov-Nikolev's novel shares some aesthetic positions with these practitioners of literary Ornamentalism, the romantic plot in *Beyond Tula* is more subtle and realistic, and it evokes some of the languid decadence, aesthetic excess, and loose sexual politics of the prerevolutionary Russian Symbolists.

Another source of tension in *Beyond Tula* is the unresolved imbalance between the real world and the world of (literary) fantasy. The contradictions begin right away, with the title: Tula is a provincial Russian city known for its samovars, but Thule calls up the medieval geographical designation *ultima Thule*, "a distant unknown region; the extreme limit of travel and discovery." Next, the word "Soviet" in the subtitle points to a very concrete time and place, in a way that contrasts sharply with the ahistorical mood of the "pastoral." In the world of the novel, however, the Soviet Union is a mostly fantastical construct, insofar as the action unfolds in a timeless countryside touched by Soviet-led progress only in menacing ways. At the same time, this rural space is in a state of rapid change, as the Soviet mining industry literally undercuts the older pastoral ways of life. The Tula district and the nearby Tolstoy estate of Yasnaya Polyana are, meanwhile, real geographical locations; their old world ways are contrasted in turn to the progress and industrialization of real modern cities like Moscow and St. Petersburg/Leningrad (or its stand-in, Sergey's hometown of Peterhof). Contrasts like this point to potential utopias, but these are undermined as soon as they emerge. Fyodor's mother and Sergey have escaped the big city in search of a pastoral paradise, but they are unable to appreciate the rustic charm of the countryside.

Egunov was close with the modernist poet Mikhail Kuzmin, and Kuzmin's masterful poem "The Trout Breaks the Ice" (1925–28) is a major intertext for the novel's motifs and plot development. But Egunov was younger than Kuzmin and more rooted in the new Soviet reality; he adopted a necessarily ironic stance toward the ideal that humanity could be improved through love or art, even as he mocked the burgeoning Socialist Realist aesthetic. Along these lines, the novel's play with different registers of Soviet and pre-Soviet language (consider the persistent musical conflict between operas, sentimental romance songs, and rousing Soviet youth anthems), the idiosyncratic numbering of chapters and transitions between them, and the abrupt and somewhat absurdist "ending," recall some of the devices characteristic of poets like Kharms, Vvedensky, and Vaginov. At times the cacophony even points toward the radical language experiments of Andrey Platonov.

Egunov's subversive attitude toward genre and literary tradition extended to standing up for the artist's right to live outside the norms of society and not contribute to its material well-being. By presenting his novel as light and frivolous, he freed himself from expectations of a weighty moral message, which in turn allowed for the interpolation of any number of more and less ambiguous meanings in the novel's plot and the relationships between its characters, including the subtle but unmistakable darkness and tragedy present throughout the novel.

* * *

After serving out his sentence of exile, Egunov remained in Tomsk until 1938, when he moved to Novgorod and began commuting to Leningrad to teach at the state university.[10] In 1941, Novgorod was occupied by the Germans, and Egunov was taken as a captive to Neustadt in northern Germany, where he was kept in a labor camp for the remainder of the war. After the Allied victory in 1945, he and his mother moved to Berlin, where he taught German to Soviet officers until he was forcibly repatriated in 1946. He is known to have taught both Soviet and American soldiers and would have been considered a traitor. In any event, in 1946 he was repatriated and, like many former prisoners of war, immediately sentenced to ten years of correctional labor, which he carried out in various far-flung regions of the Soviet Union. He was rehabilitated in 1956 (just a few months before completing his sentence) and finally returned to Leningrad. He had been married to Tamara Danilova since 1930, but they had barely ever lived in the same city; she died in 1955, and they had no children. In order to receive a permit to live in Leningrad, he married his friend Anna Gipsi in 1956. Egunov spent the years left to him once again working on translations and classical philology in a number of Leningrad literary institutions. He died in 1968 and was buried in a cemetery outside Leningrad.

Egunov-Nikolev's stylistic play creates endless headaches for the translator. Romance songs, ditties, and folk sayings are, language aside,

---

10 Exiles were not permitted to hold residence permits in large cities. Novgorod is a four-hour train ride from Petersburg.

notoriously difficult to translate into a different cultural context; the distinct speech modes of the various protagonists, which subtly convey their social status and attitude toward societal change, are hardly easier. And yet the novel's basic orientation is one of fundamental indeterminacy; this is reflected in its play with doubles, names, and genders. For example, when Fyodor or Sergey is referred to as a Shade (in Russian, *ten'*, a feminine noun), all of their actions in this guise are grammatically colored by the Shade's femininity. By contrast, when Fyodor's boss is dubbed "the Adored Management," he becomes grammatically neutered, an "it" (*nachal'stvo—ono*) and hence somewhat dehumanized; this is even more the case with the character known as the Spawn (of Hell). A dehumanizing effect is also created through the device of multiplication, as in Sergey's musing on the three characters' identical speech or the multiple references to "both Fyodors" or "Dunya, and the other Dunya." Sergey ponders at one point, *The co-op operator, Syssoyich Sazykin, and the Adored—they all speak exactly the same language. How can we know—maybe they aren't three people at all, but just one.*

Manipulating names, genders, and character trajectories is, however, a perfectly ordinary thing for a writer to do. Like his friend Konstantin Vaginov, Egunov embraces this kind of writerly metacommentary, although he limits these pronouncements to his characters, particularly the writer-character Sergey:

> Sergey did some mental calculations: if this line goes this way, then that one goes the other way. Right. But then they intersect here. No, that doesn't work. This line should slant down and create a new plane. And I bend it here like this. Fyodor should really be turned into a woman. And then he can be Signora Stratelates. And Leocadia can be a man, an Italian with the last name Leocado.

These ruminations even include several gestures toward the increasingly difficulties faced by writers in the late 1920s and early 1930s:

> "There always has to be some kind of sumptuous woman in the spotlight. [. . .] But endow her with every possible perfection: young, beautiful, attractive, a brilliant public figure, committed to building a new world. [. . .] But make sure the protagonist has some flaws: under Leocadia's influence, he'll rid himself of them." [. . .]
> "And Fyodor is the ideal engineer?"
> "Why not? But bring in a couple of negative types: the local priest, the local kulak. Don't forget that everything is happening in the immediate vicinity of

Yasnaya Polyana. All of your characters should be reading Tolstoy, but the negative ones should be reading his religious nonsense." [. . .]

"[. . .] it would be even better if you made the whole thing into a historical novel. You can leave in the mines, but make it all happen under Ivan the Terrible—after all, they were mining this area back then, too. It'll be great and no one will get offended."

The last comment is both poignant and ominous, since many Soviet writers beginning in the late 1920s and early 1930s (from Aleksey Tolstoy to Yuri Tynianov) did find that writing historical fiction was safer than writing about contemporary life. As Lydia Ginzburg wrote at the time, "For many people now, historical novels and children's books are a means of writing under one's breath [*vpolgolosa*]."[11]

Although it was published in the official press, *Beyond Tula* would be Egunov's first and last publication of nonscholarly or translated work.[12] Egunov was one of the first in a long tradition of semiofficial Soviet writers; even in the 1920s, many writers whose work did not mesh well with official Soviet aesthetic standards were beginning to give up on official publication, to write "for the desk drawer," for small groups of friends, or just for themselves. *Beyond Tula* was published largely thanks to the friendly assistance of Konstantin Fedin, a prominent literary figure at the time—without Fedin's intervention, a novel like this would never have made it past the increasingly virulent political, aesthetic, and moral censors. Even after being reprinted in the Wiener Slawistischer Almanach series in 1993 (edited by Gleb Morev), the novel remained little known, even to specialists of Russian literature. It has yet to be republished in Russia, although the text of the novel was published in the debut issue of the journal *Russian Prose* (Russkaia proza [A]) in 2011, accompanied by some supplemental essays. None of Egunov's work has been translated into English before now.

Ainsley Morse
Riverside, CA
April 2018

---

11 Lidiia Ginzburg, *Zapisnye knizhki, vospominaniia, esse* (St. Petersburg: Iskusstvo-SPB, 2002), 79.

12 It would be his only official publication for decades to come. After decades spent in prison camps and his eventual rehabilitation in the 1960s, Egunov managed to publish some scholarly articles and a single monograph. See the bibliography for more information.

A NOTE ON NAMES

In polite or formal speech, Russians address each other with name and patronymic, thus "Darya Fyodorovna" (Darya, daughter of Fyodor) or "Lev Nikolayevich" (Lev, son of Nikolai—the latter refers to Leo Tolstoy). At the other end of the spectrum, informal or intimate speech offers a myriad of variations on a single name: in the course of a single day, a person named "Sergey" might be called Seryozha, Seryozhka, Seryoga, Seryozhenka, and so on, with each variation carrying nuances of emotion, greater and lesser degrees of affection, intimacy, irritation, and more. The protagonists of *Beyond Tula*, Fyodor and Sergey, are constantly playing around with greater and lesser formality in address; since their conversations are the closest thing the novel has to a plot, the nuances are important. Generally speaking, the forms "Fedya" and "Seryozha" are casual and informal; the "-ka" suffix ("Fedka," "Seryozhka") contributes a playfully aggressive tone; further variations, like "Seryozhenka" or "Fedenka," are very tender.

PART ONE

CHAPTER ONE

The others didn't have time to answer before they were driven back by the fast-moving throng. Morningtime Fyodor hung onto Sergey's neck with one hand while using the other to brandish the latter's weighty suitcase. The blackcurrant bushes in the front garden gleamed and one leaf, struck by an elbow, spilled forth a ponderous drop of dew.

"The stars sparkle, the moon weeps, sounds fly around, disturbing my sleep. But moonlight makes me mournful—as bygone nights of bliss I recall. If only I could return those days, those joyful dreams of gaiety, if only I could feel again the blaze, caresses of love's ecstasy."

"What the hell," said Sergey. "What're you talking about the moon for? It's morning, and a pretty hot one at that. Who's over there playing the guitar?"

"Yes, it's always hot here. Let's go inside, we won't bother them. You see?"

Three marvelously good-natured dogs' muzzles peeked out from under the balcony. An old woman's voice coming out of the kitchen called, "Hey, Kisser . . . here . . ."

"*Afternoon passions,*" thought Sergey. "*Kiss me: your kisses are sweeter than myrrh and wine.*"[1]

"And the other two," Fyodor went on. "Let me introduce you: Fingal and Ossian, ancient hounds, parasites on the laboring masses, vestiges of the cursed past. Which one do you like better, Seryozha?"[2]

---

1   Sergey refers to "Sebastian Bach," a story from Vladimir Odoevsky's *Russian Nights* (1844) that features a middle-aged character, Magdalina, caught in the grip of passion in the "afternoon of her life." The second quote is from Alexander Pushkin's poem "The Fire of Desire Burns in the Blood . . ." (1825), inspired by the Song of Songs.

2   Sergey is referred to variously: "Sergey Sergeyevich," "Seryozha," "Seryozhenka," etc.— the same is true of other characters as well. For more, see the Note on Names following the introduction.

"This one. He's jumping around all shaggy and shoving his homely mug into my knees."

"That homely mug was shot up with birdshot once when he was stealing apples. Now he's reformed and quieted down, made friends with Ossian and taught him not to bark. But Sergey, you're not even looking over here."

"The quiet garden has dropped into sleep, the scent of flowers is everywhere—never before, my dear friend, were you ever so lovely. For you, for you, my idol, I will forget the contemptible world; may night and garden and moon bear witness: my soul is entirely full of you, entirely full!"[3]

The rounded corner of a guitar really was peeking out from behind the bushes, and a white batiste dress was standing a distance from the garden wall, listening to the guitar. The dress was either opening the gate or closing it after itself, producing a frantic screech.

"And here is our haven." Fyodor led Sergey into the room. "Isn't it a cozy refuge, our Mon Repos?"

"I haven't read Saltykov-Shchedrin,"[4] objected Sergey. "Who was that girl at the gate, in the white dress? Such Russia—more than you could ever ask for."

"And she has such a poetic name—Leocadia! Did you bring me the underwear and flypaper?"

"Here they are: blue, red, green; choose whichever suit you best. And here's the paper. And some of my poems, as part of the set."

"Thanks, toss it all over here."

The tabletop seemed crowded with the frying pan and its mostly eaten omelette; bottles, their insides streaked with the traces of recent milk; and cigarettes scattered everywhere.

"You can't sit indoors in weather like this! Get comfortable, Seryozha—it's better here in the shade, beneath the spruce—as for me, I have to get to work. When I get back we'll talk about everything." Fyodor started harnessing the horse. The straps slapped and the bridle jangled in the morning stillness.

"It's so quiet here, Fedya. Where are the spirits of the ancestors you wrote me about?"

"They're probably out picking raspberries. Listen up: you can hear them coming."

---

3 An early twentieth-century "Gypsy romance" made famous by the tenor Leonid Sobinov.

4 *The Refuge Mon Repos* (1882) is a novel by Mikhail Saltykov-Shchedrin.

A tiny old lady in fur-lined slippers was mincing her way along the path leading to the house. The big old-fashioned leather pack hanging from her neck by a ribbon was open, and was crammed to bursting with just-gathered raspberries. The old lady was singing along industriously in time to her little steps in a lifeless voice: *The little wind is breathing barely, the little wind doesn't rustle a leaf, not in the clear field, not a bush in the dark forest, la-la-la, la-la-la.*[5]

"Haloo, my little eighty-year-old windlet, damn your eyes." Fyodor plunged his hand into the pack.

"Don't go roving round other people's wallets, you cheerful bastard, you! What're you beaming for anyway? Awfully glad your friend's here?"

Going over to Sergey, the grandmother stretched out a wrinkled hand and introduced herself. "Stratelates.[6] Very pleased to meet you. Make yourself at home. I'm sorry I have no cologne."

She went into the house, and the guitar player emerged from the bushes. He strummed a few minor chords.

"Never you mind, we're going to get this horse unharnessed right now. How can you even talk about work when your friend's just arrived? Listen— without you here, he's fallen into hermitude. Won't go out for a jaunt and never drinks a drop, just keeps bowing out and saying: when my friend gets here, then we can have a little fun. I'll close up my shop today if it means we can go out; I'm doing business every other day anyway. Let's relive a bit of the good old days, remember how the students used to sing: *O people, the people, we share a single fate, rage blazes in our eyes and our soul rages like a thunderstorm.*"[7]

The sensitive horse twitched an ear: she thought that the guitar was going to be yoked onto her head—an unusual and unnecessary harness.

"So we'll bring the whole gang over to your place today, then," the co-op operator concluded.

"Fine. Grandma, get everything we need."

"For how many people?"

"Twenty," answered the co-op operator.

---

5 Folk song "A Little Wind."
6 Fyodor's name comes from Fyodor Stratelates (stratelates—"the general" or "military commander"), also known as Theodore of Heraclea. He was a martyr and warrior saint during the time of Emperor Licinius (307–24).
7 Sergey Sergeyevich, the co-op operator, garbles some lines from the poem "My Soul is Dark" by Semyon Frug, a minor Romantic poet of the late nineteenth century.

"Good God, Fedya!"

"Grandma, don't contradict me."

"I'm not contradicting you, of course; it's your money. But you yourself know full well . . ."

"Just give the money to Sergey Sergeyevich, he'll go buy everything himself. I'm not talking about you, Seryozha—you haven't met yet, I think"—and Fyodor set about introducing the co-op operator and Sergey. "This is my friend Sergey Sergeyevich. And this is also my friend, also Sergey Sergeyevich."

A squeal drowned out the pleasantries. Some kids were shrieking and rolling around on the grass, pulling up their smocks. Two cats politely climbed out of a basket, followed by eight or so kittens. The kittens evidently didn't make much of a distinction as to which of them belonged to which mother and snuggled up to both equally. Sergey stumbled; there was a piteous moan, and the maimed kitten crawled off like a paralytic, dragging its newly useless hind legs.

The only thing that could be made out in the muddle were the following words of the new arrival: "I was buried in Therapnai . . . they are mistaken when they say I was hanged from a tree . . ."

The co-op operator didn't see the hand held out to him.

"Give me the money, Grandmother, and don't worry: all of our stuff is official prix-fixe."

"Fyodor," whispered Sergey. "I'm not here alone, you know; where can we put the new arrival?"

"No problem," answered Fyodor. "My grandmother's a good woman, she can look after Helen, too. I remember how an old homeless woman used to live with her: she would sleep on chairs, but since the room was already cramped, they used to take out one of the lower dresser drawers, and the old lady would lie there with her legs stuck in the dresser. But never mind that, I just thought of something even better. Hey, Grisha Ermolov! Take the lady to the lean-to."

Grisha Ermolov materialized, wearing a felt hat.

A march started playing. Bronze trumpets blared.

Fyodor leapt up onto the cart and was already whipping the horse. Sergey ran alongside and jumped up to join him. "May I go along with you to work, to have a look?"

Fyodor began explaining the mechanics of boreholes and bell-shafts, but an approaching chicken shifted his thoughts in a different direction.

"My grandmother is always complaining that there isn't enough money, no matter how much she scrimps and saves. I know that she's terribly forgetful: when someone brings her a chicken, she bargains and bargains, eventually bargains them down to a ruble, and pays for it. Then the same lady comes back the next day to sell her the very same chicken, and it goes on like that for several days in a row. In the end, the chicken costs us five rubles."

"Are we really going to talk about chickens? I wouldn't have come."

"And if I want to talk about chickens?"

"I won't have it."

"Stop teasing me like some kind of monkey! I beg of you, don't quash the child's individuality."

"You're no child—you're a beanpole."

The horse took off at a full gallop, carried away by the skirmish underway in the cart.

A slightly drunken little peasant was scuffling his feet in the middle of the road. When they drove around him, he launched into conversation. "You've no hat, and I've no hat, so you won't run me over. My old lady took off to Moscow; they've put her in a hospital there. If you want, I'll sell you a bull."

A little girl was pulling him by the shirt and crying, "Dada, let's go home."

"It's strange," said Fyodor. "Around here the word 'engineer' has taken on the meaning of 'nobleman.' But what kind of noblemen are we? And you're not even an engineer. Anyway, enough is enough, Seryozhka: we've arrived. But please, if you can, try to keep quiet, otherwise you with your jibber-jabber . . ."

The workers shook hands with Fyodor. Sergey sat down on a pile of sand next to the proving winch. Rope was wound around a wooden shaft, which was supported on both sides by two struts. Fyodor put his foot through a loop of rope.

This is how giants ride around.

Fyodor is about to push off from the ground and fly off, tracing circles in the morning air. During his ascent, he'll see the whole of the area: slight hills, fields bristled with the remnants of harvested rye, far-off drilling rigs.

"Let me down," said Fyodor, unwinding his measuring tape.

"You want some wind?" The guy standing by the winch winked.

"Sure, give me a little wind."

The bell-shaft rapidly swallowed up Fyodor's legs, then his shoulders and cap. He disappeared from the face of the earth.

Indians bury people alive like that, thought Sergey, and pronounced, "Mayne Reid!"[8]

The workers glanced back and forth. Sergey bit his tongue. A hollow echo came up from the bell-shaft: "Shut up already."

The rope stopped unwinding. From the depths wafted, "Bring me up! All right. Floor of red sand. Hanging layer. About twenty meters. OK, bring me up higher. More."

Fyodor's cap emerged from underground, then his hand holding a notebook and pencil. Finally all of him jumped out of the pit. His trousers were stained all over with red.

"Everything's fine," he said. "Well, see you guys later. Seryozha, you wait here in the grove—I can't take you anywhere, you ruin everything. I'll go check out a few more bell-shafts, and then I'll come by here at the dinner break."

Sergey was let out from the cart near the white tree trunks. A brook was enjoying the midday shade. It was pleasant to dabble bare feet in it and to feel thin sand running between your fingers.

Girls came out from behind the birches.

Each of them was holding a large white mushroom. Sergey learned their names right away. They were Dunya, Fenya, another Dunya, Domasha. None of them was more than twenty, and they all turned out to be village schoolteachers.

The whole company settled down on the bank. Sergey was in the middle, lying on his back. He saw the little flowers of colorful country calico; the reddish hairs on the napes of their necks, brushed lightly by the impudent breeze; and a bit higher up—the green leaves and very bright sky covering the four girls.

Railroad engineers used to refer to tracks in the feminine: "get up on her," they'd say about the fifth track, or "she's a tough one, the eleventh." They were right, and this track of theirs fell in with other words like "ship," "moon," or "whale." Was this what had bothered Sergey yesterday, when he was gazing out at the railway couplings splayed out along both sides of the train, merging roundly with one another at the switches? He wouldn't mind

---

8   Thomas Mayne Reid (1818–1882) was an English author of young adult adventure novels. His works were especially popular in prerevolutionary Russia and in the Soviet Union.

staying a while in that unused train car turning green over on the eleventh track, next to a little ditch and patch of grass. He'd take along the necessary goods and chattels—a razor, soap, a towel, a blanket and pillow—and settle in on the lower bunk. Run to the station in the morning for hot water and fly headlong back into the train car, afraid it would take off from right beneath his nose. He'd look out the window at the motionless landscape: a potato patch, some metal detritus, a five-story building with tiny windows; and he'd entertain bizarre visions of looming cities with towers on the shore of the ocean. Walking along the corridor of the motionless train car, he'd hold onto the walls to keep from falling from the shaking of the train hurtling along. He'd read the same book over and over, whatever happened to be on hand—a book read in a train car becomes forever beloved.

The assembled company shared their bread in brotherly fashion and began drinking it down with water from the brook. Dunya scooped up water in her palms and carried it to Sergey's mouth, but her hand trembled slightly, and all the water slipped away between her virgin fingers, trickling onto her yellow hem.

Then she ran her wet hand across Sergey's face, uttering, "Here, wash your face."

Finally, everyone was worn out, the mushrooms were placed to the side, and the songs began.

Dunya and Domasha started. "Two flowers on the kerchief, palest blue and darker. Nobody knows a thing about love, but for my sweetie and me. A starlet fell from heaven on the fragrant lilacs, take me, take me, falling star, can you really be too lazy? I will sew a dress with arrows forward, go on, my sweet, come after me, like a fox after the squirrel."[9]

Fenya and the other Dunya answered. "Pinned to my breast, adorning my breast, oh believe me, my dear girl, I sing not for joy. Undo my white dress, my heart cannot breathe: he was going to my place but stopped by hers. How can he feel no shame? Where we stood, my sweetie and me, the snow melted through to the earth; where my sweetie and me kissed, flowers bloomed."

Fyodor entered the grove and took off his cap. Sergey leapt up to meet him. Fyodor, displeased, slumped on a stump.

"You're tired, Fyodor?"

"And you're not, Seryozha? You seem pretty busy here."

---

9   Folk ballad "Two Flowers on the Window Sill," unknown author.

"Oh, these men, always fighting about something," exclaimed Dunya. She plucked some nettles and began striking Fyodor about the arms, repeating, "Take that, men, don't be mean."

Fyodor pulled back, but Sergey reached out his arms. "Now do me, I don't want to be mean either."

Whole bunches of nettles were pressed into the effort. The girls were pleased that Sergey, unblinking and with pursed lips, kept his arms stretched out so stubbornly, even as they turned red and became covered in white blisters. They didn't know that Sergey was thinking the whole time about Mucius Scaevola.[10]

Finally, the girls ran off, tossing all the nettles into the men's faces.

"I love my work more than anything," said Fyodor. "Just think, Seryozha: this is the ancient Tula region. There were no Urals then, no Krivoi Rog,[11] but the tsars needed iron tools, at the very least for making their instruments of torture. How else could they torment the people? So they came here for the ore."

"And the kings?" asked Sergey. "Do you remember the Thule king?"[12]

"He was just an idiot, like all kings: throwing golden grails into the water. That's called squandering the people's property."

They gazed at the moss-covered bed of the brook. Sergey thought he could see a copper Tula samovar gleaming there on the bottom, scrubbed clean by brick.[13] He threw a blade of grass into the water and followed its floating, off toward the fields where the rye lay harvested and the bell-shafts dug out.

Fyodor gestured outward. "This is all my domain."

"So you believed my poem?"

"I don't remember your poem. This is my domain, because I work here. My oil wells, my bell-shafts. The mountains, laid bare by mining, the plant

---

10 Gaius Mucius Scaevola was a Roman youth famous for his bravery. According to the legend, Scaevola burned his hand to show that he was not afraid of suffering.

11 The Urals are Russia's largest mountain range, dividing "European" (western) Russia from Siberia and the Far East. Krivoi Rog (Russ., "crooked horn") or Krivyi Rih (Ukr.) is a city in the Dnepropetrovsk industrial region of modern-day Ukraine. It is famed for being "the longest city in Ukraine."

12 Sergey refers to Johann Wolfgang von Goethe's "Der König von Thule," a stylized folk ballad (1774); in the poem, the king keeps a golden goblet to remind him of his lost love, and with his dying breath tosses it into the sea. Goethe later made the poem into Gretchen/Margaret's opening monologue in *Faust*; it becomes clear later in the story that Sergey is currently reading the tragedy, in German.

13 The city of Tula has long been famed for its samovars, rounded vessels used to boil water for tea.

products of nature unearthed in raw form, extracted, cultivated, segregated, clarified, and subjugated to the goals of humanity—that's what interests me. What a beauty that oil rig over there is, don't you think, Seryozha?"

"You know, Fyodor, this is stupid, but I just can't shake the feeling: when you say, 'the bell-shafts sprung up all over the place,' to me it sounds like you're talking about musical instruments."

"Why not! We'll start playing them soon enough. The whole country will start ringing." And Fyodor lashed Sergey across the face with the nettles, but the leaves had wilted and faded and no longer stung.

"Did you notice that guy who was turning the winch?" Fyodor continued. "I like him a lot. When Fedya's letting me down into the bell-shaft, I feel calm: the rope unwinds steadily. By now they must have brought him breakfast—we would probably just call it cold soup, but here they call it kvass. I'll introduce you to his fiancée, Maryanka, later so you won't be bored here. Really, Seryozhka, now you'll have to come visit me every summer, wherever I happen to be working—who knows, Altai, Siberia, the Tanutivinsk Republic.

"No," said Sergey. "I won't come to Tanutivinsk: there's too many mosquitoes there."

"Not any more than in your Peterhof. Or are the mosquitoes there domesticated?"

"Tell me, Fyodor, is it true that you can buy tea here without ration cards?"

"Yes, as long as the kulaks haven't bought it all up to cause a crisis.[14] Here in Mirandino the kulaks run thick and fast. When I first moved out to start working here, no one wanted to rent me a place to live. I had to settle a ways out from the village, in a wing of the big house. The co-op is over there, see, next to the church. You go straight all the way and then turn right."

"Do you need anything, Fyodor? Some soap? A toothbrush, cologne, chlorodont toothpaste?[15] Why is it that you practically don't bathe?"

"Buy soap, but not the perfume-y kind. I have no use for cologne; that is, I always drink it with wood varnish. Well, goodbye; I have to go back to work."

---

14 *Kulak* (literally, "fist") in Soviet propaganda of the late 1920s to the mid-1930s, a word for supposedly rich peasants resisting collectivization—the number-one class enemy of the time.

15 The first Soviet toothpaste.

Coming out of the grove, Sergey noted that the dust on the road had grown whiter from the noontime heat. A dog jumped out at him from a tumbledown cottage. Scorched beams and charred planks surrounded the intact, jutting chimney of the central brick oven, where puppies were squealing.

"What's your name?" Sergey struck up a conversation with the dog. "It must be Queenie? Hey, Queenie, Queenie! What's wrong, sweetheart?"

Sergey lisped and whistled, made kissing sounds, but Queenie lifted her top lip to reveal teeth bared in a firm grimace.

"You dummy," Sergey continued. "What are you worried about? I love your puppies no less than you do; even more, of course. I don't feel like picking them up right now, but otherwise I'd play around with them for a while."

Queenie read the love in Sergey's eyes and, giving a growl, disappeared back into the ruined hearth.

With falling heart and weak knees, Sergey ran into the co-op and fell onto a chair.

"Welcome. We've got the order for Fyodor's party all ready. And what can I get for you?"

"Tea," cried Sergey. "As much tea as possible and then soap."

The co-op operator was delighted. "I get it. The yokes and the tar are just here for show; I don't keep nails in stock. My goods are as elegant as my customers: all engineers. Don't you be afraid of me, I know the remedy: when you're scared of something or get to feeling down, you have to drink a cup of cold water with three spoons of sugar right away. Though beer is even better."

Light was coming into the shop only through the open door, since there were no windows. Beauties equipped with luxurious bosoms and captions were smiling out from the soap wrappers: rose, lily of the valley, hyacinth. On the wall a green water nymph was surfacing with a priceless potion in her hands. A gray peasant blouse hung from a stretching frame. Sergey sketched in its continuation: he put bare legs below, a beard above, and wrinkled hands in the pockets—a little old man like that might have been geometry tutor to the princess.

Meanwhile, the co-op operator had shut the door tightly. Everything disappeared. The only thing left was a warm, rather sweaty hand tugging along the meek customer.

Sergey discerned that the co-op operator smelled of fresh footwear, New Way of Life cookies, and the breath of a man who did not use chlorodont toothpaste. Chlorodont squeezes out like a white fragrant sausage onto the stubble of the toothbrush. The paste foams in your mouth along with warm water, and when you gargle, you see the bathroom ceiling—it's smaller and darker than in other rooms.

"Come on, come on." The co-op operator dragged Sergey into the neighboring room, illuminated by a dim little window high up the wall.

"You were right not to live in the village—people would have lurked under your windows to see what you were up to. And you and I have secrets, after all—I'm nobody's fool. Well, she keeps saying that these days the evening light is more flattering, that she's only got three years left to live, because after forty your face only shows vestiges of the cursed past, and that's when she'll really need her innocence. But I tell her: we're not going anywhere anytime soon, don't you worry. Just don't worry. I did some secret calculations. Mitenka says, 'I'll buy a revolver: I need to learn to be a perfect shot, just in case.' But he's got it all wrong. Everything needs to happen in silence—I'm nobody's fool, after all. You aren't his relative, now, are you? You weren't at the university together? As for me, brother, I graduated from the Moscow Institute of Commerce."

When Sergey's eyes adjusted to the half-darkness, he could make out the threadbare but, by all means, mahogany furniture distributed about the room. It all looked uncomfortable, cracked and falling apart, but was of an unmistakably aristocratic design. An outdated chart with portraits of revolutionary leaders hung above the couch. The co-op operator ushered Sergey over to the opposite wall, where there was another chart with carefully traced lines:

Registration of persons having made it past eighty, by profession:
Wetnurses—2. Shepherds—3. Cardinals and bishops—6. Merchants—11. Painters—3. Sailors—2. Musicians—2. Stewards—10. Officers—21, 3 of them field marshals. Popes—1. Philosophers—18. Scholars 23. Schoolchildren—4. Soldiers—12. State ministers—4. Gravediggers—1. Doctors—6. Co-op operators—?

The co-op operator shifted his gaze from Sergey to the revolutionary leaders' portraits and snickered conspicuously. "Did you get it, about the ones on top?"

Darya Fyodorovna came in and asked whether to serve them dinner, but the co-op operator was loping dreamily around the room. A porcelain Easter egg was hanging in the corner beneath the icon case; paper roses, already very ancient, were pinned thickly to the icons.

"What a tiresome circumstance," complained Darya Fyodorovna. "The son died from scarlet fever, so they won't allow an open coffin. What do you two want for dinner?"

"What dinner? You think we're interested in dinner when Fyodor's friend has arrived? And your circumstance is tiresome 'cause you don't know how to live right."

Big Al made his entrance, smooched with the co-op operator, and started relating, "Buddy of mine, three days now I've been planning to go to Moscow, but somehow I just can't leave—there's so much cultural education to be done here."[16] The young engineer winked.

Another couple of beers appeared on the table, foamy as the engineer's blond curls. Everyone clinked bottles and Big Al continued his tale. "Romania is a shitty country. People sell all kinds of garbage right out of their houses, right out the window, all over the place; there's a lawyer in every house and his wife is up to all kinds of dirty business. When I was there, all my underwear got stolen. There are thousands of pillows on the beds, stacked up with the smallest one on top, but they think it's gauche to sleep on them. In a word—bourgeois bullshit.

"But why bother remembering war stories, that's all in the past. Let's drink to the health of today's educational front!"

After he drank, Big Al left.

The co-op operator splashed the remaining beer onto the chart with the revolutionary leaders' portraits. "I know everything, y'hear. When Fyodor Fyodorovich first showed up, Domasha went over to his landlady's place like she was just visiting, sat there for hours, and ended up staying the night. She made up her bed on the floor in the room that's in between Fyodor's balcony and his drafting studio, right on the threshold. And what do you think? Fyodor stepped right over her, y'see, very politely, and settled in to work at his desk nearly all night long. Domasha was so insulted she didn't sleep a wink either. As for me, y'hear, I got it right away: a hermit and a draftsman . . . You know, I myself am . . . anyway, I put my trust in your student's word of honor."

"I'm not a student," Sergey objected.

"Yeah, right! Don't be shy, now: that's what I've got my red corner all fitted out for."[17]

---

16 Big Al is identified as working for KULTPROS, a new Soviet government outfit devoted to "cultural education."

17 By "red corner," the co-op operator refers to his chart with the revolutionary leaders. In prerevolutionary times, the "red [*krasnyi*, also beautiful] corner" in a house was the

Sergey turned over on the mahogany, manorly divan and pinched himself terribly painfully on the cracked seat. While the pain was passing and Sergey was surreptitiously rubbing the pinched spot, he managed to take a little stroll with Fyodor. Actually, at first Sergey was walking by himself and looking at the ruts in the road. They were worn deep from all the peasant carts.

Kids were sitting atop the haystacks; mongrels were yelping at the horses, sticking out their tongues as far as possible (since dogs don't sweat, and in hot weather their tongues serve as their only air vent). Fyodor came up from behind and took Sergey by the hand. Sergey pulled him forward; at first Fyodor was embarrassed and didn't want to keep going forward, although the going was very comfortable: a splendidly swept path led toward the house. Flowerbeds with blooming roses lay to either side. But there was something still more vividly red than the roses there, and this was what had made Fyodor embarrassed.

Rods appeared, and the stripes came out after the first blow—white for an instant and crimson immediately afterward. They couldn't see the face of the young man lying prone on the bench: the hem of his shirt was pulled up over his head. No cries could be heard, either; the flogging was proceeding magnificently and did not disturb Susi's strolling beneath the shade of the linden trees, a French novel in her hands. The rounded linden leaves cast a shifting shadowy grid onto her gauzy dress. She had plunged with all of her maidenly and innocent heart into the musings of Lelia, whose unquenchable love had forced Adolphe to throw himself headlong into the waterfall.

Noticing Fyodor and Sergey moving along the path straight toward her, Susi furrowed her pretty little brow.

"Hey, boys, where do you think you're going?" she exclaimed. "Peasants aren't allowed to walk in the park."

Then Sergey realized that, indeed, he and Fyodor were stepping out in highly inappropriate outfits. At least they had on trousers instead of just briefs, but everything else was very bad: Fyodor was wearing a sleeveless undershirt, his naked armpits shone with red-gold down, and his bare feet were barely covered with perforated sandals.

Susi was getting ready to fall onto the yellow sand with a lifeless "Ah!" when Sergey suddenly got hold of himself.

---

corner where the icons hung, but the Soviet ideologues repurposed the pun. In Soviet institutions the red corner was a recreational area decorated with a red flag, portrait of Lenin, etc.

"Don't be frightened, for the love of God, don't be frightened!" he said, in French, pronouncing the words as best he could. "My friend and I, we are, of course, simple folk, that is, the unhappy victims of fate: we were attacked by bandits. However, their leader assured us that he remains tortured by the flame of unrequited passion. We left Sir Ralph sitting by the edge of the forest, weaving a wreath of wild mistletoe leaves."

"All the same," objected Susi, "you must agree that I cannot speak with young men unchaperoned. It is unacceptable. If you wish to ask for my hand, please speak to my *papà*."

By then all three had made it past the execution scene. The young man's back no longer resembled a human body, and Fyodor stopped feeling agitated. It was a hash of willow switches and flesh oozing blood.

"*Papà, papà*, it's so fine," exclaimed Susi, ascending the balcony steps. "We have unexpected guests from Mirandino, a charming *visite*."

She fluttered off to adjust her toilette.

"Welcome, guests." The old man took a foulard handkerchief from his pocket. "Come along, I shall show you my farmyard and kennels. I do hope you will consent to stay the night?"

"No, we're in the hayloft."

"Of course, of course, some people like that. The deceased Anempodist Pavlovich did too . . . Hey, Proshka, bring us . . ." The friendly old man began to fuss about. A bit blind, he hadn't noticed Fyodor and Sergey's outfits.

They wanted to respond in kind, and said, "If you come to see us in Mirandino, we could show you a photograph of your great-granddaughter with *Memento mori* written on the back. Serpukhov, 13 September 1903."

"I'm sorry, I'm a little hard of hearing. What would you like to show me in Mirandino?"

"A photograph of your granddaughter."

"I did not receive such a brilliant education, of course. Susi, come over here—what does 'photograph' mean in French?"

"It's a kind of science, *papà*."

"Ah, yes, of course. But I have no granddaughter: it's still too early for Susi to think about getting married, and Voldemar is young, too—just this fall he found a place in Petersburg, in the noblemen's regiment.[18] Though, by

---

18 The scene with Susi and her *papà* presents a caricature of the lifestyle of the early nineteenth-century nobility.

all means, Volodka has already embarked on his seventeenth year. You know yourselves how young people are. What do I know—it's possible I do have a granddaughter somewhere in Petersburg, but, if you'll excuse me, they don't teach photographies to such people; we'll never have enough science to teach it to everyone. They should all be sent to the villages, let 'em grow up eating oat flour. Heh-heh, you've given an old man a nice chuckle. I too was young once, I know: *I love the roar of debauchery, the fires of mind and speeches, the thunderous boom of champagne corks . . .*[19] Are you by any chance hussars?" The old man wiped away a little tear that had rolled out from under his red necrotic lid.

"No," answered Fyodor and Sergey.

"No? But you are, I trust, noblemen?"

"Many thanks, but not really."

The outraged old man leapt up and staggered. Fyodor reached out to support him, and his golden armpit flashed before the weak-sighted eyes of the old man, who fell as if dead onto the waxed floorboards.

"*Papà, papà*, he's dead, oh God!" screamed Susi, throwing herself onto her father's corpse.

Fyodor sang out, ". . . To the foundations, and then . . ."[20]

Everything started shaking. A faint scent of air flickered beneath the arches of the age-old lindens; the motheaten judge's robe, a white cap with nobleman's cockade, the glistening dapples of sunlight on the sand of the avenue; and all of this jumbled together with a melancholy song: *They want to wed our Paranya to a nobleman—two lapdogs in front, two lackeys behind.*[21]

"Not a bad little poem," noted the co-op operator. "But these days people don't sing those songs anymore. You know, the twentieth century—the age of steam and electricity! The subtlety of feeling among our countrymen has reached the point of: *Oh, remember, I came to you when I was sick, you were waiting for my touch—and you'll wait forever.*[22]

---

19 The old man quotes Denis Davydov's poem "The Hussar's Confession" (1832). Davydov was a contemporary of Pushkin known for his dashing charm and hardcore partying.

20 Fyodor sings a line from the official Russian translation of the "Internationale," which in 1922 became the national anthem of the USSR. The surrounding lines read "We will destroy the whole world of violence/To the foundations, and then/We will build our own, a new world."

21 Sergey hears some of the words of a late eighteenth-century ballad, attributed to a serf actress, Praskovya Ivanovna Kuznetsova-Gorbunova (1768–1803) who was indeed wedded to her noble master, Count Sheremetyev.

22 The co-op operator quotes the poem "Flowers" by Semyon Nadson (1862–1887), an extremely popular sentimental poet of the late nineteenth century and the subject of many jibes by later modernist and avant-garde poets.

"Yes," continued the co-op operator. "It's too bad Leo Nikolaich didn't write poetry,[23] but some poems are wonderful—they just go straight to the heart, especially the ones written by young ladies. The day before yesterday Domasha came by, all stern and gloomy. I took a dig: 'Wherefore this sadness on the exquisite features of a young face?' 'The sadness,' she answered, 'is 'cause I want some grub.' But I kept at her: 'Crazed, agonized, I want happiness and tears, and I love you endlessly.' And what do you think? She stayed to have dinner with me! Well, I grabbed a can of sprats from the co-op so her feelings wouldn't be hurt at dinner."

Sergey looked at the co-op operator's paunch, at his rosy little cheeks, and resolutely said, "I write poems too."

"Hurrah," howled the co-op operator. "I love students and poets. Anyway, a true student is always a poet: *Up and over, one hump down, up and over, two humps down.*[24] Could you remind me of your last name? . . . Very pleased to meet you. Are you related to the famous one?"

"Of course, I'm his son."

"Well, over there in Yasnaya Polyana Leo Nikolaich spawned a whole pile of kids, and they're all talentless; it's a real tragedy. Talent doesn't always carry over. But hey, brother, let's hear your poem."

"Sure," said Sergey. "Just a minute. All right: ready, set . . .'"

The co-op operator made to kiss him. "You're an oasis in the Arabian desert. Hey now, look after yourself, you and I still have to live for the future. So, brother, trust means trust. Scoot over. One, two, three . . ."

Sergey reckoned, *Now there's going to be a card trick, and the card I choose will turn out to be lying at the top of the deck. Then they'll start playing forfeit. The loser's head will be covered with a kerchief; he will become an oracle. Everyone will come up to him, touch the top of his head with a finger and ask what this forfeit should do. He will designate one of them a mirror, another the lighter of streetlamps, and order the third to hop in circles on one leg.*

---

23 There are many references to Leo Tolstoy throughout the novel. Sometimes he is called by his full name, given here in the standard English spelling; and sometimes by his name and patronymic, Lev (Leo) Nikolaevich (or, as here, a more informal version of it). Tolstoy's estate, Yasnaya Polyana (literally, "clear meadow" or "clearing"), lies outside the real city of Tula and near the imaginary village of Mirandino.

24 The co-op operator sings the opening lines of the chorus to a popular student drinking song, known variously as "There by the Kryukov Canal" or "From Dusk till Dawn" and dating from the mid-nineteenth century.

"See," said the co-op operator and moved the heavy table aside. The table's one leg began as a column, then widened into a red oval—smaller than the tabletop, but still large and comfortable, like a footrest.

Beneath the table, there was a ring lying in a hollowed-out depression in the floor, like a jeweler's masterpiece in its little box. The co-op operator spread his fat thighs wide. When he grabbed the ring, a secret hatch opened up. A few steps of a wooden staircase could be seen leading down into the black hole.

"Is that a grave?" Sergey was curious.

"No, it has everything you need for the continuation of life. Nothing to worry about. I'm trusting you, brother. Now go down into the crypt."

The lit candle guttered to the side, doused by the co-op operator's breath.

Down below there was a cement floor and air deprived of season. It smelled neither of summer or winter, but of eternity: lard, candies, kerosene. It was cooler down in the basement than it had been coming down the stairs, with a belly from behind weighing heavily on Sergey, and the candle in raised hand threatened to drip hot stearin onto the top of his head.

The copper candlestick was placed on a barrel.

"I come down here to enjoy solitude amid the scarce commodities. See, here in this basket I have maraschino liqueur—ordered it from Moscow. My sacred principle is: scarce commodities for scarce people. There isn't enough for the whole village anyway, so what's the sense in giving it out by the eighth or the pinch? Better for the people to suffer: it elevates their souls, and there are so few of the rest of us we need to look after ourselves for the sake of the future. A healthy stomach is the guarantor of digestion. Just you wait, we'll turn out to be healthier than everything else: it's the lot of the people, their happiness . . . You want some salami? It's pretty fatty." The co-op operator twirled his knife around.

"What am I sitting on here?" asked Sergey. "It's hard, with sharp edges."

"Get up and feast your eyes."

The co-op operator untied the sack and drew out a block of lump sugar that resembled Kazbek.[25]

"Isn't it a beauty?"

---

25 One of the highest peaks in the Caucasian Mountains and, as such, a literary cliché of the nineteenth century.

CHAPTER THREE

"But over here I have granulated too, look."

He threw handfuls of the sugar onto the floor. In the candlelight it looked like it was snowing.

"Well, what do you say—does it crunch?" The co-op operator strutted back and forth around the basement. "Y'see, I really started missing the good life. You know: a frosty winter day, a Sunday, in the morning—tea with lots of sugar, Filippov cakes, church bells; you sip on that Chinese brew through a lump of sugar, then off to Sokolniki on sleds.[26] Little bells, a patterned lap rug with roses gleaming on it even in January. And a little rose sitting next to you as well. You walk around hand in hand with her under the pines, and it crunches beneath your feet."

"I've seen the Northern Lights," said Sergey. "It was on the corner of Nevsky and Sadovaya in St. Petersburg. Violet and dark-blue stripes twining above the lights of the *Pavilion de Paris*. It was very cold, and I got on the tram."

"Who cares about sugar!" bellowed the co-op operator. "It's despicable prose—stomp on it, brother, don't be shy; and believe me when I say that Baal will be toppled and love returned to the earth! . . ."[27]

A playful twittering really was carrying down from upstairs.

The co-op operator, holding his hands like a guitar player, sang out a song of invitation, accompanying himself on imaginary strings: *A kiss is a moment of pleasure, a kiss is a moment of triumph.*[28]

French high heels appeared on the stairs—pale slippers on bare feet. Someone was coming down, backside-first and singing. The co-op operator fell upon the descending feet and, despite some resistance, managed to plant several kisses onto the flat soles. Then white batiste shot up into his

---

26 Sokolniki is a suburb east of Moscow, in past centuries a favorite spot for the city's elite to hunt, sled, and stroll.

27 The co-op operator quotes from Pushkin ("despicable prose") and another poem by Nadson, "My Friend, My Brother . . ." (1880).

28 More garbled Nadson.

hands, and the mysterious stranger leapt down onto the basement floor with a thud.

"Oh! Who's that?"

"Never mind, never mind, he's my best friend, he won't give you away . . . Listen—curses always come home to roost."

The co-op operator looked at Sergey for an instant with the same expression he had directed toward the granulated sugar.

Sergey kissed the lady's proffered hand and said, "I believe I have already seen your dress: it stood opening and closing the gate this morning. You are Leocadia, are you not?"

"Oh, so my name is already known to you? Ah, what a naughty boy! And we've only just met, how bizarre . . . So tell me, are you as much of a hermit as Fyodor Fyodorovich? I've just come by for a minute to cool off. It's hot as hell outside, and there are so few cultured people around; I've got no one to socialize with."

She smoothed her ethereal dress, which had suffered some on the headlong flight down the stairs. A ring with a turquoise shone blue on her calloused pinky.

"Oh, right," Sergey remembered. "I have to go."

And he began to make his way up the stairs, accompanied by the co-op operator's words: "Delicacy—now that's something I've always respected. Well, see you soon. Wait for me by the gate, y'hear."

Above ground, everything was very bright. The mahogany furniture stood there, bored, and the revolutionary leaders' portraits were still wet from the beer. The pit gaped in the middle of the floor, illuminated from below. Sounds were coming out.

". . . Goddess . . ."

". . . Crazy madman . . ."

After these shrieks, the light went out—all that was left was a taciturn hole. The hatch door lay nearby.

Just slam the hatch, drag the heavy table on top—in a month they'd find two skeletons down there in the vault, entwined in deathly love! And I'd walk around the village keeping mysterious silence when asked: where did our co-op operator get to? Where is the exquisite Leocadia? . . . Oh, but I'm an idiot. Sergey whacked himself on the forehead. *All the scarce commodities are down there. They could live for years and years! Though the co-op operator said that he can't stay put in any one place for more than a year . . . The squeal of a newborn baby will issue forth from below ground. They'll break through the floorboards and out from the vault will come Leo Tolstoy, all grown over with a long beard, and Leocadia will leap out like some kind of Madonna with an infant in arms. The baby will be christened "Crypt" or, as they say around here, "Cropt" . . . Oh, but I'm an idiot—there's no water down there! They'll die slowly, agonizingly, their parched lips will vainly seek the moisture of kisses. The maraschino liqueur will not cool them. Doubtless, down there underground, taciturn Leocadia will forget how to speak entirely. But the co-op operator will start digging a tunnel with his knife, and they'll crawl out like moles, blinking in the sun, somewhere in a field of grain, among pregnant reaping women. Or an underwater spring will drown them in liquid, and they'll float around, sealed in the basement like sardines in a tin . . . But I'm really on the verge of downfall*, thought Sergey, gazing at the black and silent aperture. *I only just got here and I'm already ready to commit a crime. Oh, Leo Tolstoy, save me—this is your district, after all!*

Sergey ran headlong out of the room into the open air.

But out on the porch things felt even more dreary. A horse was nibbling at the dust-covered grass with utter disinterest. Mindless, disgusting chickens drank water out of the slops bucket. Still, the far-off fields were shining, flooded by sun. Fyodor is over there, working and probably wiping away the sweat with his sleeve. There are lanes walled and arched with wooden lattices, covered amply with new shoots and the thick leaves of grapevines; walking through them, you feel like you were walking down the hallway of your own apartment. Enormous bunches of grapes hanging from the inner arches beckon the eyes and lips, and the built-in cisterns, their water flowing along canals, offer charitable refreshment to limbs enervated by the daytime heat.

Sergey sat down on the stoop and took a book out of his pocket. Against the rounded edges of the surrounding landscape, the Gothic script seemed especially tiny, sharp, and tile-roofed.

A village woman spat upon seeing that the co-op was locked and asked Sergey to read her the piece of paper hanging on the door.

"Closed for dinner? He has no shame."

Meanwhile, Leocadia came into view on a cart at the gate of the co-op building. She was sitting on something rather suggestive and covered in straw. Sergey hurried to help her and held open the squeaking sides of the gate.

"No, no, don't look at me: this light is not to my advantage, the sun is so inappropriate." Leocadia pulled her scarf over her face and adjusted her short dress, covering the straw and putting her naked thighs out on display.

"You are more beautiful than Margarethe upon the straw."[29]

"Enough joking, I'm not your Margarethe. Oh, I get it, it's from your poems—Sergey Sergeyevich told me. Give me some to read—I love fun stuff. But I don't have any time now. Goodbye! Giddyup, beast!" Leocadia spurred on the horse.

"I beg you, please tell me how to get home!"

"Come on, didn't you take some kind of road to get to the shop here? You repulsive comedian."

"Yes, but I was terrified half to death by a dog."

"Young man, I see that you don't miss a beat: you even managed to work a dog in quite neatly. But aren't you afraid of me too? Anyway, if that's how it is, I'll give you a lift—but I am putting my trust in your decency."

Leocadia stretched out her naked leg, indicating to Sergey a spot at the edge of the cart. "People are evil—I haven't trusted anyone since I was fourteen. Giddyup, you beast! But who knows, maybe you have secret intentions too. After all, you didn't come here just to grow cold in solitude, did you? And what are you staring at me so intently for, you madman?"

"I'm looking at what you're sitting on. Isn't it pricking you?"

"I don't understand your ambiguities. One more word and I'll throw you off the cart."

"Oh no, it just seemed to me that you are sitting on the same thing I was recently sitting on, down in the vault . . ."

The eyes of Leocadia's husband, who had come out onto the porch to meet the cart as it drove up, encountered Sergey, roughly thrust off the cart by Leocadia's sharp heel.

"So you're already back from work?"

The husband nodded and withdrew back into the house.

"Where are you, My Innocence?" squawked Leocadia. "Come here, I can't manage on my own. Well, goodbye; just walk straight from here and then take a right. Wait—I saw you out the window when you were walking to the co-op but didn't stop you on purpose—I thought, let him have a stroll. In Minsk they used to say that I had a slight innate demonism. What

---

29 In the end of the first part of Goethe's *Faust*, Margarethe/Gretchen appears in a pile of straw in her prison cell.

do you think?" Leocadia grinned mysteriously and held out her hand to Sergey, so high up that it was obviously intended for a kiss.

"Oh, yes," Sergey recalled. "Fyodor Fyodorovich is having a party today. Perhaps you will come?"

"For me to go visit a young man? You must have lost your mind! What do you take me for?"

Leaving, Sergey saw My Innocence come out of the house, walk up to the cart, pull out the heavy sack from beneath the straw and, preceded by Leocadia, disappear into the inner quarters.

The church—a cube of the seventeenth century, with the columns of empire pinned to its outside—stayed behind. Sergey entered the fruit orchard that surrounded Fyodor's wing of the house.

There was little shade to be found here from the short and widely spaced apple trees, but this was the kind of orchard where one could let days drag on ponderously. Plus the place offered utter seclusion, since the village folk were forbidden from entering these grounds.

Comparing it with Peterhof, Sergey found that central Russia, where he was currently wandering, was a far more southern country.[30] One could lie down on the unmoist earth with no concern. There was no heather or lingonberry, tumbleweeds grew, and the earth lay in black circles beneath the apple trees.

Sergey strolled around among the white-smeared trunks. The aggravated apple branches sketched out complicated blue figures all over the sky. In the middle of the nursery, a little pond had been planted all round with shaggy willows.

When Sergey put his hand into the water, it turned out to be warm from the sun and redolent of apples. Two or three fruits floated in it, as if stewed. It looked like fruit punch. Farther off a lean-to had been built into a purple willow. In the corner was a bed of rags that smelled of Helen, but also a cheerful sourish smell, since piles of different colorful types of apples were rotting fragrantly nearby.

How fine it is to sit and go through papers—subscriptions, clippings— when there are apples spoiling in the desk drawer.

"Mister, you can't walk around here." Sergey awoke to an arm embracing him.

---

30 Peterhof is a suburb of St. Petersburg, known for its eponymous palace and elaborate gardens built by Peter the Great in the early eighteenth century.

"Maybe I'm not saying the right thing; you're my superior, of course," continued the gardener. "But they make us answer for this kind of thing. You understand, we have suisleppers here, various pinks, idareds, jonathons, goldens—lots of temptation."

"But, Comrade Ermolov, how can I get to the lean-to otherwise? Do you expect me to fly through the air? Only a winged devil can manage that. And why do you have a felt hat, Grisha? That's a rarity in the village."

Grisha sat down close to Sergey. "This hat was brought by a girl from Dolgy."

"From Dolgy? Isn't that where the Yasnaya Polyana house was sold off to?"

"Yes, but they'd taken it all apart brick by brick. So she brought the hat to the cobbler, see, and asked him to make winter boots out of it. But the cobbler felt bad. He likes me, so he gave me the hat, and the girl started yelling at him, but you can't take it off my head once it's on. The village mugs laugh, but I think it looks good. Too bad I'm not allowed to wear it into church. The ladies all have their bright kerchiefs, but the guys have to stand there with bare heads. Our priest is strict: he watches when the girls come up to the cross, and if he catches one of them, he'll go and whack her over the head with the cross and ream her out in front of the whole church: 'Dressing like a city girl! Skirts above the knee, legs swinging free. Beast! Mother Mary didn't go around like that!'"

"I'm sleepy, Grisha," answered Sergey. "I don't know where to put myself, it's so hot everywhere. I'm bored to tears, and Fyodor is still off at work."

"Go to the hayloft; it's nicer there than in the lean-to."

"All right—bye for now."

Sergey walked past the balcony. Fyodor's grandmother was sitting in the company of the landlady and another old lady. They were talking their talk, though the old lady was silent. This was evidently the old noble-woman taken to begging around the village, whom Fyodor used to call "The Spawn of Hell." The name stuck: Grandma also started calling her The Spawn, and the word had begun to seem rather tender. The Spawn would set out every morning to visit the neighboring houses, then come back home, sit down, and immediately fall asleep. Periodically, she'd be awakened and made to tell what she had been dreaming. She also read cards, promising the fulfillment of wishes, letters, and small quantities of money.

"Fyodor's friend's arrived." A voice carried down from the balcony. "And he seems to be well brought-up. Not like the mining expert—you say to him, 'wouldn't you like another serving of cold soup,' and he just says straight, 'Wouldn't I ever!' But we're not having dinner today; I'm sorry, Spawn, you should come tomorrow."

At the word "dinner" The Spawn woke up, started sputtering and assuring everyone that it had dreamed of a wedding: Grandma was being wed to the church elder.

The landlady noticed Sergey passing by. "You'd do better to promise a wedding to that one there."

"Him? He who gets married's a fool. She who gets married is a clever one." The Spawn pursed its lips. "All right now, young man, show yourself. Want to marry me? Never you mind that my teeth are gone; I have plenty of Jacks in my deck. The one I like least is Hearts; he's always lying down with the Queen of Clubs. But I'll take him up and throw him off to the side. You're lying over here, honey, far away, and there's a wish come true. As for the queen, maybe someone else will lie down with her."

The Spawn suddenly fell asleep in front of the bemused Sergey and displeased landlady, Makarovna. The conversation shifted to other topics.

"Makarovna, did you plant peas today?"

"Just a few. Oh, and Arisha came by to see you recently, she was offering butter for ninety kopecks. Upped it by a dime. They say the Shitov lady's buying up all the butter—says as soon as her husband sells off the apples she'll settle up."

"Weasel."

"As if there's any way to get along with the womenfolk around here? Peasants is what they are. Your Fyodor's right not to get married to anyone here. My deceased husband always kept an eye out—he'd buy a girl fruit drops, hand them over: 'And now tell me how much is three pounds of raisins at thirty kopecks. Don't get nervous, do have some more. And now, twelve feet of calico at eleven kopecks.' But where are the kopecks now? Sorry, but this won't do for us. Back then everything was cheap: thirty-five pounds of meat for a ruble and twenty. Where are the fruit drops now? . . . But you and I need to negotiate." She turned to Sergey. "Are you staying here long?"

"Three days."

"In a Tula hotel you'd be paying five rubles a day, so, I won't ask for much."

"But he's Fyodor's guest," Grandma intervened.

"All the same. He's walking around on the balcony, the floor is getting worn out, and he'll be sleeping in the room."

"No, Fyodor wrote that he'd sleep in the hayloft."

"Ah, you Peterhofers! You economize on everything. You're lucky to be staying with me."

At the word "peasants" The Spawn woke up again and said, "I don't remember anything."

"How's that?" Sergey was curious. "They say that memory, on the contrary, gets sharper in old age. Can it be that incomprehensible night really approacheth?"

The Spawn spewed slobber. Her mouth proved to be not only toothless but also gumless: it was a brown hole unbounded by lips. Sounds emanated from it: *Olee and Polee ran around the green lea, while little Lida Vorontsova lies long since in the grave.*

"What are you doing waltzing around in front of me? Get into my deck—I'll shuffle you all alive." The Spawn threw itself at Sergey.

Sergey felt slender, made of cardboard, with a blue shirt on his back; a bit ragged and with dog-eared corners, since he was often played with.

Sergey lowered his eyes. Like every true Jack, instead of legs he repeated his upper half upside-down—like a reflection in water, or antipodes living on the rounded terrestrial globe, like a doubled cumulative paunch of Jacks. It became clear to him that his Jack was currently living in America, just as legless as he.

Grandma explained. "Go on now, don't vex her for no reason."

Sergey made his way to the hayloft and threw himself down on the hay.

The straw roof of the hay barn was supported by various beams and planks. Some were unstripped, and the bark on them shone white. A branch with leaves hung from one beam. The sky showed in the spaces between, and the whole hayloft was seized from outside by the heat of the sun.

In the half-darkness the flies lost their fervor and made do with peaceful walking back and forth over the face of the sleeper.

If you lie down on the floor in the Hermitage, in the tent-roofed hall,[31] the polished floors—which are ordinarily more noticeable than everything else—disappear from sight. The pictures in the side cases also become

---

31 The Hermitage is a famous museum in the center of St. Petersburg. The "tent-roofed hall" (with decorative exposed rafters) houses the collection of seventeenth-century Dutch painting.

unintelligible, with their hollows and swamps, mills and streams. You can get your fill of admiring the ceiling until the museum guard comes and asks you to stand up.

Slippers shuffled, and Grandma appeared with fresh sheets folded into quarters.

"Come down for a sec, honey: you and Fedya have to make your bed while it's still light out. Oh, so I don't forget: swear to me right now . . ."

"What, Grandma, you're demanding oaths now? What for?"

"That you won't smoke in here. This close to disaster! The landlady will demand three thousand, you'll see."

In fact, in addition to hay, the hayloft was full of ungristed grain and straw. It all glinted golden in the places where the sun fell through the wattled walls.

"It'll light up so fast you won't have time to get out," continued Grandma, roughly tossing the white sheets onto the high hay.

Sergey placed a mirror, soap, and a razor on the bottom of an overturned barrel. "Will Fyodor be back soon?"

Grandma left the barn, shielding herself from the sun with a skeletal hand. Her transparent skin showed yellow through the bones. "Soon enough now. He always comes back around six. I'll go set up the samovar. And thank you for the present."

Sergey perched at the foot of the hay bed. A Tula landscape could be seen through the open barn doors. Children were digging around in the ditch. A five-year-old boy was spitting in the face of a three-year-old girl. She started bawling after every round of spittle, but then, having wiped off her face, began waiting curiously for the next one. A towheaded kid insistently waved a very long whip above his head. A loop formed in the air, and a slapping sound resounded. He'd rashly hit a nearby apple tree, and the fruits were plopping to the ground. From outside the hayloft

CHAPTER FIVE

came the sound of chomping—a hobbled horse, free from field work, capered lamely, pining for fresher grass.

Sergey became terrified. He reviewed his grandmother's tales of evil men and Motenka: a face covered in pockmarks; he uses creams and powders himself with Gioconda powder. He goes to Tula and sells tires there. Doesn't drink, doesn't smoke, doesn't swear, but "thirsts for new sensations," and thus works as butcher for the village. When slaughtering a calf, he first sings out, knife poised at the childlike, awkward neck:

Are you still alive, my dear old lady?
I'm alive too—hello to you, hello![32]

and with that "hello" sticks the knife in. When he came into the shop, Motenka demanded cocoa.

"You've grown rich, Mitri Petrovich—will you have a drink?"

"Lumphead, only village people drink cocoa—in the city they sniff it." And Motenka opened the box right away, grabbed a pinch of cocoa, and snorted. His brown sneezing filled the shop. Everyone stepped back. Motenka was triumphant. "That'll put hair on your chest! There's a new sensation!"

Ever since then he's always carried the box with him. He used to offer it to the ladies. They would lick a finger and taste the dark powder, but found it bitter.

"So you feel bitterness even before you're married?"[33] And Motenka would try to lean in for a kiss.

---

32 Well-known opening lines from "A Letter to My Mother" (1924), by the popular poet Sergei Esenin (1895–1925).

33 Motenka refers to the Russian tradition of shouting "bitter, bitter" to the bride and groom at a wedding, encouraging the couple to "sweeten" the atmosphere with a kiss.

He could dance the foxtrot up and down, but his knees had recently started to give out, and now all the girls refused to dance with him despite all his city-boy catchphrases: *I heard down at the station that the chicks down here are cheap, the best girls. All the dandies are decked out in their djama-jean jackets; all the chicks are dazzled, the favorites.*

"What are you dreaming about, Seryozha?" Fyodor said, coming into the barn.

"About Motenka, Fyodor."

"Boy, some dream. He's an alien element in society."

"I want to meet him."

"Oh, no, don't compromise us in the eyes of the whole village. You'll leave soon enough, but I'll be stuck disentangling myself."

"I'm afraid for you, Fyodor."

"No, you'd better be afraid for yourself. This all comes from being idle. You couldn't even arrange your things decently: there's a whole geology class in your suitcase, dirty socks next to the toothbrush, a fissure between layers filled with fragments of various minerals. You should see how considerately Fil d'Écosse treats his things: he threads his cufflinks into his shirtsleeves with respect, values the knot of his tie, ties his bootlaces with dignity."

Fyodor took a twig to tease fat Fingal, who had loped over to greet him.

"Fyodor, you brazen reptile, what are you doing with my poems?"

"I want to teach the hound to sing this song—they say that the blind have very fine hearing. But you're right about my being brazen. Just ask around the village. After I got here, I once walked around wearing white Moscow trousers, and everyone I ran into spat."

"Wait, Fyodor: first and foremost we need to work out the day's program. Two excursions: to Kulikovo Pole and to Yasnaya Polyana;[34] then a fundamental introduction to village life;[35] and the rest of the time for relaxation."

"Fine. Kulikovo is about forty miles from here. I'll get a dandy—that's what they call motorbikes around here—and sit you in the sidecar. Only, you won't be relaxing anytime soon. In honor of your arrival I've decided to bathe. Come and do some work; got to get you used to it."

---

34 Kulikovo Field (Kulikovo Pole) is the site of a legendary fourteenth-century victory of the Russians (led by Grand Prince Dmitry Donskoy of Moscow) over the Mongol forces who controlled much of Russia at that time.

35 Egunov pokes fun at another literary commonplace of the late nineteenth century (and into the Soviet 1920s): urban writers going on ethnographic expeditions to Russian villages to document the authentic life of "the people."

Fyodor pointed to his face and arms, all dusty and dirty. Clay was smeared all over his coarse official uniform.

Sergey's work began: that is, the ritual of washing Fyodor. This took place in the little meadow next to the hayloft. Sergey dragged ringing buckets out of the well. Soaped-up Fyodor splashed and huffed and puffed. There was even some snuffling; but Sergey's fears were washed away with the water.

When Fyodor took the towel off his eyes, his boss was sitting before him in a horse-drawn carriage, on his way home after riding around the work sites.

Fyodor made the introductions. "This is my friend Sergey, and this is my Adored Management."

"Fyodor Fyodorovich, buddy," said The Adored. "I'm sorry. I won't be having dinner with you today. But here's an urgent bit of work for you. I need it by tomorrow without delay. It's a trifling matter: copy down the data, sketch out a cross-section of the prospecting shaft, its dimensions and the direction of the cross-cut. The inclining headways too."

Fyodor tried to protest.

"I have 105 bell-shafts," he said. "How can I do all that by tomorrow? Why didn't you think of this before, my Adored?"

"Fyodor Fyodorovich, I myself work until I'm unconscious," The Adored objected, plucking at his goatee. "I don't spare my own strength, all for the socialist fatherland. I need it in twenty-four hours! Mobilize whoever you want—your grandma, your friend—but I need it done. I, as they say, love to work," and The Adored looked straight at Sergey.

Sergey rattled his bucket and looked the other way.

Clearly, Fyodor's Adored Management was thinking, *Something's going on here; he's silent, but I've heard he said something in a foreign tongue and went to work along with Fyodor. But would an Englishman really go writing poems? He must be a* rabkor *or a* selkor.[36]

Bidding farewell to Sergey, The Adored said, "If I may, your respected . . ."

"What?"

"Your respected hand, I said. Not a mere hand, but pure gold! Of course, I've read your work."

---

36 The Adored Management refers to new types of journalists instituted in the early Soviet period: a *rabkor*, or worker-correspondent, was a citizen of working-class origin working in Soviet journalism; a *selkor*, or village correspondent, was the source of reports from the newly collectivizing villages.

Sergey dropped the bucket with the water. Fyodor leapt over to him, and his bare feet wound up in a frozen puddle, which was, however, quickly absorbed into the grass.

"There's your adoring public, Seryozhka. But we're having people over today, so there'll be no dinner—all the money went for the party . . . And I'm starving to death. Do you have any money?"

"Only for the train back."

"Now there's an idea: I'll take that money, and you won't leave and will stay here with me for ten years."

"Why ten? What if I want to live with you for twenty years?"

"No one in Peterhof will recognize you if you go back as a forty-six-year-old!"[37]

"That's true. So I'll have to leave in three days—then they'll recognize me. That is, in two days—today is already ending."

"So quickly, alas, pass by the days of happiness," crooned Fyodor, slapping Sergey across the nose with his wet towel.[38]

The day really was already waning. The samovar standing on the grass grew rosy, lit up by the sunset. Grandma was fanning it with a boot. The animals mooed, coming back from the fields.

Figures appeared out of the bushes, fortyish and clearly already soused. Georgie Gusynkin came carrying a weighty crate behind them.

"Woe is us," they wailed. "All the chicks are busy. Fil d'Écosse is leaving today, so they're having some kind of girls' night. We're all invited. But since we already promised you, we've come here first, and then we can go over to their place with the whole gang."

Grandma hurried to set the table inside. The crate was deposited onto the table.

"How come you're not eating the sprats? And it looks like the vodka's flowing weakly here too?"

"I can't stand sprats," Sergey said in self-justification.

"After dinner, it makes sense—you're full, I guess. Then it's not bad to just cool off with a beer."

---

37 This is one of the more direct references to Mikhail Kuzmin's poem "The Trout Breaks the Ice" (1928). Kuzmin was a close friend of Egunov, and the poem is an important subtext for the entire novel (see introduction).

38 Fyodor paraphrases the *Herbstlied no. 4* (*Autumn Song*) by Felix Mendelssohn (words by Nicholas Lenau), popularized in Russia in the late nineteenth century.

The co-op operator carefully chewed the oily sprats (a fishtail was slightly visible in the corner of his mouth), smacked his lips, and repeated: "He who wants to live long had better eat slowly. Each bite must be chewed twenty-four times, once for every hour in the day."

"*Pour me a glass, there's no wine in it, if there's no wine, then there's no happiness, in wine is passion and depth,*" Big Al sang out.[39]

"Well, Fyodor, let's drink to Dunya! Or is it Domasha?"

"To everyone," answered Fyodor.

"We can't drink to everyone at once. This glass is for Fenya, and that one's for Dunya."

The co-op operator began to count them out, and they ended up with eight glasses. Fyodor's hands began shaking.

"Don't try to argue, just submit." The co-op operator poured some vodka into the beer. "I know what I'm doing. Do you know the joke about 'calm down'? 'Calm down, I'm shooting, says the photographer'—not bad, dodger. And then there's . . ."

Big Al in turn told a joke about life in Romania. Fyodor blushed. His departure wasn't noticed: the conversation had already shifted to how one time, toward morning, they were making hooch out of buckwheat porridge and poured in the water left over from dishwashing.

In the dark bedroom Grandma was pressing a wet towel to Fyodor's forehead where he lay. Sergey got some pyramidon tablets.

"Don't tell them, Seryozha. I'll be right there."

"It's fine. Just rest a bit, they won't notice."

"You should go back out and make conversation; otherwise it'll be awkward."

Out on the balcony the candles had been lit and were besieged by evening midges. Toasts were underway, and a shaggy moth quivered on the tabletop in a pool of spilled beer.

"Oh, anguish!" howled the co-op operator, tracing the Mediterranean Sea with a finger. "Once upon a time there was life, and then life passed away. There was *La Belle Hélène* in Karetnyi Riad, in the Moscow Hermitage . . . Medyntseva was singing then, she would come out in head-to-toe stockings, with *jais de verre*[40] here and here . . . Her voice was a bit hoarse but jagged. . . That was a good country, the ancient Greeks: swans everywhere, little ladies, blue sky . . . Orestes would have walked around with no stockings on at all,

---

39 "Pour Me a Glass," a 1910s-era romance by Lev Drizo.

40 *Jais de verre*—probably jet beads made of glass, which decorate nineteenth-century versions of Helen's costume in Jacques Offenbach's *La Belle Hélène*.

carrying a stick . . . And plenty of plump ones wherever you look: *Dzy! La! La! Dzy! La! La!*"

"If I may," Sergey interrupted. "This year in the Hermitage they did an experiment: they rolled barbells along the parquet—carefully, so as not to hit any of the malachite vases—and dumbbells, you know, those round discs, around twenty pounds apiece: they screw onto the barbells. A crew of young men in athletic wear came in. They started looking at the paintings and bench-pressing the barbells. Scientists jotted down the influence of *The Last Supper* on muscular energy. And as far as the ancient Greeks are concerned, Sergey Sergeyevich, you're in the wrong—they couldn't have had any sugar. That came only after America was discovered . . ."

"Aw, don't go rubbing my nose in your Americas. I graduated from the Moscow Institute of Commerce . . . I don't know about anybody else, but the Greeks had more than they could handle . . . I feel I should have been born on marble, but here you can just drop off the face of the earth, and my wife—you know, she left me. You might think: look at me, the picture of health! but maybe I'm a total bundle of nerves . . . Where are the Volkonskys, where are the Sheremetevs?[41] We've all been crippled."

"I'm twenty years old and a crown awaits me."[42] Big Al winked. "But where's Fyodor Fyodorovich?"

"My wife left me too," Sergey hastened to add. "It was a strange case—it's like I heard about it somewhere, or maybe it actually happened to me. The thing is, I have a wife."

"That's not so surprising." Big Al took a gulp from his wineglass. "And she's probably young, no?"

"Oh yes—you know, somewhere around forty-eight."

"Ah, that's why you're so serious."

"So listen: I go to the bank, and there's a bunch of barred windows, and a sign up top: 'Before you sell your bonds, check to see if you're a winner.' I ask, 'Where's the exchange register?' 'What do you need it for?—are you selling or do you want to put down for a loan?' 'Well actually, I want to exchange a forty-eight-year-old for two twenty-four-year-olds.'"

The co-op operator and Big Al snorted through their beer.

"Fyodor Fyodorovich's got quite a friend here! No wife would dump a guy like you."

---

41 Famous old Muscovite noble families.
42 Big Al quotes from Edmond Rostand's *The Eaglet*, a popular romantic play about the young Napoleon II.

"But get this—she *did* dump me."

"Ah, so you get how it is, brother! It's a real insult!" The co-op operator pounded himself on the chest. "You have to understand: all the people who've made it to ninety were, essentially, married. I'll show you the statistics later."

"Yes, yes," continued Sergey. "I was just getting ready to come here, and she up and dumped me."

"How come?" Big Al got interested. "You're young, and you look pretty cultured."

"She dumped me because of lines." Sergey groaned, pouring his companions full glasses of vodka. "We had it all, a chicken in every pot, I mean every pot—everything to our heart's content. But she couldn't handle all the lines; she gets these terrible urges . . . 'How dare you,' she would say. 'How dare you disrupt my work? I really need to know where the people in number seven got trout for dinner yesterday; I have to find out why Shurochka got smacked up by her fancy-man.' I was getting ready to leave to come out here and she kept asking: 'So, out there in the Tula district, they have lines there?' 'No,' I'd say. 'Out there the co-op is kept by my best friend and namemate, Sergey Sergeyevich.' 'Well, then I'm not going,' she said, and, there you go, she dumped me just like that."

All three of them slumped over the table.

"We're dumped and unlucky," groaned the co-op operator. "Fil d'Écosse is out there cooling off with the ladies, and Leocadia is at home sleeping with her Innocence. She's put her head down on the pillow, closed her pale little eyes, and gone to sleep, my little dove."

Then they started singing, drawling and melancholy, looking out into the darkness surrounding the balcony. The co-op operator jerkily picked out unheard-of chords on the guitar: *They're falling like tears, the drops of vapor, the shades of two moments, two faded roses. There was so much happiness, like drops in the sea, like leaves on the gray earth, but all that's left is two, just two faded roses in the crystal blue.*[43]

"Ho-ho!" Somebody whooped, and veiny hairy arms reached out of the darkness toward the table. The bottle was knocked over, and the shattering glass jingled.

"Let's get on over to the girls," bawled the miners.

The arms seized the co-op operator and Big Al.

"Fedya and I will catch up to you in a second," said Sergey.

---

43 From a 1920s romance by Samuil Pokrass, "Two Roses."

The whole vision disappeared into the darkness.

Then Fyodor came crawling out of the room, the towel still on his head. Grandma trudged along after him, turned centenarian by the sleepless evening.

"Wait, Fedya, let me clear up."

"I'm starving to death, Grandma."

"Yes, we're all hungry, but who boozed up all our money on the party? What will we eat tomorrow? These leftovers?"

"Do you feel better, Fyodor?" asked Sergey.

"I'm completely fine now, and I really don't like being sick anyway."

Fyodor put his hands down on the table and immediately picked them up again. The sticky table smelled like a city bar: peas and dried fish.

Fyodor undid his turban and began to swing it around to drive away the motionless air.

They decided to carry out the boss's orders. A kerosene lamp was lit and the prospecting journals laid out across the table.

"No, Gram, damn your eyes, you can't do anything right, even if I did mobilize you—I can't work with wobbly lines. Go warm up the samovar instead."

Her arms full of kindling, Grandma muttered, "Will there really be a war with China?"

"And you're completely talentless, Sergey. Is that really supposed to be a bell-shaft? You know what: why don't you read to me—drafting is almost completely mechanical work. What books did you bring along?"

"Only three. One is really terrifying; it says that the earth is near at hand. The other one you know already, and the third is a Russian translation."

"Oh, the one we started reading together back in Peterhof? The little yellow one? But for now, read me the translation; it'll be easier to understand."

Ossian, Kisser, and Fingal crawled out from under the porch and settled down like a disheveled rug at Fyodor's feet. Vertical lines materialized on the paper.

"You know what, Fyodor? You should draw yourself in, there at the bottom of the pit."

"Don't bother me, Seryozhka. I'm working."

"Fine," answered Sergey. "But finish up quick, or there won't be enough night for all 105 pits."

"You're a co-op operator too, Seryozhka. I said that on purpose to tease The Adored. I know his character—he's always rushing; everything is always a race. I had all the sketches ready ahead of time, and I'll just finish these two right now."

"Oh, you're a crafty one! He takes after me," said Grandma, kissing Fyodor, and it became clear that they really did resemble one another—all the more since Fyodor was still yellow from his recent headache.

"Your friend reads well. I could cry out of pity for Margarethe, and that guy, what's his name?—he's so bad. Anyway, the samovar's hot, kids. And I suppose there's no way around it—I'll drink down a cuppa along with you."

"I wouldn't say no myself, Gram. And I can spin such succulent tales that even Fingal would blush."

"Hey, parasites! Come eat up."

Fyodor threw a piece of bread up into the air for the enormous hounds, who leapt toward the balcony ceiling.

Grandma surreptitiously crossed herself as she sat down to table.

"Why do you have devils in your eyes, Fyodor?" asked Sergey.

"I don't know; because of the pyramidon, probably, or maybe because of the guests, or your arrival, or Margarethe. Today turned out to be so unusual—nothing but disorder from morning on. Or maybe because I get attacks of antireligious feeling in the evenings."

And Fyodor, sipping tea, began to act out a funeral: he sang "Lord, Have Mercy" in a nasal voice and then slipped directly into the funeral march. This meant that church burials had been replaced by civilian ones.

Grandma perked up at the sound of Chopin. "Back at our place in Kozikhinsky Lane the actors used to sing for Easter. Sometimes even the ones from the Bolshoi Theater. They would put on such a show that you couldn't make out a word, and it's only later you'd figure out they must have been singing 'The Angel Wails.'"[44]

"That really suits your talent," Sergey pointed out to Fyodor, who was yowling with all his strength.

Having finished the part with the trumpets, Fyodor started a new conversation. "In church, everyone's passing along their candles toward the icons; you get tapped on the shoulder, the guy standing in front of you puts the candle at the wrong icon and the one who passed the candle curses . . ."

---

44 A prayer from the Orthodox liturgy. The Bolshoi Theater is Moscow's premier theater for opera and ballet performances.

"Don't pass the cup, this one's for you. It's no good for him to drink such strong tea, he's still a little boy, and it's already late."

"Don't inhibit me, please: I turned twenty-two last week," squealed Fyodor, pretending to play a flute. Afterward, finishing on a high note, he fell on his grandmother with kisses. "Oh my old lady, damn your eyes, you really believe in yochimania?"

"In what? Yochimania?"

"In Joachim and Anna."[45]

"How could I not believe? Everyone believes in them."

"Well, I don't."

"Oh, you scoundrel! Look out, you'll meet your own Anna one day and then you'll start believing."

"But I haven't yet, even though I've met various Dunyas here, and plenty of Marys in the city. So your yochimania's not true."

"Don't argue, you've got your whole life ahead of you. You'll definitely meet your Anna."

"And what if I meet both—Anna and Joachim?"

"You mean if she's married? Only you would wag your tongue like that. You'd do better to head for the hayloft. It's late already."

"Good night, Grandma," said Fyodor and Sergey.

They had to walk in the dark around the sloping meadow between the house and the hayloft.

"Fedya, should I close the doors?" asked Sergey, walking into the barn.

"Yes, we'd better—otherwise the parasites on the laboring masses will crawl in during the night."

Sergey pulled the two ungainly halves of the barn doors toward himself with both hands. It became even darker, but they weren't allowed to light a light in the hayloft.

"Where are you, Fyodor?"

"Over here. Walk toward my voice." Fyodor hallooed like in the woods.

Sergey crawled onto the hay, and his clambering brought the bed linens, which Grandma had laid out so carefully, into total disarray: the sheet ended up beneath the hay and the pillow at their feet. But perhaps this happened also because Fyodor, lying on the hay, had started doing Swedish gymnastics before bed.

---

45 In the Roman Catholic, Anglican, and Orthodox traditions, according to the apocryphal Gospel of James, St. Joachim and St. Anne are the parents of Mary, mother of Christ.

"All right, now let's lie here quietly and talk. What should we talk about?"

"About women, of course; that's what we're supposed to do: you and I are young men, after all. I have a vision," said Fyodor. "A leather-lined study, soft, shaded lamps. The husband is sitting at his desk, leafing through a book. His wife sits on the settee; she is in evening dress—they're about to go to the opera or to visit friends at a fun party. A long skirt and a high collar, up to the chin. She's at least thirty-eight. After all, the little Marys and Sashas are such dummies, I have no idea what to do with them. The better dressed a woman is, the better. But God, I want a smoke."

"Yes, but we promised the landlady. Maybe we should go sleep inside?"

"No, how could we! Seryozha, just think how fine it is to never once be indoors for the whole summer. We'll be locked up in boxes plenty all winter. But have you noticed how, here in the hayloft, the air is carousing through the wattled walls? Your face is cool, but the hay keeps your body warm. In socialism there won't be any indoors at all. I feel like I can already feel the fresh air of the future. You know, Seryozha, one time Volodya and I were at the races in Moscow. I know, I know, all those jockeys and their caps; but the main thing was the horses, strong three-year-olds, four-year-olds, they were straining forward. Will you quit your whining, Seryozha—isn't the hay nice?"

"Yes," answered Sergey. "It smells, and it pricks. I can distinguish beneath myself clover shoots, timothy grass, ribwort, and dandelion."

"This is the third cutting this summer already," said Fyodor. "I've started shaving more often. I have to do it at least once a week now."

"I have to do it every other day or even every day, but my skin can't take it: I get cuts or grazes every time. But tell me, Fyodor, what do you feel when you're at the bottom of the bell-shaft? Why are you tossing and turning? Maybe we should go and sleep in the yard, under the open sky?"

"No, Seryozha. I don't like the space above; it oppresses me."

"Did you notice, Fedya? We're not smoking, and it lends a certain tang to our conversation."

"I don't know, Seryozha. That's you just digging around like always. I don't think like that; I prefer math."

"Whatever do you mean, Fedenka? This relates to the 'theory of infinitesimals' too, after all."

"What, is that like your 'theory of adventures'?"

"Yes. You see, sometimes I have to leave Peterhof to go to meetings. My fellow travelers; the cows out the window; the hues of the sky. Then, when

I'm back home, I have to write up a report. So here's my Peterhof case of the twenty-first of June . . ."

"These damned infinitesimals, there's enough of them here to kill a man! . . ."

"Why are you swearing at me, Fyodor?"

"It's not you—there's masses of fleas here. We'd never have enough Persian powder to treat all this hay. Well, go on, but with more details. You must have different cases every month?"

"Right. This one's titled 'A Trip to the City and Back.'

"*On the way there*: the train car is occupied almost exclusively by either a vocational school or a foster home. Little girls and boys of various ages, two teachers. They must be coming back from an excursion—they're tanned and hungry (talking about the cafeteria). By the window sits one of the eldest: he's already old enough for a suit coat, gray, and beneath it a lightweight button-down shirt with an open neck and some kind of sash on the chest, with a green ribbon stuck through it, and he's arranging a dispute, as he puts it, speaking to the whole car in a booming voice: 'Of course, at your age there can't be any serious feelings. Maybe you feel some sparks from time to time; like for instance, you're working on your homework and you want it to come out as good as possible . . .'

"The girls adjust their dresses with self-satisfied expressions. The smallest boys make literary interjections. The eyes of the seventeen-year-old author of the dispute search the audience, he is making faces for the younger ones . . .

"*On the way back*: the train hasn't left yet. Catty-corner across from me sits a young worker guy (big coarse hands, a thoroughly pockmarked face, around nineteen or twenty, really nothing to write home about). Next to me is another guy of about the same appearance. They're talking with each other rather coolly, buying penny candies and gnawing on them. Suddenly they become animated . . . 'Look there, that's your super,' says my neighbor . . . The guy across from him brightens, leaps up, and presses his nose to the window. A man appears on the platform by the window; he's maybe thirty, wearing a shabby army-type jacket and carrying a threadbare overcoat . . ."

"I wouldn't pay attention to such insignificant details," said Fyodor.

"Fedenka, you can find adventures everywhere."

"A fine adventure; there's nothing you can say, though, really: you were just observing."

"Of course—but that's enough for me. Afterward I spend a whole week composing the past and future, pushing them together."

"If you're an adventurer, Seryozha, before we know it you'll probably go and get cozy with the local kulaks."

"Yes, Fyodor. Sometimes I don't eat for days in order to achieve my goal; sometimes I sleep all day long."

"Well, I love my work—I'm building the future, after all."

"And it's lovely, Fyodor. But here's another one of my adventures for you: the workers' Sunday day off in Peterhof . . . The end of the day. A meadow, a brass orchestra. Some of them are dancing the shimmy. The academics are looking on in disdain. A bit further off is the co-op automobile. They're selling buns with hotdogs inside . . . Oh, the fleas really are dreadful here . . ."

"It's from the parasites on the laboring masses: they sneak in during the day to lie in the hay."

"So, you see, Fyodor, I love people."

"Your head is completely clogged with junk, Seryozhka. We need to do a serious purge."

"Of course, that's just what I love: you root around in the thick of it all and find what you're looking for. And when you love, you somehow get all emptied out. You go to an unknown place, even just a mile away—and you have no idea what kind of people and places you'll find there, but you'll find something. And when you first arrive it can be depressing, but then you get used to it and don't notice anymore."

"Being determines consciousness," added Fyodor.

"Yes, Fedya, you won't even notice that at some point you just die. This afternoon, beneath the apple tree, through my sleep, I felt the green air filled with twittering."

"I also dozed off, in the cart on my way back from work," noted Fyodor. "And I woke up all covered in flies and gadflies. The bastards, did they think I was a corpse, or a lump of sugar?"

Sergey shuddered. "How do you know about the sugar, Fyodor?"

"Huh?"

"No, never mind, I didn't mean anything."

"What do you mean?"

"No, I just wanted to say how much I want a smoke."

"That goes without saying, but why did you shudder, Seryozha? There's something going on. You said yourself that you have no secrets from me, and here you don't want to tell me about a silly little thing like this." Fyodor drew away, displeased.

"Fedya, listen, this is more of a social problem."

"And you think a social problem doesn't impact me? What an irresponsible element you are, Seryozhka."

Sergey, hesitating, told him. Fyodor, indignant, exhaled heavily and calculated.

"What's tomorrow? Saturday. So the day after tomorrow is Sunday. Excellent."

"I don't think it's excellent: by then I'll have to leave."

Fyodor jumped up suddenly and rustled down through the hay.

"She rose, Seryozha, she rose!" he cried, throwing open the gate. White stripes of moonlight fell into the hayloft. Everything outside was dancing from moonlit cheer.

Fyodor and Sergey, without getting dressed, ran out into the yard and, standing in their shirts under the apple trees, began fumigating the moon. She answered their streams of smoke with sweet smiles. Bedazzled, Sergey tripped; first his unaccustomed foot got poked by something, then, hand-like, but less flexibly, it seized hold of something round.

"Look how many of them have fallen here, Fedya."

"Drop it, that's a Ponyavin, they're really sour and not worth eating—let's go over there."

The Arcade apples really were sweet, big and white, like the moon. Fyodor crawled bowlegged beneath the tree, his shirt occasionally touching the ground. Suddenly standing up, he did a pirouette, flashing his bare knee, and flung an apple at the moon.

"If only we could taste her— damn her eyes!"

They heard the apple plop down somewhere a ways off.

"Well, and now to bed, to bed, Seryozha! It's well enough for you, but I have to go to work tomorrow. Enough of this fooling around."

The doors of the hayloft closed again, and the ascension to the high berth began anew. But since this was taking place rather friskily, and the streaks of moonlight penetrated only indistinctly through the wattled barn walls, the sheets got permanently entangled with the hay.

"Hell if I know what's going on, it's poking me from all sides. I've even got grass in my nose."

"Ah, you Peterhofer, you can't appreciate life in the country. But that's enough, now, good night."

Fyodor threw an armful of straw in Sergey's face. Sputtering and snorting, Sergey responded in kind.

But the night was not destined to be peaceful: the doors creaked as they were opened, and they heard the striking of a match.

"Don't light up, who's there? Ah, Grisha Ermolov. I'll come down, hang on."

Lit up by a match, the gardener in his felt hat was seized from the darkness—he was holding out a paper to Fyodor.

"Faiginyu, Faiginyu's coming," exclaimed Fyodor, holding the telegram. "How come you're not jumping for joy, Seryozha? Does it upset you?"

"Not at all. I'm happy for you, but you must agree, Fyodor, that I have no reason to dance: I have yet to make your mother's acquaintance."

"We'll set out now for Tula to meet the morning train. I couldn't meet you because you didn't send a telegram. But let's go, quick—we'll take some tins and have our breakfast in the open fields, seasoned by the fresh spirit of the morning. Hey, Grisha, saddle us up."

"What's your mama like?" asked Sergey, already in the charabanc and hurriedly buttoning up the clothes he'd just pulled on. "There are all kinds of mothers: moms, mommies, mummies, mamas."

"No, I'm not going to tell you anything about Faiginyu; let it be yet another adventure for you—rack your brains over it." Fyodor whipped up the horse so strongly that Sergey nearly fell out of the carriage.

"What's her name and patronymic?"

"I won't tell you anything, wait till morning. Oh, well—you can always call her Comrade Stratelates."

"Yes, but then it won't be clear whether I'm talking to her or to your Grandma or to you."

"All the better—after all, we're all one and the same. Our last name is Georgian; there was some great-great-grandfather. That's where I get my slender waist and sharp nose."

"Are you a good dancer, Fyodor?"

"I can't stand dancing. Anyway, all of your fancy salon business has been outdated for a while now."

"Of course, down with the Grand Rond.[46] Does your la mère look like you?"

Fyodor didn't answer, confidently driving the horse forward into the darkness. Indeed, the entire visible horse consisted of her croup alone.

---

46 The Grand Rond is a public park in Toulouse, France, that dates back to the 1750s.

CHAPTER SIX

She was lifting her tail, and this recalled the lining of a coat or jacket, when one suddenly discovers a dryish horsehair sticking out through the material on one's chest.

Sergey was cold.

Meanwhile, taking advantage of the moon's absence, the stars came out brightly. The immense luminaries shone pink, confident in their place and their future. As usual, they divided the heavens neatly into the required constellations. The small fry, on the contrary, couldn't seem to hold their ground and kept falling, as is often the case in August.

"Are you looking at the stars again, Seryozha? You know, I don't really care about them. It's strange, because the stars are, along with the Soviet Union, the only place not controlled by world capital. By rights I really ought to love them, but I can't seem to make myself care."

"Why make yourself? You're going along the street, and a star is shining up there above the fifth story. One minute you're looking down at your feet—there are traces of somebody's nose-blowing; and the next minute you look up and there they are winking at you. But you're wrong anyway, Fedya: capital is encroaching on the stars, too."

"Do you mean the interplanetary rocketships? That's not going to happen anytime soon, anyway. Capital'll go kaput before then, and our little planet will go running around the sun even more cheerfully; or maybe she herself will turn into the sun, and everything will start orbiting around her. Her form will change: instead of circular she'll turn five-pointed. All of these Marses and Jupiters and Venuses will have to get renamed. Though we do already have planet Vladilen."[47]

---

47 Vladilen is short for Vladimir Ilyich Lenin. Fyodor is not entirely correct: in 1916, astronomers discovered a small asteroid and named it (852) *Wladilena* in honor of Vladimir Ilyich.

"Right. I wanted to tell you, Fyodor: Rothschild bought one of those newly discovered planets—some Vesta or Juno or Ceres—and named it Rachel after his daughter."

"But who'd he buy it from?"

"An astronomer."

"Venal beasts and scoundrels. Giddyup, beast." Fyodor urged on the horse.

"Look, Fyodor, there's the Little Dipper, and the North Star—Peterhof's that way. But there, look, such a clear clearing: lots of stars close together, lighting up even the dark spaces between."

"Tula's that way too, to the north of us. Faiginyu is probably just leaving Moscow now. The Kursk train station, a porter, the public perched somehow or other on the benches . . . She's wearing a fancy silk coat. Right now she must be looking at the porter's brass badge and trying to memorize the number."

"I know, Fyodor. I went into third class at the Kursk station to get hot water . . . They still say 'third class' . . . Everyone looked at me; there was a big bright rose on the side of my potbellied teapot."

"Are you cold, Seryozha? Here, put on my jacket."

"No, no, don't take it off. I'm from the north, after all. I'm actually really hot without any jacket; it's almost like back in the hayloft."

"Now the hayloft is empty. I don't remember: did we close the barn door? Fingal and Ossian have probably gotten in and are rolling around in our sheets. They must be all toasty, damn them."

"How could he have sold it? Was he really hurting for money? In Moscow once at the flea market I saw an old man, very *bon ton*, selling off his good-for-nothing star. Evidently he'd been a senator at some point."[48]

"No, Fyodor, it's something else. I think he was selling it off so easily because he didn't love it. That makes sense—I mean, this astronomer was a professional. The girl typist feels nauseated as she takes the lid off her typewriter: she knows that she's doomed to clicking away for the next six hours, and this dry tap-tap reminds her better than anything else of her thirty-one years of loneliness, no matter how often she officially states that she's only twenty-eight. The armchair philosopher turns the book in his hands with revulsion, surrounded by the bindings of solid dictionaries. So, somewhere in

---

48 In imperial Russia, high-ranking government officials wore medals according to their rank; many of them were star-shaped.

Pennsylvania this astronomer turned a lever, the roof of the pavilion opened out—and there, at least, something unexpected could happen! But no—that patch of sky was exactly the way it should have been at that moment and that time of year. A boring, familiar face. Oh, if only a pimple were to pop up or a little wrinkle furrow it! Eternal, suspicious youth, even if you were to observe it for sixty years. And there's nothing cosmic about it, really just cosmetic . . . You know, they say that Maria Fyodorovna would inject herself with enamel and appear at court receptions like an eternal doll, bent over but with a sixteen-year-old's fresh tint to her thick skin.[49] The only thing missing was a golden bracelet with twining ornaments—otherwise she would have looked exactly like her oleograph that hung in government offices and police stations."

"I don't know," said Fyodor. "I don't remember the old regime; I was only nine when it ended."

"I can't remember much either, but I've seen it in the movies: a constable on every corner. It must have been terrifying to walk around!"

"It's still like that in the West. Over in Peterhof, do you feel the West?"

"Do I ever! You walk up to the sea, throw in your cigarette butt or some other rubbish, and you repeat: go on, honey, float your way to London."

"Oh, Seryozha, you're too much . . . So what about the astronomer?"

"You know, Fyodor, he must have loved the movies too. Who needs movie stars! Astronomers don't look into their telescopes much these days: they screw a camera onto the lens—let it film the heavens as much as it wants. It's better anyway—photography doesn't lie, to begin with, and it won't ever get sick of any one physiognomy. The sky is a mechanical device, so it makes sense that it was made for other devices. And the astronomer meanwhile goes to the bar—there are lots of bars in Pennsylvania—and there he finds foxtrots and everything else the soul might desire; and the soul desires money most of all. He'd sell anything to Rothschild. The next morning he goes to his building, unscrews the reel, starts bathing the film in a little tub, and he can fantasize as much as he likes that, any minute now, the fluffy locks of Gloria Swanson will appear, her linen smile spotted yesterday in the Cosmos . . .[50] Hey, Fyodor, you're sticking your whole hand in my face. You could poke my eye out."

---

49 Maria Fyodorovna (1847–1928), born Princess Dagmar of Denmark, was empress consort of Russia as spouse of Alexander III and mother of the last Russian emperor, Nicholas II, whom she outlived by ten years.

50 Sergey continues the astronomy pun with a reference to the Leningrad movie theater "Cosmos."

"That's what the darkness is for, Seryozha. I'm going by feel."

"Are your hands even clean? For some reason they smell like tar and . . ."

"And horse. That's from the reins."

"Toss 'em, they're getting in our way."

"How would we get where we're going then?"

"By the stars. Before the compass was invented, that's how everyone got around. Look, there's Gemini, Aries, Sagittarius, Capricorn, Cancer, the Ecliptic, Boyle's law, Fyodor Stratelates . . ."

"That guy! What are you looking at him for . . . I'd rather look at you: after all, we haven't seen each other in a long time."

And Fyodor moved his face very close to Sergey's, so that his nose seemed enormous and blurred.

"That's enough, Fyodor. Keep your eyes on the road, or we'll never get there. Take the reins."

Sergey shoved his hands deeper into his pockets and tried to suppress the shiver penetrating him through the August night. They were now driving through treeless places. A breath halfway of the steppes rippled around the charabanc.

Not only did Sergey have no coat here—he had no coat in Peterhof: he'd sold it in order to come visit Fyodor, and now he clearly felt the northern bitterness of this far-off place that he'd been riding around for nearly twenty-four hours now. Fyodor, meanwhile, was speaking ever more incoherently. He was falling asleep without noticing it, which wasn't hard to believe: he hadn't had a moment of rest since the early morning.

Sergey sensed the smell of Fyodor's leather jacket very close by, and then something heavy slumped onto him.

This warm, weak-willed body continued holding the reins, but heaved from side to side with every jolt of the charabanc, which was, however, coping with the potholes quite peacefully.

Sergey supported Fyodor with one hand while trying to disentangle the whip and reins with the other. He was presented with the choice of either waking the exhausted Fyodor or taking the reins of government into his own hands, despite the now absolute darkness and strange shifting of all the stars: the Big Dipper was now to the left instead of the right, and Sergey couldn't for the life of him find the little one, though he was squinting intently with his head thrown back: evidently it'd gotten lost somewhere.

Everything's already past, thought Sergey. *My first Tula day is already over. If the moon were to rise now, collapsed Fyodor and I would exist only as shadows reaching out on the road. I'll go back to roving around Peterhof, like a shadow, thinking about how paychecks will be given out only four days from now, so I'll have to stick it out somehow and find comfort elsewhere for the moment.*

The Shadow glanced at the leaves fallen down—yellow, red, copper-colored, the last recalling samovars. But the open spaces between the trees were filled with an un-Tulan moist haze . . . And on either side of the Shadow, his companions were discussing a most relevant topic: did the name *Navarin* come from the Navarres?[51]

Opinions were divided: those on the left insisted that it did, while those on the right allowed for some doubt. However, the battle over the *Navarin* was hardly likely to be bloody, and everyone kept shuffling along. The Shadow felt uncomfortable in the silence.

"Look, the color of *Navarin* smoke and flames." The Shadow pointed toward the mist-shrouded distance and a nearby red maple.

"Yes, Peterhof is enchanting, no less divine than Rubatov's Petersburg," affirmed the local Peterhofers. Afterwards came appropriate quotations. And since they were already approaching the fountains and statues, the Shadow also offered a quotation: "*Tricks of rural simplicity.*"[52] Looking at the water jets, he added, "It's high time to rename Peterhof like they did with Petersburg."

The Shadow felt a breeze around itself—from the companions leaping away. Just as one side of the moon always faces the earth, so the Peterhofers always showed one another only one side of themselves. The Shadow had bared a different, unexpected side to them, but the companions didn't wish to follow its example.

To really drive them over the edge, the Shadow began crooning, "*Do you remember that tune of languid bliss, rushing in the room round midnight? You heeded its call, your little head against my breast!*"[53]

The Peterhofers glanced at the Shadow's paw, red from the autumn cold.

---

51 *Navarin* was a pre-dreadnought battleship built for the Imperial Russian Navy in the late 1880s and early 1890s. In the course of the Russo-Japanese War (1904–5) she was sunk by Japanese destroyers. The Kingdom of Navarre, originally the Kingdom of Pamplona, was a European kingdom founded in the ninth century, which occupied lands on either side of the Pyrenees, alongside the Atlantic Ocean between present-day Spain and France.

52 The Shadow/Sergey alters a famous line from Alexander Pushkin's 1833 novel in verse, *Eugene Onegin* (chap. 3, verse 39).

53 Opening lines of a romance by L. L. Ivanov.

Everyone sat down by the sea, having gone past the Monplaisir Garden, already emptied of the tubbed palms that had stood there all summer. They were all wearing suits as dark as black bread, and the autumn smell of stagnating water, on the shore clotted with brushwood and dead leaves, made the Shadow suddenly hungry.

"Wouldn't mind breaking a little bread," said the Shadow and tossed its cigarette butt into the water. It began tossing stones in the flat sea. One of the stones sunk the floating butt. A cart appeared in the avenue—the carter was bringing another load of sticks and brushwood to line the shore with. Evidently, they were cleaning out the park after the summer. The horse twitched its nostrils at the raw sea air.

The Shadow thought about riding horseback and selected words. "Jolly, Shining, Gleaming, Sinewy, Silver-withers and Swift-runner, Pale-legs, Golden, Light-legs, Golden-withers—these are the names of steeds; they carry knights."

"Well, this horse is hardly likely to carry them," his companions corrected him. "It's practically still a colt."

Sergey pulled with all his might, but as soon as he'd freed the reins from Fyodor's hands, the latter suddenly woke and again took control of them.

"Ugh, what are you doing, damn it? Where are you taking us? Oh ho, the big shot, the overnight expert!"

Sergey's teeth were chattering from the jolting and the deep cold; he was afraid he'd bite off his tongue. Fyodor was driving now, raised partway off the seat. He was waving the whip around, but in the nighttime muddle most of the blows landed on Sergey rather than the horse.

"One, two." Fyodor lashed, not noticing Sergey wincing from the accidental flagellation; he was unable to defend himself, since he was holding tightly onto the carriage to keep from falling out.

"Come on, Seryozhka, make lively! Enough napping! Giddyup, lazy-bones!" And Fyodor, friskier than ever, sang out, "*In heat and blaze, in the nighttime hour—*"[54]

Sergey chimed in, "*And in my teeth, I'm quite beneath, your sneakers.*"

"One!"—this blow was particularly powerful. Sergey didn't cry out, but he felt himself flying through the air with winged arms reaching forward. The hard seat of the charabanc was no longer beneath him. Then his

---

54 Fyodor begins singing Ratmir's aria from Mikhail Glinka's opera *Ruslan and Liudmila* (1842).

forehead and nose touched the soft dew-covered grass. It wasn't frightening in the slightest: this sudden gentle flight.

"Faiginyu is stretching now, approaching Tula and fixing her hair . . . Are you alive, Seryozha?" came Fyodor's voice.

"Yep, what about you?"

"Me too."

"But where are you?"

"I'm underneath the charabanc, on the grass. Come over here."

"I can't see anything."

"Come toward my voice." Fyodor continued singing in a booming voice. "*He subtly sharpens his arrows, their blows are sharp and bold . . .* That's right, Seryozha, lift up this end."

Fyodor crawled out from under the charabanc. The horse had run off with the two front wheels.

"You have any matches, Fyodor?"

"I had some, but they fell out somewhere."

"We're really out of luck. Look at these damned tomfooleries . . ."

"What are you so upset about, Fyodor?"

"How can I not be upset! Faiginyu's going to think that I forgot about her because of you. We should look and see if the pivot's in one piece."

"Did she really know that I was coming?"

"Yes, I wrote to her, though then it was only tentative, of course."

"Well, we can still fix it—we'll tell her all about everything tomorrow."

"Yes, but we shouldn't mention the charabanc: she'll be worried, even though we're fine and didn't get hurt. But I'm so hungry I could die . . ."

"Fyodor, dear friend, poor wretch, ay-ay-ay, don't tarry, do tell: where are our tins?"

"Wherever the matches are."

Sergey and Fyodor began crawling around the charabanc. Their trouser knees were soon soaked through, and the palms of their hands washed clean with dew. Finally, clambering up onto the overturned charabanc, they nestled in close, with Fyodor's leather jacket thrown over their shoulders.

"It's very nice right now down at the bottom of the bell-shaft," said Fyodor. "It's warm and there's no wind."

"Would there be space enough for the two of us down there?"

"Standing, yes, but even that would be very tight."

"You know what I'm thinking, Fedenka—why do we even need to go to Kulikovo now? Just look around: you can't see a thing. So let's just say this is Kulikovo. You know: *the field it shall be covered in corpses, the river Nepryadva it shall flow with blood.*[55] How can we know—maybe five hundred years from now theaters will be putting on a show of our night spent in the Field of Kulikovo."

"Well, I'd still prefer the hayloft."

"Just squeeze in closer, then you won't be cold. Let's watch the sunrise together."

Sergey was walking down the street near Five Corners.[56] The two-storied building that used to house the Elephant Restaurant reminded him of Moscow, mainly because it stood opposite a five-story turreted Art Nouveau. Sergey ran into an acquaintance, and they both began discussing where to go: over to Razezzhaya, to Yamskaya, or down the avenue toward Cinizelli's circus. They exchanged some other pleasantries as well.

"How's life?"

"Fine, just fine."

"Well, and how's that thing of yours—everything the same?"

"Of course, what else can you expect? Well, good-bye, see you."

Sergey woke up wearing Fyodor's leather jacket. Fyodor was dancing around the charabanc and yelling, "It rose, Seryozhka, it rose!"

Indeed, everything was already gleaming in the sun: the pivot they had talked about in the night; Fyodor's face with sprinkles of dew on his nose, as if it was time for him to blow it; the nighttime ravines that had threatened death; the ditch the charabanc was lying in; the buckwheat field, rosy at this hour; the horse with the front part of the carriage, nibbling on some bushes a little ways off; the distant many-colored hills, the clear blue mantle of the sky, the box of matches on the road.

"What's that there glinting in the rut? What a discovery! This is obviously the helmet of Oslyabya or Peresvet.[57] It was August then, too; six hundred years ago, the sun rose just as it does now."

---

55 A quote from the fourteenth-century *Zadonshchina* (The tale from beyond the River Don), a landmark work of Old Russian literature that tells of the Battle of Kulikovo (against the Tatar-Mongol kingdom) in 1380.

56 A location in central St. Petersburg. Razezzhaya and Yamskaya (now Dostoevsky St.) are nearby streets; Cinizelli's circus is located on the bank of the Fontanka Canal, a few blocks farther away.

57 Rodion Oslyabya was a Russian monk who became famous for his part in the Battle of Kulikovo. Another monk, Alexander Peresvet, who was allegedly Oslyabya's brother, fought in single combat with the Tatar champion Temir-murza at the opening of the battle (September 8, 1380), where the two fighters killed each other.

Sergey lifted the silvery tin. The horse had crushed it with a hoof, and all of the tomato sauce had leaked out of the crack. But he could still get purchase on a corner of the metal, and with the tin opened at long last, he located the herrings, which Fyodor began grabbing and shoving into his own and Sergey's mouths.

"And now it's time to warm up. Tag, Seryozhka, you're it!"

Dew fell from the bushes they brushed past, and the first birds started chattering: "*O bright-brighter and beauteous-beautified Russian land.*[58] *O skylark, bird of summer, comfort of joyous days, fly up to the blue heavens and look upon the mighty city of Moscow.*"[59]

---

58 A quote from the thirteenth-century *Slovo o pogibeli russkoi zemli* (*The Tale of the Demise of the Russian Land*).

59 Another quote from the *Zadonshchina*.

PART TWO

"I'm sorry we didn't meet you at Kulikovo Field, Faiginyu. So it goes."

"What, am I a Tatar or something? And why are you so pale, Fedya?"

"We had a wild night, Faiginyu."

"That's right," interrupted Grandma. "I didn't sleep a wink either because of them; it really was a wild night. I dreamed of a snake: it was peeking out from a crack in the floor and looking to slither out. We poured boiling water in there and saw that the snake was as slippery as if we'd poured in kerosene."

"But where's your guest, Fedya?"

CHAPTER SEVEN

Sergey appeared, covered in a bee veil and holding a bee smoker. He had been helping the landlady inspect her hives. When they lifted the lid, Sergey saw the combs: at the top were empty ones placed to discourage the bees from wasting their strength on wax production, while below were the heavyweights, already laden with honey. The many-legged herd of bees, dazed by the smoke, swarmed shaggily. Flower pollen, chewed up and spit out by the insects and smelling of their brownish bellies, dripped in yellow droplets from their narrow, rational jaws. Sergey was delighted to learn from the landlady that it was still too early to gather the honey.

"I have no guests, Faiginyu," answered Fyodor. "But there are plenty of parasites on the laboring masses. Allow me to introduce you: Fingal, Ossian, Sergey, Kisser—they're all my friends."

Fyodor's mother shook hands with one member of the company, waving away the others.

"Don't worry, don't worry, I'm not even looking at you," she said to Sergey, who was confusedly pulling off his grilled visor.

"But Fedya, I don't understand what you're calling me. What's this awful Faiginyu business?"[60]

Fyodor kissed the nape of his mother's neck with a sucking sound and mussed her dress. "Faiginyu, don't resist evil. It's your own fault: fashions and flounces, silks, sleeveless shirt dresses, babydoll dresses—I should be the one wearing them instead of you, Madame Faiginyu. They call me Fyodor for a reason, after all. I inherited your letter F; Fingal is also obviously a member of our family."

---

60   Ilja Kukuj has suggested this name might derive from an imprecise anagram of Egunov's own last name written phonetically in the Latin alphabet: A. Yegunof -> * Fojgenau -> * Faigenau, when rewritten in Cyrillic and taking into account Russian phonetics -> Faiginyu.

Fyodor's mother slapped him across the cheeks, and he started spanking her, calling it "educational methods." It all ended with a foxtrot, in which even the sluggish Fingal was forced to take part, but he soon got out of breath and disappeared. Fyodor made faces, pretending to be an elegant little dandy; this impression was somewhat spoiled, however, by his coarse work uniform.

Finally, the mother pushed her son away. "You know, I have a premiere in October. I'll be singing the Marschallin.[61] You must come."

"Fine, Faiginyu, so be it—you're the one giving out tickets. We'll bring Sergey along too."

Sergey stood off to the side, forgotten. Grandma, creaking, dragged in the newly cleaned samovar, but Fyodor refused to sit down for tea as he was hurrying off to work.

"Well, goodbye until our next pleasant meeting. Sergey is my replacement; he'll tell you all about our quiet village life. You must be tired from the trip—he'll put you right to sleep."

"Can I go to work with you?" asked Sergey.

"No, you're not allowed. You made more than enough gaffes yesterday, so today you'll stay home. *Why d'ya need a ram when ya got a Sam—lotsa fun.*"[62] Having seized a crunchy cucumber and a crust of bread, Fyodor leapt onto the cart and galloped off.

On the balcony, everyone sat down properly to table. Sergey reached for his glass, but quickly jerked his hands back. Fyodor's mother exclaimed, "What, is it too hot? Don't worry, I didn't notice anything. But why are they so swollen?"

"It's from the girls," muttered the embarrassed Sergey. "It wasn't so bad yesterday, but today there are blisters, and the tips of my fingers seem to have gone numb—guess it was a lethal dose. But it'll pass."

"Of course, everything passes, Sergey Sergeyevich. Only, you know, one shouldn't have such a free hand with everything. You must have really liked them?"

"Oh yes, very much. That is, it's a shame that Dunya wipes her mouth with her sleeve, and Fenya sweats so heavily, but in general all is well, Lamere."

"Come again?"

"Oh, I'm sorry—yesterday Fyodor and I agreed not to call you that."

---

61 The female lead in a comic opera by Richard Strauss, *Der Rosenkavalier*.

62 In Russian, part of the joke is the "Georgian" (or generally Caucasian) accent; the Caucasus is known as a land of pastoral herders.

"Well, you know, if it's already come to this, then we have to think up a nickname for you too, Sergey Sergeyevich. What should I call you? Fyodor hasn't come up with anything?"

"No."

"What about you for him?"

"No. The easiest thing is some kind of abbreviation; that's what every-one's doing nowadays."

"Perfect. I'll call you Essess. Agreed?"

Sergey was silent for a moment, then pronounced, stirring the nonex-istent sugar in his glass, "Yes, agreed. Are we going to call Fyodor Effeff?"

"No, we'd better not. Privately I usually call him 'restless angel.' Have you noticed his gait? His head hangs down for some reason, as if it's weighed down by invisible wings. Sometimes, lost in thought, he places his hand on his chest. What is he thinking about? Most likely about whist. But we've digressed. Tell me, who's the most beautiful of them all?"

"Oh!" answered Sergey. "There's this one: imagine a bolt of lightning, breaking free of black storm clouds and suddenly illuminating the earth; when the hundred-year oaks are cracking and suddenly falling; when the whiteness of curls, mixing with . . ."

"In brief," interrupted Lamere, "what do they call this Innezelia?"

"Leocadia. Fyodor and I are mortally infatuated."

"Ah, so that's how it is, you're rivals. Be careful there's no blood spilt. Have you heard, Essess, about *playing objects*? The director shouldn't put anything onstage that will not at some point enter into the action. This bal-cony that we're drinking tea on, or this Tula samovar, the glasses—all of this counts as the props of our play . . . What, you parasite, you want some bread? Here, have at it." Lamere threw a piece to the dog. "If this tubby Fingal has appeared onstage, it means we have to play him too; otherwise there's no reason for him to have appeared."

"Careful," said Sergey. "Look out, or he might decide to play you with his slobbery muzzle."

"But the most interesting part," continued Lamere, "is playing with the objects that aren't there. We staged a play that was completely without props. The first lover skillfully fenced with an absent rapier; his hand tightly grasped its nonexistent handle. The imaginary blade plunged into the breast of his defeated enemy and, passing all the way through, showed on the other side. Unable to bear this terrible spectacle, I covered my face with a made-up black veil, then threw it off and took up an imaginary apple, singing descending chromatic scales. The apple was poisoned; I knew it, and a shudder came out of it and entered me. Look: right now we have no sugar; Fyodor's salary is obviously not generous. Watch me pour sugar from a little sack into the sugar bowl, take two—no, three—teaspoons full, and drink this sweet tea. Oh, how incredibly sweet my face becomes—it's because I've been wanting sugar for such a long time. Would you like some too? Here are three spoonfuls for you, too. Wait—before you drink it, stir it all the way in."

"You're right about everything," answered Sergey. "But this sweet-ness just reminds me yet again of the cruel Leocadia. If she is an actress, then she has just one fault: she probably hails from somewhere out west, which is why she pronounces a final "g" so hard, it comes out like a "k"; and sometimes, from trying to avoid the Polish stress on words, she removes it entirely from the penultimate syllable: *it's so borink here, so borink, there's no talkink to these people, everythink is owned by kulaks.*"

"That doesn't mean anything," objected Lamere. "Old opera librettos have absurd words in them all the time . . . I will certainly make Leocadia's acquaintance . . . But I can see that you are having a hard time thinking what to talk about with me. So let's not talk, we'll listen to what my *belle-mère* is discussing with the landlady."

Having gulped down three cups of tea, Grandma was working. She had already managed to unstitch the hat Lamere had arrived in and was sewing a handbag out of the silk lining. The landlady had placed the ironing board on the corner of the trunk and the table and was taking wrinkled, rolled-up bedding out of the basket while sharing the Mirandino news: who's not getting along with his father, whose cow fell, who's getting mixed up with whom. She compared things to the old days: who used to ride up to church in a carriage; who among the local landowners used to drag village girls into his bed; who cheated his lackeys at cards; who used to calculate how many potatoes went for every dinner; whose daughter had, naturally, shot herself, while the other son served as a factory inspector. It turned out that some of the landowners here were Poles: *Pan* Dolzhevsky sobbed like a baby when he read Polish poetry, though he also used the same book to beat his wife about the neck.[63]

Grandma listened, since it was impossible not to listen, but didn't especially share the landlady's delight and was more occupied by her

---

63 *Pan* (masc.)/*pani* (fem.), which translates literally as "master" or "lord," are polite forms of address in Polish.

handiwork. Sergey realized that all of this talk had been for Lamere's sake, in the hope that long heart-to-hearts might be forthcoming. But Lamere sat silently, lost in thought, and threw no bones to the landlady, who went on insistently ironing, from time to time taking mouthfuls of water and loudly sprinkling the withered, stiff linens. The landlady rebuked the village girls, the iron moved more and more furiously in her fat hands, and the white shirt ended up with a brown burnt spot.

Sitting on the balcony, they heard that it was impossible to get anything out of the village council because of the village councilwoman; and that when dealing with peasant women you'll always end up in a spat. This was followed by an energetic declaration that "them's that don't understand reason, understand the whip," and the listeners learned that the village councilwoman was particularly skilled at inspecting heads: she had a special wooden comb for raking hair; that the landlady hated doing laundry; and, as everyone knows, young people find everything entertaining.

Finally, Isa Makarovna, waving the iron around, came up to Lamere directly. The latter raised her blue eyes to Makarovna but remained silent. Then the landlady, unable to hold back, pronounced, "I'm an orphan and was raised by the wife of a landowner from around here, God rest her soul, though she was a bloodsucker. But now, thank God, the church is failing, and even then children know no respect."

From here on, the words came thick and fast about religion: the children piled up a stool on the table, took down the icons, and started playing with them as if the icons were going to visit one another. The backs of the icons turned out to be dusty; insane and terrified cockroaches were writhing there.

"See, let's pretend my St. Varvara the Great Martyress comes to visit and says: 'Never you mind that I'm dusty: I've just been out in the fields, I didn't have time to clean off.' And then, let's pretend, my Nikola says to her: 'Like I could care! We're dusty ourselves, praise the Lord, no less than you.' 'No, I'm dustier!'—'No, I'm dustier!' And let's say they start attacking each other and cursing. And my Varvara has a heavy frame, and doesn't she just go and get hold of Nikola's mug. And let's pretend the cockroaches are Varvara's little rascals: it's a big family and there's not much to eat; let's say her husband left her and he's fooling around with the mother of God. But Varvara feels bad for the roaches. When she starts bawling, right away some little god comes up, let's pretend he goes after her: 'Don't go bawling, you dumb broad, I'll give you a reason to bawl. Wipe your nose; what a punishment you are to me.' The peasant woman heaved and sighed and pleaded with them to leave the icons alone.

Then the kids ran up to the windows and threatened to break them. The side of one of the icons was already touching the glass. The woman gave up and sat weeping quietly in the corner. Her tears fell onto the startled cockroaches."

Lamere didn't say a word in response to this, either. The landlady added by way of conclusion, "But we're working people, of course. We don't have time to indulge in empty discussions. Excuse me, if I've displeased you somehow,"—and continued on into the kitchen. Sticking her head back out, she yelled, "Where are you planning on washing your clothes?"

"I'll do it myself," answered Lamere. "It's not such hard work. Before I went to the conservatory I experienced many things in life, and I'm not afraid of any kind of dirty work. If I didn't have a voice, who knows, maybe I would be a cleaning lady, a laundress, a mail carrier. Sometimes I open my mouth and look in the mirror. I wish I could see my vocal cords. Everything I have is because of them: my earnings, my success; even Fyodor, since that stylish tenor would hardly have thought of marrying me if I hadn't had a voice. When he sang the parting aria of the Duke: *If I fall for a beauty, Argus himself couldn't look after her*, thousands of Arguses in the audience gazed at his slender legs, hugged tightly by white silk tights.[64] I was envied; in Ryazan they even called me *Signora Stratilato*. Now that's all dead and buried: the skilled *messa di voce*, the grace notes, and the tenor's legs. I've saved only the silk tights, along with our wedding candles and the *fleur d'orange*."

Lamere lowered her voice and leaned in to Sergey. "You like Grandma? She thinks so highly of you: she didn't even have time to hint, she says, and you'd already given her cologne. She's very good, my *belle-mère*, but, to be honest, I don't like old ladies: they give off a faint scent of the grave. No, *to be free, to be carefree, to dash ever in a whirlwind of happiness and know no hint of heartache*."[65]

Instead of a goblet, Lamere lifted her glass of golden tea.

"No," she said. "It won't work: for this I would need to be wearing a long extravagant skirt with flounces. I am entirely opposed to the fashions these days. We get so cold in the winter; there are so many rheumatisms. It's all your fault, you men—you created them for us. You see, Essess, there was an imperialist war, an enormous gathering of armies. Were you at the front, Essess?"

---

64 The reference is to Verdi's *Rigoletto*.

65 Lamere quotes from the beginning of Violetta's "Sempre libera" aria from Verdi's *La Traviata*: *Sempre libera degg'io/folleggiare di gioia in gioia,/vo'che scorra il viver mio/pei sentieri del piacer.*

"Ostensibly not, but you can pretend that I was."

"Well, yes—your generation all grew up under artillery fire. Trenches, shells, shacks . . . So then, Essess, take a look at some fashionable postwar couple from a distance, out walking down the street. He's still keeping his nineteenth-century suit: long trousers, and so on, that's what makes him look serious; but how is she dressed? Tights like my husband's; her legs are exposed, even her knees; a short tight skirt; something close to a man's overcoat; hair cropped, a tiny little hat; in a word, it's a page's costume, like something from the sixteenth century. The fashions require a flat figure. Where are the wide hips promising fertility; where are the breasts, heavy with milk? This ambiguous angel foxtrots, forgetting the long falling folds of women's clothing. However, I think these fashions will pass along with the acrid fumes of war."

Thus reasoned Lamere. Sergey was meanwhile taking a mental stroll to yesterday's grove, though no longer with Fyodor. When they got to the top of the hill, naturally, they met the girls. They gazed curiously at Lamere, or more likely at her dress. Not a single pattern and no pansies could be glimpsed upon its smooth material. They inquired as to the state of Sergey's hands, but he shoved them into his pockets and changed the subject. There was no need to search for a pretext: the girls sat in a row on the log, downcast and melancholy. Dunya's black bangs had not even been curled.

"He left?" asked Sergey. "You're sad? Sing something like yesterday—that was nice."

But Fenya, Dunya, the other Dunya, and Domasha gazed into the distance instead of answering: Tula was hiding beyond the far pine forest, blurred in the sultry air. The kulak village, in contrast, was wholly discernible and, paradoxically, looked entirely innocent: brick huts, silos, cattle sheds, fences.

"*I went out to suffer on the hill, so that my sweetie'd hear it. I'll pass Tula, I'll pass the city, my sweetie's sitting, the gates embroidered—go see my sweetie in his workshop,*" Dunya began. The girls exchanged glances and started whispering: *the suffering songs, the suffering songs.*

Like yesterday, they divided into two camps and began singing by turns.

It was seven of us suffered, but they spoke for just the two. Oh comrade dear, tell us which one you're suffering for. Believe me, sweet girl, the pillow's all wet from tears. Oh sweetie, let's suffer some, we'll learn what love is like.

"More, more please," said Lamere, who had been listening very attentively. "But who are you suffering for, who is it that left?"

"For Fyodor," whispered Dunya, blushing scarlet. Her face looked more full of suffering than all the others'.

"But he's here, he hasn't gone anywhere. If you want to see him, come have tea with us. Essess will tell you about the beauty of Leocadia."

"Oh, she's sure suffering, she has a reason to." Dunya burst out laughing. "But we could care less, we're a side story."

Fenya gave Lamere a wink and spun around, her skirts blowing about. "*Sufferers, sufferers, don't bluff the mothers. I have a new sufferer, my sweet, a king of diamonds; plus there's my Mishka—my suffering lad of seventeen.*"

Fenya ran off ahead of everyone, Lamere and Sergey also took off down the hill. Everyone got covered in dust. As they went along, Sergey explained to Lamere, so that she wouldn't be confused, that Mirandino had three different Fyodors: Fil d'Écosse was also Fyodor, and in addition there was the so-called other Fyodor, a worker.

Lamere answered, laughing. "Of course, here in the village there might be ten Fyodors and ten Sergeys; do you really think I won't be able to tell which one is my son and which is his friend?"

Having finished her tea, Lamere was really laughing now. "But this did turn out funny, Essess: I wanted to find out all about you, but in the end just blabbed on about myself. Fyodor did write to me about you, but it was all of two lines, and I couldn't understand how you make a living."

"Signora Stratilato," Sergey replied. "You are of course aware how the Italians make their living: they borrow from each other."

"No, Essess, really, what is your profession?"

"I run engines."

"You don't say? In the train on the way here I imagined all sorts of things, but would never have suspected that. Do tell, is it dangerous to ride with you?"

"Lamere, you have been misled. I am the eighth wonder of the world, the adornment of our [Soviet] Union: I am the only girl typist of the male gender, and I work in the office of the Peterhof palace museums."

Lamere frowned. "But how did you find your way to such a life?"

"Through education. Mine was unusually subtle: I am a specialist in ancient Icelandic literature. I flutter amid the blossoms of culture and cannot find an application for myself. Even if it were Norwegian literature, I'd be better off—Norway is a country of hardworking peasants, its capital city is Oslo."

"So that's how it is," said Lamere. "And have you met the local peasants?"

"I should think not. Everythink's owned by koolaks, as Leocadia puts it."

"Essess, you're playing objects again? Wait, I'll look into Leocadia on my own. Bear in mind that this, your second day of Tula life, will be female. Yesterday you and Fyodor spent time together in solitude. Today is livelier: all the bulbs are lit; the operator directs the spotlight; and we, the women, walk out into the blinding light of the stage. In the middle of the first act we drove up to the theater, walked through the empty aisles to our dressing room; for an instant, the stage flickered at us through the sounds of the orchestra, the warmth and the song and the work. The painted bush standing behind the curtains showed off its linen underside and wooden crossbar. We saw the fly and the set builders and the hammers. But we have nothing to do with the first act. We get made up and dressed. Now the second act begins: the queen's coloratura aria, the female chorus, and the ballet. The high-society dandies would usually come right on time for the second act, to look at us."

"I don't know," Sergey objected. "I came right on time for the first act. I generally don't like being late to shows."

"I think," said Lamere, "that I hurried to get there on time too. Just imagine, Essess, what would happen if the prima donna was late: the curtain has long since been lifted, the prelude's been played, the chorus sang its part, the men have completed their *recitatifs*, but she's just not there. Even the audience notices the agonizing pause. The conductor attempts to save the situation by giving the signal for the orchestra to play what they know by heart. The public ceases its grumbling and, sitting up, listens. Those who didn't have time to read the evening papers before coming to the theater begin thinking there must be important political news in them. Finally, the prima donna, hurriedly made-up, runs out breathless onto the stage. Her nose is smeared with blush, she has no eyebrows, since she forgot to draw them in, and her tight Renaissance bodice is fastened on top of a short modern dress. The high collar is bouncing down her back. Everyone understands that the queen is truly in a terrible state of confusion . . . When receiving her paycheck, Marguerite de Valois is fined for tardiness, but the director smacks his forehead: he's struck by the thought that only in this state can queens make sense to the contemporary theatergoer.[66] His next

---

66 Lamere refers to a staging of *Les Huguenots*, a grand opera by Giacomo Meyerbeer with the sixteenth-century queen Marguerite de Valois (the Queen of Navarre) in the lead role.

show is staged entirely in line with this aesthetic . . . Well, Essess, what do you say? It seems like Fyodor's right: *what dya need a ram for, you got Sam."*

Lamere went down from the balcony and stopped, illuminated by the sun. "The footlights are shining right into my eyes. I can't see anything. Above me is the blue, the midday dark of the heavens. This is an open auditorium; the watchful warmth of the restless crowd wafts over as they wait for my first sounds. The orchestra between us is building a resonant fence from below, out of its den up to the ceiling. I must break through this palisade to get to those for whom I exist, and so I throw my first, still quivering note to them across the stockade."

"You really still get nervous when you go onstage?"

"Do I ever! Always. Even now. But I love that moment of walking out onstage."

Lamere extended her arm in a familiar operatic gesture, indicating the dark cupola of sky. Her blond hair glowed in the sun. Gazing straight up with fevered eyes, she seized the opening note, which began a melody unknown to Sergey.

We cannot know whether the audience sitting there in the dark heavenly auditorium was pleased. Of course, those in the front rows had higher salaries; some were already balding, although we couldn't say with absolute confidence that they ate dinner every day. The gallery housed the young and the shrieking, though all of the above were card-carrying union members. As soon as the singing began to be broken up by interludes, filled by the orchestra, muffled conversations immediately could be heard.

"Maria Petrovna came by some splendid stockings through dark channels."

"Have a chocolate. I unexpectedly came by two."

"Thanks, I'll take it home instead: we haven't got a speck of sugar in the house."

"Look sharp during the intermission, Petya: we've got to be among the first to get to the buffet in time for the pastries. I wore one of my worst dresses on purpose: it's sure to get smushed against the counter when everybody hurls themselves at the cheese sandwiches. You didn't forget the box? They say you can buy up to three sandwiches. The kids are staying up waiting for us, after all."

Perspiration broke out on the singer's forehead. Having finished, Lamere stood in a pose natural for receiving applause. But everything was silent, even Sergey.

Rain suddenly came down in torrents, an utterly summery rain, astonishing for the month of August. Silver nails were falling, heads down. The freshness and cool and cheerful drops' falling caused Sergey's bewilderment to pass.

He cast a few more preliminary glances at Lamere, who had hastily come back up to the balcony, and said: "Great! Bravo! Now I will tell you about myself. First and foremost—I am a born-and-bred Peterhofer. We have the Marly Palace there, a cozy little white house, 'Marly's House,' as they call it in Peterhof. You know—we have stores called 'House of the Book,' so this is 'House of Marly.' As soon as I entered its lower *halle*, everything outside became obscured by a whitish light rain. The resonant stone floor echoed my footsteps. There were no visitors besides me. During Peter the Great's reign, the *halle* served as a warehouse for gardening supplies and stores of fruits and berries. Next to it is a Dutch kitchen, where one might enjoy sitting and reading the fifth volume of a slow-moving novel. Capons would be roasting on a spit; plates with fine blue designs would already be placed around the table. Everyone would sit down and eat: an entire chicken would be appointed for each guest's breakfast. And afterward there would still be dinner and supper. I had the thought that, in our time, I would be satisfied with a single chicken leg or wing for the whole day."

"Don't be overly ethereal, please. Judging by your complexion, you could probably eat, oh, I don't know, half a chicken," noted Lamere.

"No, I assure you that afterward I went up to the second floor. It was empty there too. Senya Larionov was doggedly sticking out his shift among the Petrine chairs, next to the rope barring access to the carved Pineau study. If you lean far over the rope, you can see, in a glass case on the tabletop, the horse tooth Peter the Great himself pulled out of some grandee. Senya and I walked hand-in-hand through all the rooms on the second floor, saw the wardrobe, the motheaten greatcoat and unbelievably enormous dressing-gown, and the blackened paintings on the walls. 'You know, Lesnoy—it's just outside Leningrad,' Senya explained. 'You can get there on tram number . . .' One could distinguish the whitish speckled croup of a horse, a crimson soldier's coat, distinct tiny leaves on the branch of a tree overhanging the center of the battle . . . Afterward Senya and I looked in the mirror together. Stripped of their quicksilver, dark and no longer reflective, its eighteenth-century spots were right in the middle of Senya's nose. He laughed and refused candies, assuring me that the museum workers had already fed him to bursting and that today alone he'd made his way through a whole pound of hard candies. Nevertheless, he devoured a few mocha bonbons as he described the antireligious show at his high school and how he, as an eighteen-year-old, had been given the role of the priest: they stuck on a brown beard and small horns. Through the open balcony door a white vase in the park and some illegible trees could be seen, swathed in softening gauze. When, finally, the rain stopped, we tried to get up from the Petrine chairs, but this turned out to be trickier than we thought: we'd gotten stuck to their antediluvian leather. Senya explained that this was our punishment for having broken the rule: no sitting on museum objects. I went down the rounded oak staircase. It was impossible to make out anything on the tarnished ceiling besides the elongated legs and pink heels of the bustling heavenly world. But Senya laughed down from the upper landing and waved to me . . . Back home, when I looked at the wall, I discovered that I'd spent no less than three hours in that 'Marly's House,' and for some reason I had the feeling in my mouth that Senya and I, arrested by the rain, had been chattering away the whole time not in Russian, but in Dutch, or—in a pinch—in English."

Having heard out Sergey's story all the way to the end, Lamere became agitated. "Oh, Fyodor, Fyodor, he's out in the fields now. He'll get soaked through, the poor boy."

"It's all right," Sergey said to comfort her. "Fyodor'll go down the bell-shaft, they'll cover him from above, and he'll listen to the rain pounding down on the wooden lid. It's lovely to sing down there; you have a thirty-meter-tall tube—excellent resonance."

"That may be, but you still owe me more stories. I'm going to number them. This was number one."

Lamere got lost in thought, working her fingers absentmindedly through Kisser's shaggy coat, where fleas were jumping around visibly.

"Everything runs through your fingers, everything we make a grab for falls apart, everything drifts apart like steam. A wild goose chase! And indeed, how is it possible that I was once little Rezi?[67] Soon everyone will be saying: *Look, there goes old lady Rezi.* Time, Quinquin, is an astonishing thing; it flows between me and you, wordless as an hourglass. I often get up in the night and stop all the clocks. One must be light, with a light

---

67 In *Der Rosenkavalier*, the Marschallin, whose name is Therese, is known intimately as Rezi; her lover Octavian, who betrays her, has the nickname Quinquin. Lamere's soliloquy echoes themes of the opera, including that of the Marschallin's anxious awareness of her approaching old age.

heart, light hands for holding and taking, for holding onto and giving up . . . Octavian . . . Bichette . . . he's already grown up—Fyodor . . . Fyodor . . ."

"I know that," said Sergey.

"Really? But it hasn't been shown in Moscow, though the orchestra did start rehearsing."

"Fyodor and I liked it very much."

"Oh, that's right, you're from Leningrad."

"Pardon me, from Peterhof."

"Pardon me, I'm forgetful. I suppose I'm getting old. One musn't give in to it."

"How old are you?"

"Ay-ay-ay, Essess. And Grandma considers you well brought-up! We are never older than twenty-nine: we are twenty-six for six years in a row, the same for twenty-seven. After we turn twenty-nine, the order starts to go backward—twenty-eight comes around again, and so on into infinity."

"But Fyodor," insisted Sergey, "is right about to turn twenty-two, no matter how you count it—Gregorian or Julian."

"How about you?" interrupted Lamere.

"I'm twenty-six."

"Well then, you and I are age-mates."

Lamere abruptly twirled around the balcony; she tripped and would have fallen from the uneven planks of the unfenced balcony, but for the support of a new arrival. Lying with her legs still on the balcony, but shoulders and head on the one holding her, Lamere managed to finish her aria without turning her head. Then she got up, fixed her hair, and looked around. There was reciprocal embarrassment.

The new arrival, however, mumbled, "Quite a song—but what's it about? The people?"

To give the new acquaintances time to tidy themselves, Sergey began translating: "*I used to say long ago, beneath the fragrant branch of lilac it became unbearably airless, and I dropped to my knees before her.*"[68]

"Oh," answered the co-op operator. "Sergey Sergeyevich has been my best friend since yesterday. Not too chatty; self-absorbed, like all students; but you won't get bored around him. The main thing is, you know he's one of us. Sparing in his gestures, but comes across as expressive—like in the

---

68 Sergey quotes from a romance by Krestovsky and Paskhalov, "Beneath the Fragrant Branch of Lilac."

movies when they bring her the corpse and she just moves a finger and her brow shivers. Weaknesses, too, of course; but every woman is a world unto herself, after all. But I won't say anything about that in your presence, Madam; I'll just join your salon here on the balcony. I flew over here to you on wings, y'hear, with an order."

The co-op operator's back really did look darker than the rest of his shirt: evidently he had run over, bent double, and the rain had soaked him only on one side.

Lamere took the proffered note and unfolded it. "With your permission?"

"Read it, read it, why not. I know what's in there anyway, without reading it. Well, and the woman in question, I have to tell you: as tasty as they come. And she's educated: she finished all of them, not just those two or three steps—the whole stairway, you could say. But I can't go, alas—I have to go distribute the herring."

Lamere began reading the letter out loud like a tongue-twister (Hermann reading Liza's note, the scene in the barracks).[69] When she finished, Lamere asked, "Is it far from here?"

The co-op operator winked at Sergey. "He knows the way already—he's nobody's fool either. Such a beauty, and not too heavy either; I guessed her weight, after all."

His final words were meant for Lamere, who had stepped away to fix her hair. Grandma treated the co-op operator to tea. It quickly became clear that he remembered her very well: she used to visit the church in Kozikhinsky Lane where he had sung as a boy in the chorus. They began adding up who was how old, and how many years ago this or that must have happened. Then the conversation shifted to the local Father Alexander and the Old Testament forefathers. It turned out that Abraham, a man with a great and decisive soul, had lived 175 years, while handsome Joseph had only lived to 110.

"Beauty takes its toll, I guess," noted the co-op operator.

Grandma started worrying about Fyodor. The co-op operator comforted her with the fact that prophets live even shorter lives: Elias was just ninety, Simeon only eighty, and there were plenty of exceptions.

"Now your beauty struck me back then on Kozikhinsky, even though I was still just a boy back then. You used to make the sign of the cross so

---

69 A reference to *The Queen of Spades*, an opera based on Alexander Pushkin's eponymous story.

beautifully, with your luxurious bosoms and stern brow, while all around us were candles, glinting gold, plumes of incense."

"Beauty, ha." Grandma shook her head. "Even back then I was already past fifty."

"So what—Sarah bore a son in her 127th year," the co-op operator protested. "But why did you get so animated when we started talking about women?" He slapped Sergey on the back.

"I'm more interested in the actresses," he answered, not noticing Lamere frowning. "Like, Luceia was still working onstage in her 119th year. When he embraced her, Abraham didn't know if he would conceive a son or enter a toothless grave, smelling of chlorodont. Then you have the dancer Coppala, who greeted Pompeii with a bouquet of flowers ninety years after her first debut."

"Yes, that's right. Medyntseva couldn't have been less than forty then but, you see, there's all those costumes, the stage, and, most important, the proper lifestyle. What do you think a man looks like who's predestined to a long life? His parents have to have been healthy. My father and mother are lowlifes; but this guy, he's got a proportional build, medium height; his face is neither pale nor red, his hair's more blond than black, his head isn't overlarge, his shoulders and belly are rounded, full cheeks, he has complete harmony in all his parts. He's open to feelings of hope; he's at the height, one could say, of his strength; calculation, envy, and rage are unknown to him; he loves quiet reflection and opposes the dark masses; he's around forty, so still young; a friend to science and the people; an optimist. Does that sound about right?"

"Sure," confirmed Sergey.

"And your friend has a beautiful mother, a real *belle-mère*. And I approve of her having come to our village: life in the countryside, amid the trees, is more prolonged than in the city. A landowner probably once leaned on this poplar; its leaves are somehow mournful. If we can just live long enough, live on through!" the co-op operator repeated, gazing at the autumn caravans of birds, forming a black triangle in the sky. "Lucky ones, they're already flying off. *Oh my dove, let us dash off to the lands where all, like you, is perfection . . .*[70] Let's fly off, Madam," the co-op operator addressed Grandma.

She answered, "Can you really not be sorry to leave nothing behind? Fine, you're no longer young, but it's fine to lie in the grave when it's drizzling

---

70 Sergey Sergeyevich quotes the beginning of a Baudelaire-inspired poem by the Symbolist poet Dmitri Merezhkovsky—correctly, for once.

up above. I can't complain about my health, my stomach functions well, everyone in our family is doing fine. The little nuisances don't matter: like how Fyodor forbade me from having Father Alexander over to visit."

At these words Lamere went inside to rest up after her journey, evidently assuming that the conversation was guaranteed to flow on without her assistance. Grandma continued, "Fyodor says: invite whoever you want, only I won't have any priests. And here we are with no sugar, flies, mud, snot-nosed kids. I'm sick of it here. Our landlady sleeps in her clothes in one bed with two children and four kittens. How is it she hasn't smothered them in her sleep yet, I don't know! But that doesn't really matter, it's just that, you know, every year there's spring, winter, summer, autumn, every day there's day and night. You have to get dressed, get undressed, eat. Whether the tea has sugar or not, it's all the same taste; I've known it since I was a child. If only I could eat something new, something I never tried before. I've never had a sweet tooth or been a glutton, but now I think: God willing, in the next world I'll get to eat something tasty. I'll stuff my mouth full and start chewing, like we used to with chocolate when we were little kids. It's incomprehensible how a person can live on this earth for 190 years. You get bored after just half that time. When they start reading from the Book of Hours in the church, you think that time has gone away for good and there's no hours anymore either. The church elder wanted to put a stool in the corner for me, but Fyodor shoved him away. If it weren't for Fyodor, our life would be a little boring. When you manage to get used to living, Lord knows it's hard to break the habit. Even though I'm old, I've got used to all this stuff nowadays because of Fyodor. I agree with all of it. He's so red-cheeked, our boy; his hair's still baby-soft. Sometimes I want to give him a bath in the trough, like he's still little; watch him squint his eyes against the soap."

"Why on earth didn't you tell me you haven't any sugar? I thought you were serving the tea like this on purpose, to be healthy. I'd do it for you in an instant, in memory of Kozikhinsky: in thought and deed help friends in need! Tell Fyodor to come by and see me."

Sergey, sitting a ways off with a book in his hands, flinched on hearing his friend's name.[71]

---

71 The co-op operator uses the rhymed expression *dlya milogo druzhka i seryozhka iz ushka* (literally, "for a good friend I'd give the earring [*seryozhka*] from my ear")—thus in the Russian Sergey flinches on hearing *his own* name.

"Give me some sugar, any amount. Like 815 pounds," he whispered into the co-op operator's ear.

"Look, if you show some respect to Leocadia, brother, like how we should, like students do; then I might toss fifteen hundred over, depending on your services. She'll let me know herself," the operator answered, also in a whisper.

Astonishing—he's not jealous at all, thought Sergey.

"Listen, brother, here's my advice: use as much production strength as possible; nights on end, consume hot drinks, smoke; pile on the worries, concerns, and woe. It's easy to remember: if you want to go on living, always do just the opposite . . . But I've got to run. Norwegian herrings! Well, gentlemen, a good journey to you. And good luck." The co-op operator winked at Sergey.

He ran off, and in the silence they could hear the regular pounding of chains: Makar and Ustinya were threshing on the little threshing floor next to the house. Ustinya was notable for her baldness, visible through her few neatly combed hairs, and for her love toward her husband, whom she was constantly advising to take a rest. At some point Makar had gotten used to considering himself rich. Now as he threshed, he looked as if he was beating against the hateful, deceitful Kerensky banknotes.[72] The only words that Sergey had heard out of him were the following: "We don't have one of those, sir: we go to the bushes."

"Enough cooling off. Let's go," said Lamere, glancing at her watch.

Along the way they exchanged bows with the deacon, whose wife had thrown him out. When he raised his black straw hat, the sun caught the gold of his wedding ring. Beside the co-op they met yesterday's maidens. They really did look tired.

Sergey began comforting them. "I know, I myself suffer from loneliness. But never you mind: Fil d'Écosse is thinking of you; he asked me to tell you hello. He said he'll never forget you in a million years, and next summer he'll be sure to come, so, you see, everything is all right."

Sergey shifted his gaze from Dunya to Fenya, to the other Dunya, to Domasha, trying to guess which one of them might be particularly interested in his invented hello from Fil d'Écosse.

---

72 So-called Kerensky banknotes, or *kerenki*, were issued by the Russian Provisional Government (led by Alexander Kerensky) in 1917 and by the new Soviet government until 1919. In the situation of hyperinflation that reigned during the revolutionary and Civil War periods, the notes became essentially worthless and unredeemable.

"Well, I could care less about him," said Fenya.

Dunya just sighed.

"You're suffering?" Sergey was cheered. "Leo Tolstoy was right: there is so much suffering on this earth."

"I'm suffering," said Dunya, "because I didn't get assigned to do a stretch at the university. Fenya's the lucky one: this fall she'll be in Moscow apprenticing to Fil d'Écosse. Just try staying here, messing around with snot-nosed brats; then the bad weather'll start and the roads will all be shot."

"And why aren't you suffering?" Sergey turned to lucky Fenya.

"I'm not suffering because I got the assignment. It must be nice at the university: parties, outings. But I'm still suffering because my St. Nicholas icon will stay here and get mixed up with all kinds of riffraff."

"Hey, Fenka, don't go looking at me—pot calling the kettle black!" Domasha perked up.

"Aw, I'm not talking about you. As if he'd want to get mixed up with you."

"But maybe he would? How am I any worse than you?"

"Worse 'cause you aren't me."

"Ay ay ay, and I suffer," wailed Domasha, "'cause of the mole on my lip. I tried to burn it off with vinegar essence, it didn't work, I just got all bloodied. And I also suffer 'cause this riffraff here is making fun of me."

The maidens were already ready to start seizing each other's hair. In any case, squealing was already underway. Beneath the raised arms, armpits darkened: sweat had soaked through the patterned calico in the heat. The co-op doors suddenly swung noisily open. The co-op operator ran out, breathing heavily. His eyes met a disheveled scene.

"Girls! Brother! My tired and suffering brother, whoever you are, don't lose heart! Don't be a loser. You tell your heart, 'listen up, you bitch, don't lose and don't go tingling.' C'mon, come on into the shop, I'll treat everyone to some candy—I just got some fresh ones, Red Navy brand."

The co-op doors closed behind the entering throng.

Lamere looked carefully at Sergey. "I've been thinking about our landlady—she'd make a good abbess: white, thick elbows. She must be a capable woman. These maidens ought to be put under her supervision. But tell me, why is he called Fil d'Écosse?

"There's a certain Grisha Ermolov here, he wears a felt hat. Fyodor claims that the departed gentleman once referred to Grisha's hat as 'made of fil d'Écosse' and that the name stuck. I don't know; maybe that's not true."

"It's true, it's true, but how fine it's become since it rained. These work uniforms are very high quality, I didn't get wet at all." Fyodor's words rang out as he came out of the hollow. He was carrying a canvas briefcase with papers.

Fyodor walked in the middle, holding hands on one side with Lamere and on the other with Sergey. His companions were forced to trudge along in the ruts of the country road, while he strode playfully along the grassy strip in the middle. At first everyone was silent, surrendering themselves to the air grown light after the rain. But Fyodor couldn't hold back and, squeezing his companions' elbows, began to sing loudly. *"Drum-de-dum, bang a drum, what a treat, to feel strong heartbeats! All day long I'm a king, but at night I'm a ding-a-ling."*

"Fedya, quit."

"Fedenka's doing it bébé-style again, he needs a picture book: lady-bugs, bang-a-drum, time to eat your soup."

"This isn't bébé at all, I just wanted to have some fun before we get to Leocadia's—it's always so *borink* there."

"That depends on us—you can have fun anywhere. Let's distribute roles: Fedya, as long as you're singing about banging drums, you have to go after Leocadia: neither you nor she will find it *borink*, and in the end even I think it'd be nice for you to 'feel strong heartbeats.'"

"So, now this—you're teasing me like a monkey again. Back in June I felt more heartbeats than I knew what to do with. A bunch of girl students came to measure temperature averages. And wouldn't you know, they were all tall and skinny. Fil d'Écosse called them 'the thermometers.' One time I walked one of them home. After that they gave me no peace. But what did I have to do with it? They were all feverish for Fil d'Écosse. So let Seryozhka take care of that, and I'll just play with Leocadia's little boy."

"I'm afraid Essess won't pull it off—he's too much of an Icelander."

"You're mistaken, Lamere."

"Well, we'll see."

"So what role do you have in mind for yourself?"

"I'll throw off all roles and appear as my own self; I'll be Fyodor's taci-turn, tragic mother."

"In that case it's too bad you're not wearing a high-necked black dress."

"Faiginyu and Seryozhka," cried Fyodor. "You must become friends. We will live in peace and harmony and establish a distribution of labor: I will work in the fields, Grandma will make meals, Faiginyu will be silent to let her voice rest, Seryozhka will daydream in the barn. Boy, it's really hot. In this kind of weather corpses decompose well."

Lamere answered, after a few moments' consideration. "I'm game, but only if it's really all three of us together: the ram and Sam and Essess. Otherwise—no."

Three kids with squeals and chortles pointed fingers at the approaching party. Sergey's Panama hat, bought at some point in a commission store, amused them.

"It's all right, it's all right," Fyodor said to comfort Sergey. "We're in a period of transition now, but the hat is really not bad."

But Lamere turned out to be right: everything passes. The kids' laughter passed too. A few cabins were already drawing close, stuck to the nape of either a hill or a large burial mound; they were surrounded by fields of motley flowers. Further on lay a circle of greenswards. Two roads came out from the little square: one led to Akreika, the other to Shizdrovo. Leocadia's house could also be seen. The shutters were open, but the windows were caulked up with something from inside. The porch was woven over with inviting ivy. Fyodor knocked three times on the half-open door.

Without waiting for an answer, they entered the dark hallway.

What would it be like to never part from Mirandino, thought Sergey. *By all means, there is a way to do it, even a very simple one: to stop existing and to move here to live among the local inhabitants. And what am I anyway? I see, hear, jot things down—nothing more.*

Sergey suddenly felt that he loved Leocadia. Yes, he loved her passionately.

"Have you prepared your opening lines? Though, actually, you should listen to what your heart tells you," Lamere whispered to him.

Sergey didn't answer and still had time to think, "*Algernon, tell them to give me a cup of tea, I'm terribly hungry*"—*that's how English aristocrats talk. I'll drink and eat as much as possible. A good appetite and imposing stature are refined.*

Everyone banged against the low lintel and were rubbing their foreheads when Leocadia came out into the hallway, holding up a kerosene lamp with bared raised arm. She froze on the threshold, demonstrating her batiste dress. The second that she stood there recalled the color postcard illustrating *Quo vadis*—"Ligia on the Threshold of Vinicius's House," Salon de Paris, 1899.[73]

"Ah, good evenink, good evenink! Did you hurt yourselves? It's so dark out here. There's nothing to be done—we have to live here in this rustic cabin," she went on profusely, leading the guests into her keep. "I cleaned it up as best I could, but in the end what can you really do? It's a Russian village, after all—it's no Minsk, am I right?"

Sergey gazed at the wall decorations. Strawberries and cornflowers peeked out of plaster wreaths, hung all over the place with pink and pale blue ribbons—this was doubtless Leocadia's work. She had also adorned the ornate country-style icons that filled one corner of the cabin with little bows of ribbon. On a side table beneath them, a naked plaster nymph stood, her right hand reaching toward the silver-plated icon of Nicholas the Martyr hanging above her; painted green, she supported a round toilette mirror with a massively inflated thigh.

"But everything here is really very elegant," said Lamere, sitting down. "I don't understand, though, why you have stopped up all the windows with blankets. Why do you have the lamp and the church candles burning? It's still day, after all—just dinnertime."

"Oh, stop; you big-city types are always judging. I practically didn't bring anything with me, you know, so that there wouldn't be excess baggage. So I just brought along a few doodads. But it seems to me, Madam, that you and I understand each other: after the age of sixteen it's better to suffer from too much heat than too much light, and a little perspiration is even rather piquant."

Fyodor and Leocadia's husband combined tea drinking with examining sketches. Lamere was silent. Leocadia's child reached for the table, which was covered with buns, cookies, and the finest sorts of chocolates the local co-op had to offer. Leocadia slapped him across the hands.

"He gets up before five and it's impossible to get him to sleep during the day. It's just torture with these children!" She moved the sweets farther away from the insistent boy.

But at this point Fyodor got involved. "Come on, Boba, let's make a bet over who'll fall asleep faster. You know, a race. The prize is this here chocolate." And Fyodor, taking one of his mother's hairpins, pinned the candy to

---

73 The reference is to the leading lovers in a historical novel, *Quo vadis: A Narrative of the Time of Nero* (1896) by the Polish writer Henryk Sienkiewicz, later a recipient of the Nobel Prize (1905).

the wall. It seemed as if one of the wallpaper flowers had suddenly ripened into a weighty dark fruit.

In a few minutes a pacified regular breathing could be heard from the neighboring room.

Leocadia smiled and, leaning over Fyodor's shoulder, whispered, "Boba's already asleep. Now it's your turn. Why aren't you sleepy? Why do your eyes never close? Tell us your secret, you madman."

To drown her out, Leocadia's husband began reading out loud from the prospecting journals. "*Spread investigation . . . exposing seams . . . deep and shallow drilling . . . diamond drilling.*"

Leocadia giggled. Fyodor grabbed an eraser and started erasing something in the prospecting journal. Sergey got up and had time to notice that Fyodor's eraser was directed toward the second of the following lines:

brownstone
come tomorrow?

Leocadia shrugged and stepped away.

"Tell me instead, are you very interested in Romania?" Leocadia squinted one eye. "I already know all about you. They say you and your wife don't get along and that you have dealinks with boyars."

"No," answered Sergey. "I said that before just because. You know, at my age it's awkward not to have a wife. And I never even think about Romania. That was just yesterday in the co-op."

"Whatever do you mean, in the co-op? How do you dare!"

"No, no, that was Big Al . . . He was just talking. That is, I don't know what his name is. The co-op operator just called him Big Al. Maybe you know his full name?"

"How should I know? I've only known him a month. This morning that disastrous madman left. Oh, everyone is leaving: him, and Fil d'Écosse too. Now all our hopes are pinned on the present company, who no one talks about. When he was leaving, he left me a book and, can you imagine, it's a very interestink writer—a Romanian, must be a smolderink brunet. I love a little literature."

"Are these the 'sharp marks of your nails'?" asked Sergei, leafing through the battered volume and unwillingly reading the marked places.[74]

---

74 In Alexander Pushkin's *Eugene Onegin*, the heroine Tatyana leafs through the title character's library, looking for the interesting spots he'd marked with his nails.

Leana left the train car. Adrian sensed in her a woman to the mar-
row of her bones, and instantaneously flared up like a campfire. In his head
everything spun with rabid speed; his heart leapt in his chest like a lion gone
hog-wild in its tight cage; his boiling blood poured like flame throughout his
whole body, from the mane to the claws of the beast. And not for naught. This
devilish young filly had, it seems, been forged in the raging inferno of desire.
The flexibility of her body recalled a snake. The poor guy's mouth went dry
from the irresistible desire to bite in. His eyes were clouded by a thick veil
raised up from his unrestrainedly blazing innards. He sank his face into her
neck and, disregarding her babble, hungrily, like a dog, drank in the scent of
her skin with his nostrils . . .

Sergey continued, "Why did this Romanian writer waste so much fire?
I like some of the other parts. You didn't notice them?"

"Why?" Leocadia repeated after a pause. "Well, it's all of your ilk; you're
all hidden volcanoes. You blink and there's a fire. I know, I can see right
through you: you're a streetlight, blazink with fire inside—everything's lit
up all around, am I wrong? Hey, don't be so quiet, it's immodest!"

Sergey saw that Lamere was biting her lip more than the cookies, and
Fyodor, leaning over the draft that he was showing Leocadia's husband, was
somehow tracing out one and the same line for far too long.

Sergey opened his mouth. The air was already moving from his lungs
to his vocal cords—in a second he would say something, and he waited
curiously to see what was about to sound forth from his mouth.

"Oh, your singing, your singing, Leocadia Innokentievna!" Sergey's
raptures rang out unexpectedly.

"Oh, I don't sink." Leocadia was overjoyed.

"Little Leocadia really doesn't sing," intervened her husband, breaking
away from the drafts. "Fyodor Fyodorovich, Sergey Sergeyevich, mama—I
don't know your full name—give me your glasses. The tea is very good—
Extra brand. Have two lumps, it's fine."

"I always have it without sugar," answered Fyodor.

Sergey fished a huge chunk out of the jar, one still not broken into
smaller pieces, and started spinning it around in his hands. "This reminds
me so much of the virginal nature of the Caucasus, the snows, Kazbeks,
passions. I really love Georgians, ardent Caucasian huts, dances, daggers."

"If you love it all so much," Leocadia began and, without finishing her
sentence, dropped Kazbek into Sergey's glass. The displaced tea spilled all
over the flowered saucer.

"Oh, that low, agitating voice," insisted Sergey, looking at the lamp, the green nymph, and the plaster wreaths.

"Sergey Sergeyevich, I don't understand what singink you're talking about—alas, I have no talents."

"What do you mean, no talents? That is, you're not Shakespeare, of course, not Aivazovsky, I'm not here to flatter you.[75] It could be, of course, that you don't have a voice for the opera, but that's not the point, the main thing is how it moves you, the main thing is *l'expression*! . . ."

"*L'expression*? Oh, you flatter me!"

"Yes, that's the key: some women have stronger voices, but you know, there's something missing, how can I say? . . . But you have it."

"You're awful, just awful." Leocadia slapped Sergey across the wrist with her handkerchief.

Now Sergey tried to grab her handkerchief, which started to tear, ready to split in two. Leocadia's face depicted the tragic conflict of passion and duty: on the one hand, there was the threat of loss in the form of a torn handkerchief; on the other hand, Sergey's manner and mode of action were captivating in their indubitably cosmopolitan style. Ultimately, passion won out.

"Hmmmpppphhh!" Leocadia tugged the handkerchief toward herself most coquettishly. The fabric split with a ripping sound. Sergey raised to his nose the half that remained in his hands. It smelled of co-op laundry soap and something burnt.

"This is *Rêve végétale*, of course," he asked, kissing the scrap in front of Leocadia's husband's gaze.

"Oh, no, it's a bouquet of country hay." Leocadia waved her scrap around. A bunched-up thread bounced along its uneven edge. "There are strange incidents," she continued. "Last month about thirty city Komsomol kids showed up and, just imagine—they were all little blonds.[76] Of course they couldn't find anywhere to sleep. You know, they were on some kind of cultural excursion or the like. They spent the night in the barn, on the hay. And, you know, that night the barn just went up in flames—not one of them survived."

"I was so engulfed by your singing that I can no longer distinguish between aromas, as you can see," Sergey continued.

---

75 Ivan Aivazovsky was a famous painter of the late nineteenth century.
76 The Komsomol was the Soviet Communist youth organization.

"So, you were there today, I presume?" Leocadia asked, lowering her voice.

"How could I not have been there, if you were there! But tell me, the co-op operator won't have anything against it?"

"Well, we'll check to see if this is really true. Describe this grove to me. And don't worry about him: he's pretty scarce himself. I'm sick of him, he talks about old age all the time. But excuse me, you were sayink: about the little grove."

"I don't know, it's just a grove."

"No, don't try to get out of it, tell me what kind of trees were there."

"All different kinds—oaks, birches . . ."

"Now that's not true—there were no birches."

"Leocadia Innokentievna," Lamere intervened, "Sergey Sergeyevich is from Peterhof and is such a city boy that you can't expect him to distinguish between trees; he can't tell the difference between rye and pines."

"Oh, you awful city boy!"

"Oh, that grove," Sergey went on. "When you flitted by between the bushes, I thought that I wasn't here in Mirandino but rather in Versailles, in the Trianon. You know: *On the banks of the crystal brook, the shepherdesses, the lambkins . . .*"[77]

"You're makink it all up—there were no sheep there, thank heavens, and I'm not some kind of shepherdess. It's such a desert here, of course; but in Minsk we have not just Great Lipki, but also Little Lipki. Anyway, I noticed right away: and then you asked me to give you a lift."

"You're right, yes. But your songs! You are a siren purer than this nymph." Sergey gestured toward the green mirror-bearer. "Anyone wishing to remain unharmed must stop up his ears with wax."

Leocadia looked curiously into Sergey's ear: turned toward her, it was rather large and had hairs peeking out from inside.

"Would you like a cookie?"

"I desperately want one, if it was produced by your hands!"

"I never used to cook; you know, there's no sense to it when there are cooks and dishwashers. But here I have to."

The shortbreads on the proffered dish revealed flourishes, knots, hearts, rhombuses. Sergey picked up a heart with two fingers, demonstrated it to everyone at the table, then pressed it to his chest.

---

77 Sergey quotes from a controversial historical drama by Dmitri Merezhkovsky, *Paul I*. In the play, the reference to the shepherdesses is acidly ironic.

"To the left, lower," intervened Lamere.

Sergey broke the heart cookie in two with a loud crunch, staring at Leocadia. "*So carelessly you touched my heart . . .*"[78]

"He's a comedian, and a poet to boot. Read us something, one of your poems."

"Only if you will sing to us as my reward."

"Well, tough luck. We don't have a piano here anyway."

Fyodor shuddered at these words.

"But you sang in that grove—there was no piano there either."

"Oh! I was just trying to get away from Boba. You know, children can be so annoying."

"Well, fine—you still owe us the singing. Now I'll read you my poem. This is from the champagne cycle."

Sergey raised his eyes heavenward, that is, to the blackened ceiling of the peasant cabin, overrun with cockroaches, and recited in a quavering voice. "*Our meeting—Victoria-Regia, rarely, rarely in bloom . . . You will come, I am dying from tenderness, and the hope just might, I shake in flight . . .* Will you be in the grove tomorrow?"

Finished, Sergey let his head sink. Leocadia laughed throatily. Suddenly everyone leapt up, and the drafts were quickly cleared from the table, which was swimming with streams of tea from an overturned cup.

"Excuse me," intoned Leocadia's husband.

Everyone began to make their farewells. Sergey reverently kissed Leocadia's hand, which had been jabbed into his mouth.

Leocadia didn't respond to Fyodor's bow, twisted her lips, and whispered to Sergey, indicating Fyodor with her eyes, "I'm imaginink how destroyed he'll be when he finds out. It's his own fault, anyway."

"Don't be angry," answered Sergey in a whisper. "He has a beauty as well."

"You don't say?"

"Yes, a beautiful rig, around the 105th bell pit."

"It's all right, come back anyway." Leocadia's husband invited everyone. "Sometimes it's nice to spend time in company."

"Oh, yes, gentlemen, so that you don't forget," said Leocadia. "Today there's a ball at the priest's wife's. Not Father Alexander's wife—she died

---

78 Sergey quotes a poem by the homosexual poet Aleksei Apukhtin, "The Broken Vase" (1883), a loose translation of a poem by René Sully-Prudhomme.

a whole year back—the one in Bogucharov. So we'll see each other again soon. My Innocence will be stayink home: he doesn't know how to behave himself in company."

Sergey asked whether Motenka would be there.

"What do you want him for? Isn't it more than enough that I'll be there? And I don't recommend you make Motenka's acquaintance; he's not of our breed. The public here is generally uneducated, it's awkward invitink them over: when they leave, they stuff their pockets with cookies and sweets. Not exactly high society, you know. Anyway, see you later."

They walked away from the house slowly, listening to the muffled voices, echoing out from the caulked-up windows: laughter, wails, squealing, the crash of broken dishes. The spouses were evidently having it out with each other.

The friendly trio strode on toward home, waving away the dogs that leapt up along the way. Fyodor went in the middle again, his arms around Lamere and Sergey. After the stuffy inside air and kerosene fumes, it was pleasant to breathe in the dusty air of the village road and to realize that it was not yet evening, but day at its peak; the apple trees stood, weighed down with fruit, and looking gray from the heat.

At the base of each apple tree lay a black patch of loosened earth. This moved Sergey to encircle the trunks with a metal grate and feel the asphalt of a boulevard, soft from the heat, beneath his heels. Any minute now he'd smell gasoline, and a bus would pull up and stop here, right beside the orchard.

Sergey would get on and, sitting down on the leather seat, start stealing handkerchiefs: the thickset office worker digging around in his wallet would never suspect that Sergey was filching his thumbnail and putting it into the still unfinished fifth line of his poem.

From Fyodor, who was squeezing his elbow, Sergey purloined an entire arm—he'd take it back with him to Peterhof. The smell of his skin would also come in handy. He'd take it as a souvenir.

In these minutes of enlightenment Sergey completely understood how dogs distinguish between women and men, children and old people by smell.

Sergey envied Queenie: she would be able to tell who had just passed by this dusty road. At the moment, she'd holed up in her oven and was utterly blissful: she'd eaten off the leg of a newborn foal. Comforting her infant, the mother horse stuck a piece of straw into its mouth.

The smell of sweat-soaked clothing and a cigarette-stained beard was strongly felt. It was—

CHAPTER TEN

Ivan Vasilyevich Shishkov greeted the walkers and treated them to apples. "One early autumn in Moscow, at his house in Khamovniki, Leo Nikolaich was munching apples and gushing, 'Now these are some real apples. Why don't I have apples like this in Yasnaya? You would think—I have a big orchard—almost a hundred acres. Where did you buy these?' 'At Bolota,' answered the lackey. 'Go there and ask the fruit sellers what orchards these apples are from.' In the evening, when Leo Nikolayevich was writing a reply in English to a foreign sympathizer, and Sofia Andreyevna had summoned the cook to the living room and was finalizing the menu for tomorrow's dinner, hesitating between sauté and boeuf braisé, the lackey returned and reported. 'The apples you ordered me to ask about,' he said, 'are from the Tolstoy orchards, in Yasnaya Pol—'"

"Ivan Vasilich," Sergey interrupted. "Why are you so dark? Are you a Gypsy?"

"My granddad was a Gypsy, but I worked as Leo Nikolaich's gardener for my whole life."

"Oh, you really ought to write your memoirs! You could make a pile of money."

"It's not our business to do the writing. Leo Nikolaich already wrote everything we need, and I work on the apples here in the co-operative."

"Now, that's the ticket," Sergey said approvingly. "There's no sense in writing about Helen, the lean-to, or Grisha Ermolov either."

Instead of answering, Ivan Vasilyevich showed them his living quarters. Beneath the ancient lindens, where Susi had once wandered about with her French novel, there stood a bright, freshly planed little plywood house. Lamere sat down on the bench by the entrance. Inside, there were three pallets: the middle one was for Ivan Vasilyevich; his assistants lolled about to either side. Shotguns hung on the walls.

"So this is how we sleep, without getting undressed; if y'hear so much as a branch rustle, you take down one of the shotguns and tiptoe on over. P'raps you might like a sip of water? We have good water here, tasty. Down by the river yesterday I saw 'em tugging over a boatful with three naked fellas. I asked 'em, 'hey, water carry off your clothes or what?' 'No,' they said. 'We're tourists; we've swum here all the way from Smolensk.'"

Ivan Vasilyevich fell silent, listening to the song carrying over from the garden. It was evidently Grisha Ermolov singing: "*Oh garden, my garden, my garden, my green vineyard.*"[79]

"Were they men or women?" Sergey inquired.

"No telling—they all had short hair, and all in the same loincloths. Wasn't like—well, excuse me, to put it bluntly . . ."

Ivan Vasilyevich really did put it bluntly. Fyodor blushed and looked down. The guys lying on the side pallets chortled.

"It's a good thing, a commune is," finished Ivan Vasilyevich. "But walking around naked, well, there's no cause for that. Leo Nikolaich wrote a lot against debauchery: he says that it is lawfully pleasant to see a naked girl, right, but a naked guy—that's enough to make you spit. You want to spew from the filth of it, like you stuffed your gut with unripe apples."

Ivan Vasilievich's gob of spit hit the rounded edge of a red apple lying on the ground.

"I'm tired for some reason," said Lamere.

But they were not far from home. They walked in silence. Fyodor's Management came along in a horse-drawn carriage. The Management tactfully turned away from the walkers, muttering, "I am blind in both eyes."

But Fyodor stopped him, leapt up into the carriage, and they both raced off to the sites.

Sergey walked Lamere to her bedroom and tarried for a moment in the landlady's room. A crocheted lace tablecloth covered the chest of drawers. Several framed photographs stood among the plaster kittens (one of the frames was from Crimea—made of seashells): Isa Makarovna in her youth, holding a rake; with her husband by the seashore (he seated in a bamboo chair, she standing and, evidently, expecting a child). Then a group shot: four women, a tea table with a samovar, the paralytic lady of the manor, sitting in a wheelchair and squeezing her children close. A young man in

---

79   Folk song, "Oh You Garden, You're My Garden."

a Russian peasant shirt and high boots with buckles, with cowlicked hair and an intelligent face, was very conscientiously stirring his tea: he was secretly already reading Buckle, pondering the female question, and had nothing but scorn for the assembled company. The last photograph showed the monument to Gleb Uspensky in Tula, the work of Riesenberg (on the pedestal: a lyre and one-fourth of a horse).[80]

Sergey approached the mirror and saw what he looked like in a Panama hat. The fly-blown glass reflected the bent rim of his hat and the tilt of his head, now thrown back, now hanging to the side.

"Could it be true that I'm demonic, too? Maria Semyonovna said something about it to me back in Peterhof."

Sergey knitted his brow and tugged a devilish lock of hair out onto his forehead from under the Panama hat. All of these exercises made him hot, all the more so since the windows were shut tightly and the sills covered with flowerpots with some sort of growths, a Mexican cactus and a lemon tree, which was specially covered with an upside-down glass (creating the hot atmosphere of Sicilian wild orange groves). Pink earthworms puttered about in the rich loose soil of these flowerpots. This was the very same earth that out there, out of doors, was birthing rye and barley, and covering the ore horizon already tested by Fyodor. Because of this earth, the peasants had routed the landowners' estates.

Sergey wiped away the sweat and thought, *It's very hot right now. The dust, the sun, I, the gangly grasses, summer, mothers, Fyodors—this always was and always will be. But the selection of statuettes being hawked by the little boys in Tula—that changes. Kittens, nymphs, puppies, Napoleons with stock plaster spines—I remember it all from my childhood. Now some new busts have joined that tired old crew. I wonder what they'll be hawking a hundred years from now?*

Just then a moment occurred that was doubtless of central importance to Sergey's life: he saw a vaguely bourgeois patchwork quilt on the landlady's bed. It was a bit stained, but the patches were still bright and multicolored, with dark lines separating them.

Sergey walked up closer. A blue square of diagonally patterned fabric seemed to hail quite possibly from a gendarme's trousers,

---

80 Gleb Uspensky (1843–1902) was a prose writer with populist-nationalist leanings. He was born in Tula and got his start as a writer under the tutelage of Leo Tolstoy.

CHAPTER ELEVEN

the brown fabric with white lilies from an old lady's fancy holiday blouse. Other scraps were girlishly soft and pink. Satin gleamed alongside the calico; nocturnal velvet was pleasant to the touch.

It seemed to Sergey, leaning down, that the quilt smelled most of all of cats and of something else, not unpleasant, but more historical: the stratification of generations, coffee, family happiness.

Sergey traced a finger along the patches, traveling from one color to the next. When he hit the satin, he shuddered spasmodically: it had the same effect as running a fingernail along wallpaper.

Scrape me with your saintly scraping on my soul and body—this prayer had been composed because the screen of the iconostasis made a grinding sound while closing: *the rings rusted*—that was Fyodor's take on it. Now, standing over the quilt, Sergey understood Fyodor's antireligious inclination. Of course, today would be the same thing again. The sunset would serve as a signal: the sun would lower behind the poplars; Lamere would eat buckwheat porridge with milk—a hygienic and moderate supper. Fyodor would come home in a good mood, anticipating the evening. The evening would be heralded less by the lowering twilight and fresh silence than by the faint languor following a full day's work out in the open air. How pleasant to sit in a chair and swing one's heels; to chat with one's neighbor, to stir tea with a little spoon; and even more pleasant to stretch out afterward in the hay.

"You're really letting yourself go today—is it because tomorrow's a big holiday?" Grandma will say to Fyodor when he asks for a fourth glass of tea.

"Yes, Grandmama, damn your eyes, of course that's why."

"Oh, don't put your elbows on the tablecloth! You've gotten so spoiled here."

Fyodor will take his arms off the table, raise them menacingly heavenward and declaim, "*Weep, o parent, and moan: your son is a scoundrel; your son is a socialist.*"

"What's that from?" Lamere will ask.

"Oh, it's just . . . And then there's '*Noble lads, this day is the illest-starred of all our lives: our Sovereign Emperor has met his end through a villainous bomb.*' I will draw an astonishing analogy for you between our Lord and the Sovereign Emperor, who lies at rest in the elder bushes. '*O Lord, forgive them, they know not what they do,*' said the Lord. '*A fine crook, stop the thief,*' said the Sovereign Emperor. '*O Lord, I deliver my spirit into your hands,*' said the Lord. '*Take me to the Winter Palace,*' said the Sovereign Emperor.

Grandma will listen, furiously gnawing at a crust of bread with teeth eighty years old, but still intact.

"'Noble lads'—that'd be a good name for cats," Sergey will say.

"Don't bother them, Seryozha, they're already sleeping, and we don't want you to cripple another kitten with your love."

"I don't understand how it's possible to love cats: cunning and treacherous creatures. Even piglets are better, if you have to love something," Lamere will intervene. "They actually have very beautiful eyes, pale and screened with white-blond eyelashes."

"By all means, I agree—piglets are pretty, especially under horseradish. But cats are better. The co-op operator and I share the same name. He already quoted something; now I have to," Sergey will say and begin to recite a sonnet about cats, with feeling.

"Nothing is sacred to you, Sergey Sergeyevich—it's the night before a church holiday and you're jabbering away in French." Grandma will be outraged and, incensed at her grandson's laughter, will be compelled to set down her saucer. "Everyone knows that the French nation is the most indecent: they just want nightclubs and beelzebubs—but as of now vespers still aren't over, so it's a sin."

"And it wasn't a sin for you to treat us to half-baked apples today at dinner?" Fyodor will ask.

"Wasn't my sin that they didn't bake all the way—the oven's to blame."

"No, that's not the point. You picked up those apples in the orchard on the path, so they're stolen. And you're going to get roasted for that in the next life for sure."

"Well, if I'm lucky they'll only half-bake me, like I did those apples." And Grandma will pull her saucer back toward herself again.

After that it should come as no surprise that Fyodor's Adored Management, riding past in his horse-drawn cart, will think, *Heh-heh-heh, see, big-city tricks. And they set it all up so neatly: first Fyodor's friend supposedly comes to visit—his friend, right—that's no shocker, we know that one.*

But then she comes, you see, from Moscow for a summer rest—tired from the opera, she says. Can you really get tired from opera? Eugene Onegin, now that's a good opera. No, she must work in operettas. These society types, damn 'em all to hell—they're probably all talking French among themselves.

The Management will fix the bandage on its forehead: it had a boil and is being treated by the local lady doctor.

Sergey will think of the Adored, *He's probably a fake expert and is just pretending with his bandage. Probably in the old days he just managed somebody's estate. It'd make sense if he turned out to be one of those Poles.*

The quilt gave off such a dense odor that Sergey started trying to catch it with his fingers.

Meanwhile, Isa Makarovna entered the room, with a parting phrase to those still sitting on the balcony. "Yes, so they really did go and lose that girl for two quarter-barrels of liquor. Ah, why are you all so polite? I'm not used to it."

She gasped when she noticed Sergey, who had lifted a corner of the quilt and was tragically observing the dark space beneath, absent of sheets; immense fleas frolicked there.

Embarrassment occurred. Sergey thrust the quilt away, blushing, leapt away from the bed, and was now standing in the middle of the room, demonstratively whistling, like a man in an exceptionally good mood and sporting an exceptional Panama hat.

The landlady, carrying a stack of ironed shirts, stood deep in thought. The lowest shirt was threatening to tumble out of the stack. Sergey recognized Fyodor's shirt, the one he'd worn in Peterhof.

"Let me help you." Sergey grabbed the edge of the shirt.

"It's fine, our Lord had to carry a heavier load," the landlady answered submissively and continued on into the kitchen. Through the door she could be seen beginning to fuss over the black troughs, tossing the linens into a basket.

The kittens stuck their little muzzles into a saucer of water whitened with milk. Sergey wondered about the fate of the kitten he'd crippled. Would he leap about on March rooftops? Would he be squeezed aside by burly cat stallions? Would he have to amputate both legs above the knee and, in a little cart, holding wooden false limbs, would he ambulate along the sidewalk, gambling on the piety of the retrograde strata of the population and coquettishly exhibiting from shortened trouser legs the red, ham-like excision sites, already grown over with a thin layer of new skin? Would a sensitive young passerby walk up to him and ask, "In view of certain circumstances, would you be so kind as to tell me your name and where you live?"

The invalid would arrogantly throw back his collapsed nose. "I've done been registered. I'm not begging, just walking along Nevsky no worse than you. But I'm sure glad to make your acquaintance."

Sergey thought that the kittens would hardly be happy if he joined their squeaking company, got down on his knees by their dish, and started lapping up milk. So he went off on his usual route over to the hayloft.

Now began the most exhausting hours—until dinner, which was late (counter to the country manner), because of waiting for Fyodor to return from work.

Sitting on the hay, Sergey counted up his wealth: Indian tea in a green wrapper; Chinese black tea, no. 1, in a dark-blue wrapper; no. 2, in a brownish one; Ceylon tea, no. 95; Central Union, in red; Chinese tea, no. 100, in purple. Why not buy up, as long as there's an open market?

Sergey had intended to devote himself to his usual hayloft ponderings but leapt up, bitten by a fly. She wandered around on his shirt, flat, greenish, and hefty. It was easy to catch her, since she wouldn't dream of taking off. In a firm grip, she didn't squash like an ordinary fly. She had to be placed on the base of a nearby barrel, the one where Sergey's toilette was arranged, and there carefully crushed by the octagonal end of a pencil. Sergey did this mechanically. The landlady's words about the good city of Aleksin on the Oka stood in his head. A pine wood, Kudeyar's well.[81] The landlady yelled at the children, "Enough of your caterwauling, get lost! . . . Go chase the sheep in."

At the same time Sergey was counting up how many seconds there are in a human life—he ended up with about a billion, which meant he had time to read a million pages.

The fly crunched under the pencil and turned into an inkblot. Sergey came to his senses and leapt up.

What is to be done? How to be? Leo Tolstoy says that killing is bad. But maybe it's good. Nothing makes sense. Why am I here, in the Krapivensky district? Why is everything so stupid? I must be stupid myself. One must love animals.

---

81 According to local legend, Kudeyar was a member of Ivan the Terrible's guard who went rogue and became a successful bandit, stashing all of his booty in a well somewhere between Tula and the neighboring city of Kaluga.

Sergey took the landlady's book from the barrel. *There is no doubt,* he thought, *that it means a lot to read something exactly where it was written: the climate and the air have stayed the same as they were before. The author leaned up against this tree trunk while strolling. This page was written after drinking tea, when his gums still remember the warmth of tea with milk. The Borodino battle was created, of course, after a fight with Sofia Andreyevna.*

Sergey dozed off without noticing and dreamed a hand. The black fur coming out from the shirt sleeve sprouted on the powerful muscle beneath the pinky as well. The men of Peterhof usually shaved their body hair once a week; their arms came to resemble women's arms, just magnified in size and more powerful. In German "fist" is *Faust, die Faust*—astonishing that this is a feminine noun.[82]

Sergey woke to the sound of hoofbeats. The worker was placing his equipment in a corner of the barn. The fellow greeted Sergey and told him that his workday was already over, but that Fyodor had gone to inspect the farthest-off bell pits.

"Hey," Sergey asked him. "How can I meet Motenka? Will you sponsor me?"

The worker, running his hands over the end of a rope, laughed and, instead of answering, told him about shovel turning, about spalling the ore down to the size of a fist, to a chicken's egg, to a large nut, to a pea.

Lamere, freshly bathed, came into the barn. "I wanted to come entertain you, Essess, so that you wouldn't be bored, but I can see you're not lonely here."

Sergey introduced her to the worker. "This is Fyodor's mother. Wait, don't go, Fyodor Fyodorovich—I need to tell you something."

Sergey got up in the middle of the hay barn, raised his arm high, toward the grooves in the roof, and gave the following speech. "Listen up, Fyodor Fyodorovich, or, if you will, the other Fyodor; or Fyodor number two. This lady—her name is Lamere—and I, we are both infected with petit bourgeois ideology. Do you understand what this portends? The multicolored glass-bead figures we get when we shake a kaleidoscope in our soft, white hands. But you, the other Fyodor, you're not myopic or farsighted—you're nineteen or twenty years old, you're obviously not made of glass. You're a

---

82 Sergey's observation has an additional layer of meaning in Russian, since "fist" is *kulak*—also the word used to describe the better-off peasants who were public enemy number one during the period of collectivization of agriculture, underway at the writing of this novel.

worker, so you're not cracked. Am I right? Come here, let me give you a feel."

Fyodor answered that he was a simple guy and easygoing. He laughed about the glass, but didn't have any problem when Sergey sat down very close to him. Lamere took out her lorgnette and observed the whole scene.

"Quit talking nonsense," said Fyodor, moving Sergey's hands away. "Are you from Leningrad or something?"

"No, I'm from Peterhof," Sergey objected. "It's cleaner there. Six-story buildings, all the windows lit up in the evening; doors everywhere, stairs, people in every room. Do you like people? You see, every one of them has two hands, a nose, two eyes—it's interesting. But all the heads are full of fragments swarming around. Early in the morning on the twenty-eighth of June, Catherine opened the door—they were already expecting her. The beast-like monarchy was shooting wild game from the pavilion."

"You were right about that lot," the worker interrupted Sergey. "Well, lay it out, what do you want?"

Lamere intervened. "I know what he wants. He wants workers' control.[83] He wants to read you excerpts from his Peterhof diary and the letters that Fedya wrote to him—to hear what you think, of course. I will listen too—I'll be the audience. Don't be shy, Essess. It's always useful to read out loud; it develops your lungs. Get on with it, here's your folder of papers. I'll lean back here; it's so nice to loll about on real hay, not just a prop—you can always feel the stage beneath the prop hay. One time I even scratched my décolleté back on that awful fake grass. And it can be hard to sing lying down, but nowadays the directors make you. We'll test it out—see whether you hayloft people sleep well here."

"Well, go on then, read. If it's about the civil war, then it'll be interesting. I didn't get to be in it, I was still too little."

Sergey confusedly leafed through the papers, glancing at his audience. But there was no longer anything he could do. He couldn't think of any pretext for refusing. The listeners were looking attentively at the lecturer, who had just given a fiery speech but was now entirely flustered. But Sergey still managed to mentally don a pair of horn-rimmed glasses.

---

83 "Workers' control" refers to a system instituted in many factories in the early Soviet period, in which the workers played a central role in managing their own workplaces.

1. Dear Sergey Sergeyevich! I'm alive and didn't die and, as You can see, am writing to You with my chicken scratch.[84] I received Your postcard and was very cheered by it, although I was sorry that it wasn't a private letter in an envelope. I've gotten pretty well set up here: I have two rooms with a balcony (that's what they call a veranda here), and my house is in the middle of a big orchard (fifty-two acres). A spruce avenue leads directly up to it. There's woods here, where they say mushrooms can be found, but the best part is the rye fields. The rye this year is gorgeous; in some spots it comes up to my shoulder. Life here is quiet, peaceful, people are nice, so You'll have an easy time getting fattened up. The weather has gotten fine now, and the wild strawberries are out; they've started collecting honey and there'll be fresh combs soon. Really, Sergey Sergeyevich, come visit me soon. Write and tell me when You're coming and I'll come meet You in Tula. I hope You won't be scared off by the long journey, and that You'll arrange to come see me in the shortest possible time. Tell Murusa that I am doing my utmost to write her a letter, but for technical reasons I cannot bring this benevolent intention to its conclusion (I fall asleep). And thus, Sergey Sergeyevich, I await You impatiently. The spirits of my ancestors have already made all the necessary preparations.

Faithfully Yours, *Fyodor Stratelates*
(A shock of rye was included with the letter.)

Unsent draft of the same letter.
. . . Yesterday I received your postcard and was sorry that it wasn't a private letter in an envelope with poems included. Now I can only hope that, trusting in your word as in a granite cliff, I will hear these poems in live performance no later than in August of this year.

---

84 Fyodor writes to Sergey using the formal you (*vy*), which is often capitalized in written correspondence. In the course of the novel, the two address each other using this form, an overt affectation considering the intimacy of their relationship (compare, for instance, their use of diminutive forms of each others' names). And in the "unsent" and "unwritten" drafts that follow, Fyodor addresses Sergey with the intimate you (*ty*), here rendered through lack of capitalization.

It's very nice here, although inevitable expenses have partly taken their toll: the woods have been partly chopped down, the ponds drained, and the spruce avenue has also been leveled. But that can all be fixed in time.

Work is in full swing—there's been more ore discovered about thirteen miles from here. I've already read all the books you gave me. Come visit soon, we'll go out wandering. The crowns of the surrounding leafy groves, which whisper softly upon the gusts of a light-winged zephyr, are filled in the nocturnal calm with the song of nightingales (actually I'm not sure about the nightingales, but there's definitely an oriole), but still more affecting for a sensitive nature is the sight of fertile fields of rye, as high as my shoulder . . .

2. Seryozha, I just got Your letter, and although I have not yet had time, like You, to read it ten times over, I think that over the next two or three days I'll manage to exceed that prewar standard. Seryozha! What do I need to swear by that my invitation wasn't "impulsive"? I think in our day and age all these pathetic phrases are outdated and sound strange at the least, so I won't try to convince You for the hundredth time of the sincerity of my invitation—I am just sending You a blank page with my signature, so that You can write your own formal invitation, well fertilized with oaths, sensitive expressions of friendship, and so on. It need not necessarily be written in prose.

Now I turn to business matters.
Answers.

1. The spirits of my ancestors will be delighted to see You, and Your presence will cause them no trouble whatsoever. I won't tell You who they are right now, in order to pique Your curiosity.

2. Describing my workday would be very long and difficult, since I have a lot of obligations, and the work is entertaining and not at all monotonous. It's nice to know that you're doing something for the common good. I've gotten really exhausted in the last while, but now I should have a little more free time, and if You would be so kind as to bring me that book—you remember

the one—then You would be as charming as always. We can keep reading from the place where we left off in Peterhof. Bring me Your poems, some underwear, and about sixty pieces of flypaper. And one more request: bring all of Your equipment along, since unless You get sick of me, I won't let You leave anytime soon, and I hope You'll stay with me until the cold weather begins. The weather here is fantastic, and I'm living in seventh heaven—there are lots of young ladies, the flag is waving, and I sleep in the hayloft now.[85] Can you imagine such luxury, sleeping on fresh-cut hay? In a word, Seryozha: I am waiting for You impatiently and counting the hours until You arrive. By the way, we'll make an excursion to Kulikovo Field and to Yasnaya Polyana, which isn't far away—about twenty miles. Come as soon as You can. I wish You all the best.

Your *Fyodor Stratelates*

Don't torture me with waiting and answer me and come as soon as you can. (A page is appended to this letter: Fyodor's invitation to Sergey.)

Unwritten draft of the same letter.
  . . . Damn your eyes, Seryozhka, if you don't want to come then you shouldn't.

On the nineteenth of June, 1929, when I was looking out at the streets and Uritsky Square floating past, I thought: how these twisting streets are dear to me, the endless sewer construction that drags itself out all summer, the passersby in their secondhand and cobbled-together suits—the bit of undershirt peeking out from under a blazer.

In the streetcar, seeing the rubberized overcoat, bare knees, ankle socks, and lacquered pumps of a smoking maiden, I remembered a different face: yellow, recently grown familiar.

The coachman was openly shocked when I agreed to his exorbitant price without much argument. His smile continued for the whole mile and a half, regardless of attempts to blame it all on the high price of oats these

---

85 Fyodor quotes a famous ironic description of the good life from Nikolai Gogol's play *The Government Inspector*: "I'm living in seventh heaven—there are lots of young ladies, lots of music, the flag is waving" (Act I, Scene 2).

days; he couldn't stop even in the room, where he solicitously brought the suitcases (one of them yellow, lacquered, from the Baltics; the other of vulcanized fiber, from abroad). I slapped the coachman on the shoulder, and his smile increased from this friendly and unaccustomed treatment. Even the next day, when he was driving some lady past my windows, he nodded to me affably.

The linens lay in a pile on the table, mixed together with forks and newspaper clippings, but I hurried to make the rounds of all the places where we had been nearly a month ago today.

The statues are walking down the stairs and losing their gilt as they go. One of the legs of the upper naiad, sitting with her back to me, ends very appropriately—in a mermaid's tail. But the other leg? Its stump ends directly in gilded flourishes. The naiad probably got her leg blown off during the imperialist war. In the avenue, conversations about Dushanbe—exotica, and Sarts.[86] On the street:

"I don't believe in these governesses, et cetera . . ."

"Maybe, maybe."

"We'll see, but for the time being I still have to live through another whole month. I'll live on milk, just like Balzac," and I gazed at the newly risen moon with pride. Palmate spruces lent it an archaic, Roehrich-like look.[87]

Many years ago, I was crossing this sea from Kronstadt, on my way either to Oranienbaum or to here.[88] The weather was foul, and the waves were lashing the bag, which was hiding a longed-for bar of chocolate with nuts. In the end, though, it hadn't suffered much from the Finnish waters. At that time, everything seemed big to me: the statues and the fountains and the chocolate bar, and even my own stupidity. My peers, even the girls, were certainly smarter than me, and I suffered.

Stackenschneider, Nicholas I, Menelaus—life in the pseudofarmer mode, the pseudo-Gothic style of the pseudoexalted.[89] A little church in the

---

86 Dushanbe is the capital city of present-day Tajikistan, previously a Soviet republic and before that, part of the Russian Empire. The Sarts are a group native to Central Asia.

87 Nikolai Roerich was a turn-of-the-century neo-Romantic Russian artist from St. Petersburg.

88 Sergey refers to several locations in the vicinity of Peterhof, west of St. Petersburg on the Gulf of Finland.

89 Aleksey Stackenschneider was the chief court architect under Emperor Nicholas I and responsible for the eclectic style of many prominent palaces in St. Petersburg. Menelaus was a king of Sparta and husband of the tragically beautiful Helen of Troy.

park, also Gothic, so as not to spoil the Walter Scott-ish mood of the most noble vacationing parishioners. In Petersburg, Nicholas I would leave for work in the morning: on the streets of the capital he would seek out those visiting provincials who didn't know his face. He would get very tired, but would always return to the palace with a provincial goose, feed him dinner with the royal family, introduce him to his wife and ask the guest's pardon. "And here is my wife, she was born Lutheran."[90]

Afterward he would go into the next room, put on his crown and mantle and return to his guest, who would by that time have gotten to feeling very relaxed, would be regaling the others with tales of harvesting hay, decoctions and toothache.

"Do you recognize me?" Nicholas would exclaim. "I am the emperor of Russia."

Hiccuping in terror, the guest would fall to his knees and beg for his life.

The next day the papers would print a new sketch from the life of the sovereign.

But in the basement of the Winter Palace he had a traditional Russian bath installed. The little Smolny Institute girl he'd fallen for, who'd been raised to adore the monarch, was delivered there by Benkendorf himself.[91] She cast uncomprehending eyes over the wooden buckets, sponges, and birch brooms and adjusted the kerchief on her breast.

Suddenly, completely naked but for his crown, the emperor appeared before her.

She recognized the adored face, fell to her knees, embraced the hairy legs, begging for her life. Later she was married off to Gorchakov.[92]

Regardless of my musings about Emperor Nicholas, I am having a nice time in this little room with its highly placed semicircular window: you and I rented it together. I've already hung a few pictures on the wall: an image of Hecate, with three faces and torches (torn out of a textbook Mannstein

90 A garbled quote from Anton Chekhov's story "Fat and Thin" (1883). Meeting his "fat" schoolfellow after a prolonged absence, the "thin" character cordially informs him of the wife's Lutheran background, but immediately changes his manner of speech as soon as he learns that the "fat" character has now become a high-ranking official.

91 The Smolny Institute for Noble Maidens, Russia's first educational institution for women, was founded in the mid-eighteenth century by Catherine the Great. Benkendorf was the notorious chief of the secret police under Emperor Nicholas I.

92 Alexander Gorchakov was an influential foreign minister under Nicholas I and his successor, Alexander II.

edition), a map of this town, and a view of the church in the merchant's quarter in Novgorod, which I drew awkwardly myself many years ago, when I was interested in thirteenth-century frescos and had no idea that it would have another meaning one day.

Everything is fine. I'm drinking my milk, going through clippings and notes.

I can hear military trumpets off in the distance. They're rehearsing: "*Oh ma bayadère . . .*"[93]

The hopes of the future are swarming beneath the window and making sand pies.

The health-resort inhabitants are indulging in innocent games: wearing a blindfold, you have to whack a block with a club. A girl in a white dress, very mysterious, since her face is bound with a towel, is beating some cheerful and happy guy about the head.

The bright air warbles audibly, the birds chirp cozily, the milk is nutritious. This is how it will be for another whole month . . ."

"Quiet, Essess, finish up your reading. Don't bother him. I'll have to recommend your diaries to Boba, too."

Lamere got up and leaned over the sleeper.

"So young, so blond, and hardly older than Fyodor. He could be my son."

"And his name is Fyodor too."

"So he's another Fedenka. Only you can see he's stronger, healthier. That's from the physical labor. But maybe his parents too . . . He certainly doesn't suffer like Fyodor does from hereditary migraines. He's overheated, all worn out."

Lamere pulled out a very delicate handkerchief and began to dry off the sleeping Fyodor's forehead. The lace went gray from the sweat and dust. Without waking up, the boy turned over, away from Lamere. He thrust out his right hand and squeezed a handful of hay. The nails were covered in reddish clay.

"Sergey, don't sit there idly. Here's your diary—I like that it's large format. Now, fan Fyodor. You see, he's perspiring, and there are flies here. And I'm going to see Grandma about dinner."

---

93   *La Bayadère* is a ballet set in India, which was originally created for a celebrated Russian prima ballerina (Ekaterina Vazem) in 1877.

Turning back, Lamere added, "Well, you got your answer, Essess. There's your workers' control."

Lamere left. Sergey tossed about the barn, finally couldn't resist, and crowed like a cock, waking the sleeper.

"Get up, it's morning already! Time for dinner. But first, tell me what you thought."

He woke up instantly.

"What I thought? You had it right about Nicky Palkin, but it was awful boring.[94] Nothing ever happens to anybody; they just write letters—a waste of stamps. Anyway, I'm thinking about marrying Maryanka."

Sergey swooped in. "Oh, tell me all about it, tell me how you feel, how she feels."

"What's to tell about that." Fyodor laughed. "Everyone knows about that already. Well, bye, maybe we'll see each other again here."

"You're really not staying for dinner? It should be very soon now."

"No, I don't want to eat Fyodor Fyodorovich out of house and home; the Management already tries to worm its way to dinner every day. And anyhow it'll be more fun at home than with the old ladies here."

"I'll walk you," said Sergey to the boy. "I want to get to know you. Fyodor likes you, right?"

"Yeah, Fyodor Fyodorovich and I are working out fine. He's a noble laddie for sure, but he's a serious comrade, and in our crew he'll get fixed up in no time. Maryanka approves of him too."

"So who's your landlord: a middle peasant, a poor peasant, or a kulak? I know all about the stratification in the villages. I read the papers."

"He has seventeen horses alone," answered Fyodor.

"The poor guy, how does he deal with them all?"

Fyodor just laughed in response.

The hut where the worker lodged wasn't far from Leocadia's house. Walking past, they saw her sitting dreamily in the window. She was cracking and spitting sunflower seeds, but when she saw Sergey and Fyodor, she turned away, pretending to be examining the sky.

The hut's owner came out to greet them and, seizing both of Sergey's hands, dragged Sergey toward him. "Welcome! We're always glad to have guests."

"I'm not here to see you—I was just walking Fyodor home."

---

94   Disrespectful nickname for Nicholas I.

"Hey, kid, don't mess with other people's business," the landlord shouted at Fyodor. "And please come in, if you'd be so kind. I've heard, I've heard everything. You're here as a friend of Fyodor Fyodorovich? He's a good man."

The front room into which Sergey was led turned out to be quite comfortable. There were no flies at all: screens had been installed in the open windows. A bicycle leaned against the wall. The city-style plush furniture was grouped around the table. There were pictures, too: *The Ninth Wave*, then *Magdalene by the Lake*, and a third depicting a hunting dog with open maw, very white fangs, and drool dripping from its canine gums.[95]

Sergey quickly shifted his gaze away and contentedly rested it on a poster decorating the partition wall. A peasant woman grinned out at him, encircled by a ring of dancing letters (*The radio is the path to a new, cultured village*).

Sergey sat down on an armchair and felt surprise: in the last day and a half he'd already grown unaccustomed to soft furniture. He could only remember the hard benches of the train car: sitting on them, you start to feel the bones inside you, and you change your position, wiggle around, look out the window, but there's nothing you can do to suppress the knowledge that you are a skeleton. Then he remembered the pinching furniture by the red corner, too.

Sergey sprawled out with a feeling of great pleasure. To entertain him, the landlord brought out a postcard—just one, for some reason. It was a landscape, something like a park. First the landlord suggested Sergey just call him Syssoyich, and second, asked him to guess what was on the postcard.

"Trees," answered Sergey. "You can't fool me: birches, oaks, pines."

"Wrong. That is, there are trees there for sure, but they're not the good part. This is a forest, but it's foreign. I was a prisoner-of-war for three years outside Cassel. I learned how to talk with the boss. But over there in their villages the streets are paved, and the houses have two stories. If you're a good worker, then you're treated well. But you should quit with this Fyodor: he's not going anywhere. The village councilwoman sent him over to stay here with me; she said it's close to his work. So let him go to work; it's no skin off our back. But tell Fyodor Fyodorovich that he shouldn't believe him

---

95 *The Ninth Wave* is Aivazovsky's most famous painting. *Magdalene by the Lake* is probably the painting of Christ and Mary Magdalene by the Finnish painter Albert Edelfelt.

when he goes saying Sazykin did this, Sazykin did that. He lies all the time. Now Leocadia Innokentievna—she's a different story. A solid lady."

"Who's this Sazykin?" Sergey asked curiously. The landlord, chuckling, stroked his smooth-shaven chin, poked himself in the vest, and suggested they listen to the radio.

Sergey, gripped by a steel band, heard Moscow: *To forget, the full moon, the quiet rustling of the blinds . . .*[96]

Blushing, Sergey took off the headphones.

"What, it got you all hot and bothered? That's culture for you!" The landlord was triumphant. "Our whole district is cultured. Leo Tolstoy, you know, he's ours too. They don't have anything like it over in the Bogorodsky district—the Tatars were there at some point, so everyone there still has wide cheekbones and sits around flipping coins. So you just tell Fyodor Fyodorovich, as a friend, that he should do his digging a bit farther off. It's up to him where they dig, after all. The other people can't see what's underground; they'll drill wherever he says. And I'm planning to build on a second story next year. I get it: we're bringing the city and the village together. Used to be, everything came from the city: thick coats and gramophones and nice couches—all for our milk and our grain. But now they can't get us that easy. In Cassel, y'know, I got mixed up with the landlady's daughter; when we were done kissing, she just kept going on about bees, said they'd taken our Russian bees to Australia, to the warm climate. The first year everything went fine. Then the bees figured out that there was no winter out there and stopped making honey: no reason to stock up, they figured, so long as the weather's fine all year round and not right for us. So the Australian people had to go without sweets; they just get by on the warm climate. But hey, where are you off to? Sit a while, have some dinner—we love having guests. I'll treat you to some Ukrainian fatback."

But Sergey was hurrying outside. Behind the house a garden had been laid out, with red phlox in abundance, city-style. Syssoyich's red-cheeked wife, wearing a short skirt and with her neck bared, was walking between the flower-beds.

"When the black-eyed susans bloom," she was saying, "that means autumn's started. I love wallflowers. I've been dabbling in them ever since

---

96   A poem by Aleksey Apukhtin, set to music by Pyotr Tchaikovsky (with whom Apukhtin was romantically involved).

the tsar died. I ought to go to a nunnery; such a shame there aren't any nearby."

Saying goodbye, Syssoyich was still going on about warm regions, about a hunter there who was always climbing trees but finding only holes and no hives—all the bees had gone back to the wild. The hunter kept on climbing, fell into one of the holes, and drowned in honey.

"A sweet death," objected Sergey.

"Sweet for some; there are all kinds of deaths. You just tell Fyodor Fyodorovich to keep away from us." The landlord winked.

Sergey turned away and saw the sun, far off on a hill. It was already waning and shining through the leaves of the walnut tree.

Sergey decided he'd walk down to the river to have a swim. The river was probably just behind that hill. Once atop the slope, Sergey looked around: the surroundings looked artificially Russian, with rolling hills and forests on the horizon. From here Mirandino seemed tiny and unfamiliar. Every once in a while came the cry of the muleteer, chasing the mules working the plots of garden vegetables. Whole flocks of birds flew past, hurrying toward the cool of the river, skirting the fruitful plain.

"Am I really here for the second day already?"

The river was flowing desertedly. Sergey remembered whirlpools, fast currents, quicksands and so on. Then he imagined that, as he bathed, someone in the midst of this unspoiled wilderness would creep up and steal away his clothes, even though they were minimal because of the heat, but still, Sergey would have no way of returning to Mirandino. Or, while he swam on his back in the middle of the darkening river, gazing up at the sky, flat and absurd, if you look at it from that position, suddenly he would hear the cry, "Motenka!" and Sergey, with no time to think where the cry came from, would hide beneath the cool water. And so, although the river was already very close, Sergey turned back, trying not to look into the distance—the vast space frightened him.

Right in front of him were black clumps of turned-up earth, a tramped-down path running through the tilled field, and on the path, a pile of horse manure and broken sticks. Something carried through the warm air, redolent of earth: it was either a cry, or Sergey's ears were ringing from the heat. He walked on without stopping. It gradually became clear that someone was yelling Sergey's name. This was unremarkable: this name is found all over the place. Finally, Sergey lifted his head.

On the opposite descent stood Fyodor, waving his hands. Sergey hurried over to him.

"Did something already happen, Fyodor?"

"Well, yes, a terrible tragedy: it's time for dinner, and you're nowhere to be found, so I went off to fetch you."

"After work? But aren't you tired?"

"I'll say, but now mostly from yelling. I've lost my voice completely. Everyone's already at table, but I decided we couldn't possibly start without you."

"I picked raspberries along the way for you."

Sergey gestured to his full hand. Fyodor leaned over and, like a calf, began taking the berries with soft lips and licked them all up.

"So, what do you say, Seryozha? You like it here?"

"Very much."

"And you didn't want to come."

"What do you mean, I didn't want to?"

"It's that simple; you're just trash."

"And you're a scoundrel."

They were now walking through the golden rye, a narrow strip that hadn't yet been harvested. Everything seemed yellow, from the sun above to the ears on either side. Fyodor had shed his work clothes and was wearing a net shirt consisting entirely of holes. Funny words like *vermin, lowlife, idiot* went echoing throughout the field. Then, holding hands, they took off at a gallop through the stubble field: *Walking through the stubble, it ain't no trouble, opa-la opa-la, with you, my modest friend.*[97]

"So is there ore beneath Leocadia's house—that is, I should say, her castle? And beneath Sazykin's house too?"

"It's everywhere. We found it there a while ago, and the seam isn't deep at all; we'll just have to take off about a meter—the other Fyodor told me: he hit on it when he was digging in the garden. In another year you won't recognize this place. It'll be way more lucrative to work that ore than an orchard. Why are you so down in the mouth, Seryozha? Are you sorry for the orchards?"

The orchard really was giving off moaning sounds. Having eaten more apples than was wise, Georgie Gusynkin was rolling around on the ground.

---

97 The boys sing a modified version of "Autumn Day," a 1909 poem by the Symbolist poet Alexander Blok.

His wife was yelling at him sarcastically from the kitchen porch. "Oh, Georgie, Georgie!"

"I don't know," answered Sergey.

"Oh, come on, Seryozha, what's threatening me? Your poems or your departure? And I'm still hoping anyway that you'll stay . . . What do you want?" Fyodor asked the approaching peasant. He was complaining of damage to his crops from a bell pit being dug.

Fyodor waved his bare arms dismissively. "You know the law! What, you think you're the first? All the damages will be paid according to the law. You don't understand that these mines are better for you."

The peasant made some reference to Syssoyich and followed the pair with a displeased look as they walked away: the one of them apparently an engineer, but dressed strangely, and with arms as white as a girl's; the other supposedly an engineer too, but walking around without boots like some kind of beggar; both of them without hats; leaping around like goats, chattering and laughing. The peasant spat, cursed them both as shameless, and turned back.

They'd already sat down to dinner when the carriage with the Management drove up.

"You're having dinner? What a strange coincidence."

Noticing the German book next to Sergey's cutlery, the Management leafed through a few pages (Grossherzog Wilhelm-Ernst Ausgabe, in yellow leather) and said, "You're always reading in French, young man—that's admirable. In my youth, I also used to read in five languages."

Grandma's expression showed that she was used to coincidences. A place was set for the Adored.

Fyodor leapt up from the table under the pretext of needing to wash his hands. "Seryozhka, come wash me. You'll hold the soap and the towel."

However, by the well they didn't so much wash as give themselves over to mournful reflection. Fyodor lamented, "What bad luck, he's back again. It'd be better if one of the workers would come and have dinner with us. But they won't come. Leocadia's right: we're the local intelligentsia. Seryozhka, you're our last hope—make conversation with him."

Sergey, holding the soap dish with a pink nub of soap surrounded by foam, thought, *How fine it is to mark the passing of the day with dinners, suppers, and teas. The co-op operator, Syssoyich Sazykin, and the Adored—they all speak exactly the same language. How can we know—maybe they aren't three people at all, but just one. I really ought to look into this more closely.*

Since Sergey experienced light tremors each time Fyodor took the soap from the soap dish, put it back, or tugged the towel from his shoulder, he felt himself to be a marble washstand—gray and veined. The marble shelves surrounding the oval mirror held a mug for gargling with a yellow cellulose toothbrush in it; a little blue box with mint-scented chalk and a beauty on the lid; three kinds of soap—sandalwood, fern-oil, and Dr. Pomelov's trade-marked sulfur-tar soap—a rubber sponge and a rough nail brush. Gray soapy water dripped down the pipe into the slops bucket beneath. Fyodor's discontented face was reflected in the water-spattered mirror.

The Management praised Fyodor for his hygiene but did not itself follow his example, taking a dish of cold cucumber soup from Grandma with dust-covered hands.

The first conversation to get going was about groceries, but only Grandma and Fyodor took part.

"Tomorrow's Sunday, we have to go to church."

"I won't let you go."

"You said yourself that you went by the chapel in Leningrad."

"That was to get rice, Grandma. A certain woman there whom I adore told me: the rice in the co-op is trash, but in the chapel, they've got it coming out of their ears. I'll have to remember to go to St. Isaac's for the white cheese."[98]

The Management, however, didn't take the bait and went on gazing attentively at Sergey, hoping to comprehend the expression on his face. Sergey looked very intelligent and twice repeated, "The quilt . . . the quilt."

Then Fyodor threw a napkin over his head, and for a moment Sergey found himself in a whitish half-darkness.

Leaning over to Sergey's ear, still half-covered by the napkin, the Management whispered, quite clearly, "Tell me, how does that expression go: menazh for three?"

The soup gurgled in the mouths of those sitting and laughing.

"You live well here," said the Adored. "All friendly and fun. But I'm here without my family and just weak from hunger. Many thanks to your grandmama, who sent me a leg of lamb—I gobbled the whole thing up in two days. I'm also thinking of ordering myself a pretty little lady from Moscow—it's boring living alone, you know."

---

98 St. Isaac's is a massive cathedral in central St. Petersburg. *Tvorog,* a kind of cottage cheese, is associated with certain holiday rituals of the Orthodox Church (especially Easter).

Fyodor tried to change the subject.

"Bore pits," he said. "Crown support, the value of extending the bore pits . . ."

"Later, later. Don't start talking about work, Fyodor Fyodorovich; when eating, one should talk about something pleasant to aid digestion. Once upon a time I had me a little Rose. She was, you know, I couldn't take her on the tram—everyone ogled her, her shoulders were that alabaster."

Sergey looked into his soup plate: in the kvass, whitened with milk, bits of green onion were floating in the glinting waters, winding around cliffs of boiled potato and fibrous segments of dark meat. Stirring his spoon around, Sergey made a gale in his plate: everything crawled onto everything else, and one could pluck the most succulent bits out of the whirlpool and feel the taste of cold soup in a refreshed mouth.

Meanwhile, the Management was already talking about Leocadia. "An interesting woman. Well, I just had to employ her. Let her make sketches of bell pits—it's like fancy needlework, or how people used to sketch in albums back in the old days."

Sergey sighed and raised his gaze. "I too witnessed an interesting case, though it wasn't here, it was in Kamchatka."[99]

"In what capacity were you there?"

"Do allow me to pass over that question in silence, I would consider it immodest to speak overly much of myself. They know their volcanoes well in Kamchatka, but they had never heard of love. The poverty of nature was not conducive to the development of feelings; their fields grew only onions, and the growth of the population was extremely slow. A durable reindeer skin, a good bottle of fish oil—these things were of far greater importance to the Kamchatka natives than that which was undertaken hurriedly in their dismal yurts, reeking of blubber. And so it continued until the third decade of the last century. As we know, this was when the notorious feud between Metropolitan Platon and Emperor Alexander took place. It all happened because the metropolitan, bearing in mind high society's enchantment with all things French—including Catholicism— decided to counter this by conducting the Russian Orthodox service in French. 'One can come to know the glory of God in every language,' mused the metropolitan. 'So why not read the litany in French; it will thereby touch sooner the hearts of the ladies, with their high waists and

---

99   Kamchatka is a peninsula with a forbidding environment in Russia's Far East.

coiffures *à* la grecque, and the incorrigible brains of the aged Voltaireans.' The metropolitan began to translate the text of the liturgy himself. The long-awaited day arrived. The deacon came out to the altar of the Kazan Cathedral, shook his locks, and roared forth: *Beni, despot*—thus the metropolitan had translated 'Bless us, o Lord.' Arakcheyev, who was present at the service, convulsed.[100] Young men of a disgusting appearance, wearing evening dress, greeted the deacon's ejaculation with applause; the walls of the cathedral had never before observed such enthusiasm on the part of the worshippers. The service turned into something political. But when the boys' choir, wearing Polish caftans and having some difficulties with French pronunciation, struck up in their seraphic voices *Seigneur, ayez pitié de nous, 'tié de nous, 'tié de nous*, and the basses picked up with *Toi, seigneur, à toi, seigneur*, the St. Petersburg chief of police himself had to intervene and, declaring a state of emergency, brought the enchanting service to a close. The next day, Metropolitan Platon was most imperially exiled to Kamchatka. There he immediately set about learning the local language and enjoyed such success that one month later, in a stinking yurt referred to as a cathedral, he read a sermon in this language before a group of forcibly gathered Kamchadals and Aleuts."

---

100 Aleksey Arakcheyev (1769–1834) was a Russian general and statesman.

CHAPTER THIRTEEN

"He had taken Apostle Paul's text *Love is patient, love is kind* as the topic of his sermon.[101] In exquisite Kamchatkan, rivaling Bossuet in its circular periods, the priest extolled the virtues of love in comparison with faith and hope.[102] 'If I have not love,' the priest exclaimed—he was no longer the metropolitan of Petersburg and Ladoga, but the bishop of Kamchatka and Aleutia—'then I am become as sounding brass or a tinkling cymbal!' And he struck his breast with such force that his Mother of God icon really did give off a metallic sound. The natives, hiding their faces in their furs, giggled every time the consecrator pronounced a certain word. Afterward it transpired that he, having learned the local language through and through and adhering scrupulously to the requirements of rhetoric, had been using the sort of synonyms that in literal translation might only be seen in Russia in the form of scrawled graffiti on fences. The consequences of the sermon read by Kamchatka's enlightener made themselves felt right away. Not a year had gone by, and the population of Kamchatka tripled."

The Adored Management listened with its lower lip hanging open. Saliva glistened in the corners of its mouth. It was thinking, *A red journalist or not a red journalist?*

"Yes," it said. "I work here from dawn till dusk, with no time limits. Sometimes, of course, engineers are negligent, but I get on with the workers like I'm their own father. I fight the kulaks, right?" It turned to Sergey. "But I saved the best for last. Madame, in light of the irreproachable work of your son, I will be petitioning for his advancement to the rank of superintendent of the works."

Lamere, who had been silent for the duration of the entire meal, suddenly exploded in laughter. "Fyodor's a superintendent! Congratulations."

He fell upon her with kisses. "You see, Faiginyu, good deeds are always rewarded, but vice triumphs."

---

101 1 Corinthians 13:4 and later 13:1.

102 Jacques-Bénigne Bossuet was a seventeenth-century French theologian, famous for his exquisite oratory.

The Management, waving goodbye, drove off. Fyodor the worker came up onto the balcony. Sergey was cheered. "Are you here to see me?"

"No, you're not interesting," the boy answered. Both Fyodors started whispering in the corner. Sergey tried as hard as he could to listen in.

"Don't worry about Sergey Sergeyevich: we've figured all that out. We should have an answer from Moscow as soon as today or tomorrow. But about . . ."

Sergey, having heard his name, came closer.

"No, no, Seryozha, you can't hear this; you're too talkative."

Sergey was offended. "What kind of secrets are you keeping, Fyodor? You and the other Fyodor are having a laugh at my expense?"

"Yeah, yeah, me and the other Fyodor. But you have to wait till tomorrow."

"Bye, Fedya."

"Bye, Fedya."

Grandma dragged out the samovar.

"The worst thing ever in life," said Sergey, "is not having enough tea. This winter I somehow used up all my tea, but you couldn't get more with the ration books for a whole month. I bought a bottle of red wine and tried to color hot water with it, but it didn't help. At that moment, I happened to be deeply in love—I don't remember with whom. I only know that it was my number nine, an all-devouring passion: love and the lack of tea."

"You're just trash, plain and simple," Fyodor remarked in response.

"Fyodor, Fyodor." Lamere stopped him.

"Why, Faiginyu? I also love tea, its astringent taste. Can you feel it tugging on your gums? And it's hygienic for the stomach as well. Give me your glass, Seryozhenka."

Fyodor poured out of one teapot. Taking the golden glass, Sergey said, "Connoisseurs always drink tea without sugar, so as not to suppress the aroma."

But Fyodor waved his chocolate bar. "Old-regime chocolate! We could only get this one bar. The co-op operator sold it to me on advance. He said he'll show me the rest—that is, the sugar allowance—tonight. Well, we'll see about that. Who should I give this to, an advance toward Leocadia?

"You—you're an experienced seducer and lover of antiquity." Fyodor extended the chocolate toward Sergey.

Grandma got sad for some reason.

"No, Grandmama, damn your eyes, of course it's for you! He just gets the wrapper."

Sergey learned from his present that Georges Borman had received the *grand prix* at the international exhibition in Paris.[103]

"Only mind you," Fyodor continued. "You have to eat all of it right here, right now. We have to keep an eye on Grandma. When you give her sweets, she loves to hide them. Then, when someone wants something sweet and there's nothing in the house, Grandma takes out her box of chocolates—turns out there's a whole year's worth, all dried up, stuck together and smelling of mothballs. Well, Grandmama, to your health: the co-op operator swore that this chocolate came out in 1904."

"Yes," Sergey added. "Old wines have the most wonderful bouquet. Where does it come from? They say that time is just a category of judgment. But it does make things smell."

Grandma leaned her chin on her hand and pronounced, addressing Lamere, "Oh, I was once as young as you."

Lamere began protesting, peeled back the silver foil and broke off a piece of the graying bar.

"Give me some tea quick. Ugh." Fyodor spat. "I always said that the old regime was foul. Mosselprom is much better."[104]

The bells for vespers had already rung out. Noticing the approaching darkness, Fyodor went into his room, announcing that he had to do some sketching. Through the window they could see him light a candle and, laughing, draw something on the paper.

"While Fyodor is sketching, let's go for a little stroll, Essess. It'll be good for you to dip into the Russian Tula element. Otherwise you're entirely cut off from life. Your friendship with Fyodor helps: he's a producer and an enthusiast of modern times; you should stick close to him. In general, I think your composure is feigned. You're really not very well adjusted. Fyodor isn't either. When he was about ten, he was fascinated by chickens. He would call them—*goo-lu, goo-lu-lu*—and would sprinkle grain on their heads with such love that they ran away in all directions. Finally, there was nothing left to lure them with: they went feral, started flying around and spending the night in the birch trees. A hunter we knew shot them all

---

103 Georges (Zhorzh) Borman was a St. Petersburg chocolate maker founded in the mid-nineteenth century by Grigory Borman.

104 Mosselprom (the Moscow Trust for Processing Agricultural Production) was a major Soviet production organization in the 1920s.

down, at our request. I bet that's your kind of thing: hunting wild chickens. So, tell me, how did you spend yesterday here?"

"I don't know," answered Sergey. "Fyodor says that I'm an antiquarian. I really do love history, the heroic achievements of times past: the capture of Perekop, the battle of the Arginuz Islands, Germany's war of liberation against Napoleon."

"Come on, hurry up: story number three, I'm keeping track," said Lamere.

"And the last one," Sergey assured her.

You see, the plot takes place in 1813, in a German village. The French have mobilized the peasantry; many have deserted. A peasant is awakened by a rustle. He walks closer and listens: uneven breathing, like that of a young animal. It is his son, covered wetly with the frost of a damp night. The peasant seizes the limp body with firm fists and shakes him.

"Are you alone?"

"No, Father, there are others here too."

"How many?"

"Ten."

They had gutted the bottom half of the big haystack that filled one side of the barn, building a roomy cavity-cave in its center, where all eleven of them had crowded in. The peasant passed them provisions through the top and carefully covered the shelter with hay.

The boys pawed each other in the darkness like young blind dogs. They shoved each other around, sneezed, spat from the warm, sweet air, swore, and, gradually becoming intoxicated, finally fell asleep.

They crowded around the peasant like pigs when he came to their hiding place with food. They stood in the shed above the troughs and rubbed their faces, covered in a layer of filth.

"I don't want to hide anymore, Father."

The old man seized him and shook him like a sheaf of straw. The youth began weeping, quietly rubbing his neck.

"Why are you keeping me here? The others don't want to anymore either."

The old man could hear from the sound of their voices that they hated him like a jailer. He felt as though the enormous haystack was lying on top of him and suffocating him.

Rumors started to spread through the village that the old man had some kind of a tumor in his stomach that was sucking up everything he ate, so that he had to constantly buy enough provisions to feed a dozen men in ruddy health.

The young men started crawling out of their shelter and hanging about on the threshing floor. They straightened out their deadened, twisted limbs, ran back and forth, filled their lungs with the clean night air. Intoxicated, they rambled, embracing, jostling one another and wallowing.

Due to the long hiatus, they could no longer control their voices, and wild sounds tore out of them, harsh barks.

They started eating a week's worth of provisions in a single day. Water no longer satisfied them. One of them made his way to a tavern and brought back a pitcher of beer.

The peasant thought, *What terrible sin did I commit that I must suffer so much?*

The French would hang him for harboring. Just a spark, and the whole hay barn would disappear as if it never was.

The father fought his son. The rain fell in thin streams. Both were weakened: the old man by worries, privations, and fever; the young man by his long internment in the cramped shelter. They beat each other rather feebly about the face and the head, throttled and dragged each other back and forth.

The young man was soft and warm and smelled like a young animal; the hairs on his chin had grown wildly and hung fluffily about his flabby cheeks. The thick dark auburn hair on his head, matted with pieces of hay, protected him from his father's blows; the latter's angular skull was given over nearly defenseless to the authority of his son's fists.

Lying in a wet puddle, they gnawed on each other, feeling the esophagus cartilage beneath their thumbs.

And that's it. Sweet and cozy Germany one hundred years ago. Everything there is close at hand: these guys are wallowing in the ditch, while two feet away there lives young Pfeffel, suffering from eyesight problems. Out of compassion for him, the daughter of his landlord, Margaretha Cleophe, serves as his secretary. One day Pfeffel dictates to her, "You are the mistress of my heart. I bless that heavenly hour when you first began taking down my dictations. Can I dare to hope that you might one day feel something more for me than the feelings of a secretary?" The letter was finished. The girl asked quietly, "How shall I write the address, sir?" "Fräulein

Margaretha Cleophe Divoux," answered the young man just as quietly. They were married and, despite the blindness that struck the young husband on the first day after the wedding, they were entirely happy. Their family gradually became populous: twelve children brought them the liveliness they desired.

"Look, the sky's already gone all starry. Evening and silence. The hayloft will be fine on a night like this." Sergey finished his story.

"Don't forget," Lamere objected, "that we're still invited to the priest's wife's. Essess, on top of everything else, you're sentimental. This morning I decided that you have Baltic skin and hair, but now I see that even your soul is Baltic."

"Obviously, nature is just having a little fun," Sergey objected. "Though I really wouldn't complain if right now, instead of Mirandino and this visit to the priest's wife's, we suddenly saw the huts and cottages of Weimar: tile-roofed and overgrown with ivy, their windows covered in delicate dense casements. We'd light a candle and you would sit down to play the spinet."

Lamere responded, "How is our little wing of the house any worse than Weimar? The unsteady balcony, the tilting roof, the windows covered up by piles of last year's manure. The moon looks down upon it gently. And anyway, isn't it true that you and I enjoy an ideal everyday routine here? Don't you agree?

"I can only answer as Fyodor once answered me in Peterhof: perhaps, perhaps."

"Listen, I need to warn you when it comes to Fyodor. Of course, he's very kind, responsive, friendly. And, have you noticed that raised upper lip? Even though I'm his mother, I still think it's beautiful. But you should know that he is capable of the most unexpected acts. This last winter he lost both of his coats. He'll go into a cafeteria in Moscow, take off his coat and, when leaving, forget to put it back on—he'll just be surprised that it's so cold. Right now he's all caught up in his work here. If only he really could become an ideal production worker! When he was about seventeen, he organized a debauch in our apartment when I was away. You can imagine: his comrades, some damsels—the most innocent children possible; and of course, wines and liqueurs. The little ones had decided to become grownups: they got terribly drunk and were lolling around on the floor, kissing—and not enjoying any of it in the slightest. I know him, after all. It was just an experiment. Then the superintendent sent someone to ask what was going on. We had to say that we were rehearsing for a new opera. At one point, he developed a passion for playing *préférence*. Luckily, he didn't have any money. I'm telling you all this as a friend, you know it all already anyway. I always try to keep him from plunging into the next infatuation. I hope you'll help me."

"Seems like Fyodor takes after you," Sergey responded. "He really shouldn't be an engineer."

"If only he had a voice! If only he had been able to sing Octavian. His look is just perfect. Otherwise you have to go around embracing some portly matron dressed up as a page. You squeeze close to her and feel how the silk is ready to split beneath the force of her corpus. Just look at how beautifully the moon is slipping out from under the rim of that hill. Now she's all big, fattened up by the day, but when she gets up into the heavens she'll suck in, grow smaller and brighter. Well, I'm going to go change my clothes some; you stay here with Fyodor for a while, he's done sketching now. See, here he comes . . . You know, Fyodor, the gods were unkind to you. You've got first-class looks but no voice."

"I have no desire to be a tenor or a mezzo-soprano. Don't inhibit the child's individuality, please. It's strange that my jokes fall flat in the presence of the Adored or the mining technicians, but I'm an engineer, and you're both under my orders here. Faiginyu, Seryozhka, it's so fine that you both came to visit. I was so bored. Noble lads, arise! Obolensky, a real individual. Obolensky, give us the throne speech of the Sovereign Emperor . . .[105] Hm, it's so hot out—must be in honor of your visit."

Indeed, regardless of the moon, there was no cool: heat was rising from the earth, which was slowly blurring in the light pouring down from above.

They sat down on a hillock and didn't talk at first, listening to the silence. Then Sergey said, "What era are we in now, Fyodor?"

"A great one!"

"No, Fedya, I'm not talking about that. See, this light is so dim, your oil-rig beauties have disappeared; the village has disappeared, our house and hayloft; nothing's left except these white fields and the full-flowing light above them. So isn't it true that this could be a thousand years ago or a thousand years after us? Do you actually feel that right now, it's such-and-such a year instead of some other?"

---

105 Fyodor refers obliquely to a popular literary legend involving the poet Alexander Pushkin and his circle of friends, including the Classical Greek scholar Vasily Ivanovich Obolensky.

"I don't know about the year, but I feel that you're about five years older than me."

"You know, Fedya, if we were three thousand years younger, we'd be running around in Crete. We'd take to the hills, we'd have a little javelin, we'd make our way through blackberry thickets, and our calves would be scratched to pieces."

"To hell with you and your Cretes! Really, Seryozha, it's time to quit fooling around. You say you can't see anything, but you can still hear: listen to yourself for once. Industrialization is beating inside all of us, even in you, Seryozhka. We are filling out this land exactly how we want." Fyodor stood up and pointed toward the half-darkness flooding in all around them. "Do you really think you could be what you are now if we lived in another time? Just look: your Crete and blackberries and all that nonsense are nowhere to be seen, but you and the beautiful oil rigs do exist. Maybe you don't want it that way, Seryozhka, but that's how it is."

Leaping up, Fyodor plunged into the play of the moonlight and, blurred by it, scampered about the hillock.

"Wait, Fyodor. Do you really not want to walk around naked, eat grass, moo, burp up your cud, and, with your head finally emptied, somersault around and give somebody a good slap on the back? What do you think?"

"What does it matter? I'm a student technician, a production worker. But you—do you understand what the revolution did for you? Well, forget it, Faiginyu's coming."

Lamere really had emerged from the half-mist. She was wearing a lavender silk dress and golden concert slippers.

"You're having fun here," she said. "But it's already after nine—time to go. Georgie Gusynkin already has the horses bridled. Fyodor, go get dressed. You can't go in your underwear."

"What if I want to go like this?"

"Don't be stupid. Go put on your pants. And don't forget a shirt. All your mining technicians are sure to be in their velvet caftans, edged in fur."[106]

"How you inhibit the child's individuality, Faiginyu!" Fyodor squealed as he left.

Lamere and Sergey were left alone together.

---

106 Lamere refers to clothing typical of old-world Russian merchants or even boyars, medieval Russian nobles.

"The child," Lamere repeated. "When he was little, he would always say 'grandiose' instead of 'graceful': 'Mama, look how grandiose that cat is.' The first time he said it, I even took fright: imagine what it would be like if our ordinary cat was ten times larger! A monster, a fierce tiger!"

"I love cats," noted Sergey. Beneath his heel, enormous, ten times larger than usual, he felt the legs, that is, the hind paws of the kitten; they were warm and edged with white fur. A monstrous kitten, roaring, dragged them along the ground and writhed beneath Sergey's tiny heel.

They heard a merry voice coming from the direction of the church. As if someone had yelled, "Motenka!"

So it seemed to Sergey, and he became flustered. Fyodor came out of the house all ready, even wearing a collar. A beautiful Soviet Aviation badge was pinned to his chest.

Adjusting his tie and getting into the cart, he grumbled, "I don't want to go see this priest's wife. I know what they're like—they're the first to admit that they 'mystically represent and sing the thrice-holy hymn.'[107] Plus these shoes and trousers and collar are tight and unbelievably hot. If I had my druthers, I'd have gone just as I was. Ah, wait! I almost forgot the most important thing."

Fyodor ran back to the house and came back right away, hiding something in his pocket.

"*Billet doux*?" asked Lamere.

But the cart had already rolled out onto the road, jolting over the potholes. All three of the riders fell onto each other.

"Careful, don't get pricked. I have cufflinks in my pocket," Fyodor warned.

"Keep it down!" said Grandma, appearing at the window in her nightcap and wool vest, a candle in her trembling hand.

They passed the row of little houses huddled around the church. Their windows glimmered weakly from inside, and it wasn't clear what time it was in there—perhaps the 1850s. It got dark, since the moon had set.

They'd already ridden past Queenie's tumbledown cottage. The dark monolith of the co-op appeared. Sergey thought, *Probably when they were building the co-op they immured some girl in the wall. At first, she was going along with a pitcher to get water, then they started heaping up the bricks: her legs disappeared, then her breasts, her nose, the top of her head. Her wails*

---

107 Fyodor quotes from the "Cherubic Hymn," which is sung at the Great Entrance part of the Orthodox liturgy.

echoed dully. But in the new economically built houses the contractors pile up
all kinds of trash into the walls.

Suddenly Fyodor stopped the horse and leapt down from the cart.

When he came back, Lamere asked, "What was that all about?"

"Nothing, Faiginyu, I just wanted to buy some chlorodont and tooth
powder—Sergey insists that one must clean one's teeth. But it's already
closed."

"What do you expect, at this hour? Fyodor, I can see that you feel like
pulling some tricks—be patient, we still haven't gotten to the priest's wife's."

"Faiginyu and Seryozhka," Fyodor answered. "There are great secrets
hidden here. Everything will be explained tomorrow, so you have to be
patient. Lean on me all you want now, have no fear: the cufflinks are gone."

They drove about five miles to an unknown village. Along the way
Fyodor kept stopping passersby and inquiring where the priest's wife
lived. Sergey felt cart-sick, and Lamere was frowning heavily at the whole
escapade.

"Now I understand," she whispered. "Here in Tula 'to suffer' just means
'to love.' And that's that."

Out of politeness, Sergey pronounced listlessly, "In 1810 the same
thing was said by . . ."

They fell silent, suddenly bored. Jolting along, they started dozing,
then finally came to a stop.

Arriving late and entering the spacious front room, they found a big
crowd already supping at a long table of varying heights; it had been cob-
bled together out of smaller tables of different sizes.

Fyodor whispered to Sergey, "Question: 'But how shall all the dead on
the day of the Final Judgment fit into Josaphat's valley, it being so small?'
Answer: 'In tiers, my son, in tiers.'"[108]

The newcomers were squeezed in wherever possible. The tea glasses
were obligingly filled with vodka.

"Oh-ho, they made sure to arrive in style, later than everyone else.
Must be city folk." Spontaneous greetings were voiced all around them.

A nearby woman in a pink dress immediately asked Sergey for a cigarette and, lighting up, put on the mien of a cigarette salesgirl and twittered,
"He sez to me, and I'm like about to keel over, ya know . . ."

---

108 Fyodor refers to the statement in the biblical Book of Joel in which the Lord pledges to
judge all nations in this valley.

Sergey didn't see why she was about to keel over, since the turkey served right then sent his pink neighbor into a new flood of twittering. "Now that's what I call luxury! Just try to hold me back!"

Then Sergey had the feeling that whitish eyes were looking at him through the gaps between the bottles standing on the table. He lifted his head and said, "Oh!"

Indeed, vis-à-vis sat Leocadia, and these eyes belonged to her. Evidently, according to her plan, these orbs were supposed to be *those black eyes, those burning eyes.*[109]

"To your health, Leocadia Innokentievna!" Sergey, clinking glasses, poured nearly all the vodka from his glass into hers.

Flattered, she pronounced, "What health? *I fade with every passink day, but against you not a word I'll say . . .*"[110]

"What an intriguing pallor!" Sergey confirmed.

"And my shoulders?" objected Leocadia.

"Divine shoulders! The modern fashions suit you so well."

Meanwhile, a raucous chorus was rumbling toward them from the other end of the table: *Our engine steams ahead; we're armed with sturdy rifles.*[111]

As well as could be determined through the haze of tobacco smoke, the co-op operator was leading the choir, holding a half-liter bottle: *Along the waves, along the waves, here today and there tomorrow.*[112]

He really was coming along toward their end of the table, toward Leocadia.

"Why aren't you joining in the singing?" he asked her.

"Ugh, vulgar Soviet songs."

"Right, it's just awful—waves and more waves, without a break: *Quick as the waves are the days of our lives.*[113] These students today—what can you say! But when I was studying at the Moscow Commercial Institute, I still remember: *Gaudeamus isicum juven esdum suumus.*"[114]

---

109 "Black Eyes," a famous Russian romance, first written in the mid-nineteenth century by Yevhen Hrebinka.

110 "Chrysanthemums," a romance by the Baroness Radoshchevskaya.

111 "Our Engine," a revolutionary-era song dated to Kiev, 1917.

112 "Along the Waves," originally written in the 1830s, was taken up during the First World War and then became a song of the Soviet navy; the words changed, but the chorus (here) stayed the same.

113 A student song of the 1830s written by Andrey Serebryansky, "Wine."

114 The co-op operator garbles a popular Latin commencement song, also known as *De Brevitate Vitae.* His version translates as "Let us sausage/While we and young"; the

"Listen," continued the co-op operator, turning to Sergey. "You're a student too, right?"

"I already told you I'm not."

"Yeah, go on, keep talking and I'll believe you! You're a good kid." The co-op operator winked in Leocadia's direction. "I approve and sign off on it. Citizens, come on, let's drink to the health of Fyodor's friend and to our collective accomplishments. Hurrah!"

The toast did not, however, make the desired impression: everyone was busy with their own business. Only the people sitting nearby took it as a convenient pretext to drain their glasses and fill them anew.

The co-op operator gazed with dismay at his glass and gave himself over to reminiscences. "Milk is the wine of children, wine is the milk of adults. But do you remember that little tavern in Moscow on Trubnaya Street: herring *au naturel* for an *hors d'oeuvre*, plus the 'Lost Time' waltz."

"Of course," Leocadia intervened. "City life is somethink else entirely. In Minsk, for example, I worked on the Hughes telegraph machine: Russian and French writink. That is, I had no need to work, of course, but, you know, I just felt like it, because I love art."

"Art, the art of voice!" Sergey groaned and winked at Fyodor, who was barely visible at the other end of the table. The winking meant "come here." Fyodor got up, staggering. He hadn't yet learned how to pour the vodka from his own glass into others' while toasting, and his eyes reflected the amount he'd drunk. Dunya, the other Dunya, Fenya, and Domasha, sitting nearby, grabbed hold of him.

"Hey, girls, listen: let go of Fyodor." The co-op operator's shout came just in time.

Fyodor, wiping off sweat, settled in next to Sergey, and they both started staring motionlessly at Leocadia. The co-op operator had obviously set his sights on her bared shoulders, but for the moment limited himself to stroking her arms.

"Today I shall sink," Leocadia pronounced dreamily, draining her glass of vodka.

"Beauty, goddess, empress," whispered the co-op operator, Fyodor, and Sergey.

---

actual lines are *Gaudeamus igitur/Iuvenes dum sumus* (Let us rejoice therefore/While we are young).

"Girls, give us the guitars," the co-op operator took charge, arming himself and handing two more guitars to Fyodor and Sergey. The latter two couldn't play at all, but began randomly plucking and pulling the strings, directed by the co-op operator's singing: *Ah, that was a waltz so far-off and away . . .*[115]

"*My dear, your eyes were so full of love, it gleamed in them so, so full of care and passion.*"

"One-two-three, one-two-three, one." Everyone at the table kept time with their heels.

"L-u-u-u-uv," Leocadia exclaimed, leapt up, lifted her leg, and jumped atop the table.

Their hostess, that is, the priest's wife—Sergey decided she must be the chubby blackish person down the table—evidently had nothing against this and continued peacefully eating her turkey.

"*I love you, and you'll believe it when a Gypsy girl says so. I'll love you to the death—as long as there is fire in my soul.*"[116] Leocadia stamped on the table, its boards starting to come apart. Kerosene lamps illuminated for the benefit of all present the azure stockings on her skinny legs and her bulky flat feet in homemade satin slippers. Higher up everything was lost in darkness, and only the breeze from her shaking dress confirmed the existence of a continuation.

"*Black bread for my dinner and supper—nothing can quench my passions—I need hot kisses: the Gypsy blood inside me burns!*" Leocadia stepped into the platter of turkey. The opposite end of the platter smacked against the table. Everyone jumped up. The men carried Leocadia out into the next room, and for a minute everyone could see that a piece of turkey had stuck to the sole of her foot. Out in the narrow passageway, uneasiness set in. Lamere had gone off somewhere, and Fyodor and Sergey had been ejected from the vanguard carrying Leocadia. Looking back, she had noted this. "*Let him betray me, let him leave me—I won't shed a tear, for I am young. He'll be replaced by a new suitor, too bad for him, but what do I care! Let him go off lookink for eyes that are blacker, caresses more tender, lips redder than mine! I know he'll come back to me, come back cryink . . . Oh, how I'll laugh at him when he returns!*"[117]

---

115 A romance with words by N. Listov: "I Recall the Exquisite Sound of the Waltz."
116 "When a Gypsy Girl Says So," a traditional Gypsy melody.
117 Leocadia sings a garbled version of "Let Him Betray Me" (1849), a poem by Evdokia Rostopchina.

"My, what a thrilling, low voice you have." The co-op operator was pinching Leocadia's shoulders.

"Bite my ear! Don't you know, Italian women say that he who doesn't bite, doesn't love!"

In the general muddle the unwieldy co-op operator, supported by two of his salesmen, stretched himself toward Leocadia's turquoise-burdened earlobe.

"Hey, you batty boy, careful now." Leocadia put on a modest air. "You're likely to bite the whole think off."

"O caddy, Leo-kitty-caddy, my goddess!"

The maraschino appeared, carried in baskets extracted from the co-op cellars, and the white liquid was poured into teacups.

When everyone had unanimously tossed back a cup for the health of the goddess, Sergey heard a sudden silence. It lasted just a moment—frozen wax dolls; Russian peasant shirts with embroidered patterns, sweaty locks on foreheads, trousers rolled up atop laced boots, aroused flies crawling along naked maidenly shoulders, and Fyodor with eyes somehow distracted, lying like a corpse on the sofa amid the village schoolteachers.

"Spring in Paris, a foxtrot!" Sergey commanded, unbuttoning his collar. "*The boulevards are bustling, her poor mouth like a child's, pairs wandering and laughing, all of springtime Paris bursting with people, our veins flow with fire, and anything could transpire, a basket on her narrow arm, in the flames of spring she's selling springtime violets.*"[118]

Everyone stamped their feet and fell heavily against one another. The sawdust inside them got jostled. Fyodor danced with the drooping priest's wife, who was quivering all over like jelly beneath her pink dress. Faint-hearted Dunya turned away out of modesty. Fenya and Domasha chortled into their handkerchiefs at this Parisian spectacle. The priest's wife was worrying the hem of her silk with two fingers—a chubby crooked pinky—revealing a grayish, stained underskirt.

"I'm an honest woman, but if I took the material for an officer's hat and didn't end up with two, then you could just spit right into my mug." The priest's wife fanned herself heavily, falling onto the chair next to Sergey. Fyodor was still holding her arm. "Don't you worry, my angel; I'm pretty practical, I won't make things hard on you." Then, turning her gaze to

---

118 Sergey sings a garbled version of "Spring in Paris" by K. N. Podrevsky and B. A. Prozorovsky (first published Leningrad, 1927).

Sergey, she added, "Why won't he leave us alone? So stubborn, it's disgusting. Is he a Latvian or something? You'd think one lady would be enough for him. But you, Fyodor Fyodorovich—I like you for your innocence."

Fyodor, his eyes like they were when he was working on his sketches, leaned his head onto Sergey's shoulder. They didn't say anything to each other, but if they had, it would have been:

"Well, babe?"

"Yes, Seryozhenka!"

"And you have nothing to worry about as far as music is concerned." The priest's wife continued, "Our whole family is very musical. My sister Sonya is a terribly talented conservatory student, and just imagine! When she gets up in the morning, she doesn't even brush her hair or wash her face, she's off right away."

CHAPTER EIGHTEEN

Rah-zim-zim,
Rah-zim-zim,
Zim-la-la!

PART THREE

The next day was a Sunday, and Fyodor could sleep in, although he was bisected by the shafts of light coming through the thatched walls of the barn. Yesterday's maraschino had left him pale and insensitive to the flies walking insistently across his nose.

Sergey had long since gotten up and was sitting on the balcony, driving away the bees and wasps by smoking. Lamere drove up on a rattletrap cart.

"How did you get home last night?" she inquired. "Fyodor's unresponsive corpse is still in one piece?"

"It was fantastic," answered Sergey. "I had never driven before in my life, but I boldly took the reins. They seemed sticky to me, and at first I let go of them with distaste. After that my hand smelled like something, probably wheel grease. I wanted to kiss my hand. The rest was very simple: the horse found her own way home. I looked after Fyodor instead of her. He was raving in his sleep: *reports . . . millimeters . . . whoa, my eagle, to the sky in an hour . . .* I put his head on my knees so that he wouldn't get bounced around, and we got home just fine—you can see for yourself if you go over to the hayloft."

"No need, let him sleep it off. I myself slept very poorly; I suppose this is the curse of all haylofts."

"What do you mean?"

"Well, they put us all down to sleep in the hayloft. I went to bed fairly early, a while before you two left, and I would have slept fine if it weren't for Leocadia."

"Leocadia again!"

"Yes, it's like in Fedya's anthem: *In the heat and the blaze, in the evening haze, she is everywhere.* I was suffocated by nightmares: something collapsing on me and sweating. I woke up and in the light of the early dawn, gushing in through the open doors of the hayloft, I recognized Leocadia to my right and the lady doctor, Sara Bernardovna, to my left. They were both raving rather incoherently, but Leocadia seemed to be going on about some 'scoundrel' and, well, the doctor was talking about officer's hats, of course."

"She was talking about hats too? Why are they all so obsessed with these hats, the priest's wife and the doctor too!"

"What priest's wife? She wasn't even there: she was frightened off by the party and left for the neighbors' early yesterday morning. But Sara Bernardovna really does sew officers' hats to earn extra money; everybody knows the salaries for medical personnel aren't very good, and she got trained in hats by her deceased husband a while back. I made an attempt to extricate myself out from under Leocadia and started climbing over her. I had almost succeeded in my ascent of Leocadia when she suddenly woke up in terrible agonies—the evening had taken its toll. I started waking up the doctor. She was displeased and woke up swearing: 'Damn them all to hell, won't let a person get a decent night's sleep, giving birth every goddamn night, good-for-nothing miscreants.' She took no comfort from the fact that Leocadia had an entirely different problem. We performed coercive first aid upon her. When the vomiting abated, we lay back down and began peacefully conversing, though I remained silent. Sara Bernardovna and Leocadia cursed the hayloft: according to them, the hay pricked even through the sheets. And then they inquired of each other how each had gotten married: 'Well, and then what did he do? And what did you do then?'—'So how did you answer him then?'—'And what did he do after that?' Next commenced bilateral homilies: 'If I were you, I would have told him . . .'—'If it was me, I'd . . .'—'Throw me into the river, but if I were in his shoes . . .' I fell asleep to their breathless whispering and woke up much later, not entirely believing in the reality of these nocturnal events, if it weren't for certain vivid evidence . . . Isa Makarovna, get the basin ready in the kitchen: I'm going to bathe today."

"Just a minute," said Sergey. "Do you know what the co-op operator did? When Fyodor and I were leaving, he jumped out to escort us, giggling, then started helping—that is, he tangled up the reins. Suddenly I smelled a powerful wave of maraschino and vodka: 'Congratulations, brother, and thank you,' and the co-op operator swooped in to kiss me. But since the horse had already taken off, his hot kiss fell upon my cold ear . . . But the samovar has already stopped singing. The tea will get cold; time to go wake up Fyodor."

On this pretext Sergey, who had felt a sharp pain, left the balcony. He tripped over the root of a nearby tree, staggered, but still managed to maintain his course toward the hayloft; then he suddenly veered off to the left into the bushes and was there for some time. A few raspberries, very large and overripe, had remained intact beneath the lower leaves. And this was where Sergey had the following imaginary conversation with Fyodor.

"Get up, Fedenka. It's unholy to sleep this late."

"Unholy? So it's good," grunted the sleeping Fyodor.

"Well, not unholy, but sinful—after all, it's my last day."

"Well, you'll go on to live to seventy, so sinful must be good too."

"Look out, Fyodor, I'm going to get hissy. Come on, get up already! Let's go for a walk."

"Yes, yes, a walk," Fyodor turned over and set out across unknown meadows into the distant forest beyond the horizon. A cool gust of sweet-scented wind from a shady grove of flowering trees was the pinnacle of joy after so much exhausting heat, and evoked delightful ruminations. Breathing in the piney aroma, Fyodor exclaimed, "Oh, how good it is, Seryozhka!"

All sorts of small fry was nestled beneath the tall pines—adolescent spruce and birches. Some of them were utterly oblivious to autumn; others fostered a youthful fondness for throwing off all their leaves and acquiring brand-new ensembles in the springtime, since last year's always turned out to be outmoded. The trees grew significantly taller during their period of nakedness.

"He's sleeping like the dead; seems a shame to wake him," said Sergey, returning to the balcony. The habitual phrase came out accidentally, but could no longer be taken back. "So that's where all that absurd agitation yesterday was coming from. Everyone is aggravated. I know: there's a struggle going on in the village. True, the village is four miles away, and I haven't been there. But we can feel it here, too. What I ought to do now is drink a glass of water with three spoonfuls of sugar. Leocadia says: the koolaks, the fooools. It's clear as day."

Looking through the gaps in the balcony floor, Sergey saw the earth that had once belonged to wealthy landowners. The balcony basement gaped darkly, and Fingal's shaggy paw, nesting beneath the boards, reached forward clawingly.

Fyodor will demolish the wing and this garden. At night the earth, deprived of apple trees, will grow entirely damp. In defiance of the kulaks, bell-shafts will be dug everywhere. A stunner of an oil rig will rise up in place of this landowner's outbuilding. No longer will it be possible to trip over a gnarled root and to stagger, not knowing for an instant whether you'll keep your balance by throwing one leg quickly forward, or hit the ground nose-first. If you fall into grass, you'll feel the warmish earth beneath it. Fyodor will be lying on this same earth, but forty meters down. And just as when the maraschino put him to sleep, an incorrigible fly will stubbornly walk back and forth across his pale nose. A whole swarm of flies will rush down to the narrow base of the bell-shaft and, banging against the walls, will hover above him in circles. The bellies of these flies will grow thickly furred, like the bees that Sergey saw in the hive. The shaggies will pile stick-ily together, vying against one another in their race to the fresh treat. And among them, greenish and lacquered, a manure fly will gleam.

Of course, Fyodor was coming home from work like always, with his "restless angel's" gait (as Lamere puts it), filled with another one of his insignificant ruminations (whatever angels usually muse over—cards, or the fact that he'll have to get up early again tomorrow). The fields stretched out before him were indecipherable in the darkness. Of course, they snuck up on him from behind, when he was drawing up to the fifth bell-shaft, and the foreman had, of course, forgotten to cover it with the wooden cover. Though it's also possible the cover had been carried off for firewood. Fyodor, indignant, stopped by the round opening, and Leocadia's sugary hand pushed him in. Then she jauntily shrugged her angular shoulders and, arms akimbo, took off. Or the elusive Motenka, powdered heavily with Gioconda, shoved Fyodor into the pit with an unfamiliar but characteristic gesture, before heading off to Tula to sell some tires. Meanwhile, Syssoyich was at home waiting to treat everyone to some celebratory cognac. "The kulaks bought up all the soap and gave Fyodor the rope"—that's how the song will go.

Fyodor would fly down, past the layers he had but recently measured: the red sand upper layer, the red sand sole, about a quarter meter, then still farther, past the quartzes, past the ore. Finally, his head would hit the bottom with a crunch, and his arms, twisted above him in the same move-ment with which he once answered the peasant man complaining about the damage to his crops, would be delicately smashed. The ore is red, but the red engineer is also red, lying legs-up at the bottom of the round hole.

Lying face down, Sergey would feel the viscous and unyielding taste of the earth with his teeth. In this instant, he gained a fresh understanding of the truth that one should not eat earth. But on the other hand, one should also not be a dawdler. It was time to act—perhaps Fyodor was still alive and writhing around at the base of the shaft, trying to cry out like that time in the woods.

"Hey, little typewriter! Hey, *Genosse Sergius!*"[119]

And what would he say if Lamere asks at morning tea tomorrow, "Fyodor's unresponsive corpse is still in one piece?"

Sergey would dash off to the mining boss, forgetting the dogs that had so terrified him. The window, its oil lamp glimmering, was closed, and Sergey broke the glass with his fist. "Come quick, boss, come quick! Murder!"

Shards of glass dug into his bloodied hand, sharp glass triangles jutted out from the frame of the broken window.

Movement would stir in the room. First, something with unkempt hair would dash by with a squeal, shuffling barefoot to the door. Then the mining boss, hurriedly pulling on pants, would appear at the window. "What? Where's the fire?"

"Come this way, boss, come quick!"

The boss would leap dashingly through the window and start looking around for the blaze. In the darkness Sergey would grab his bare shoulder and drag him along. By the black hole, Sergey would stick his foot into the rope loop, the boss would turn the winch. After the cool night air above ground, Sergey would be enveloped by the warmth inside the bell-shaft, despite the fact that the boss was "giving him some wind"—*the little wind is breathing barely*—as he lowered him into this deep night.

"Well?" the boss called out from above, "is he there?"

But Sergey would go on flying down, clutching the rope, hearing only the cable cutting at his foot.

Above him, through the black tunnel of the bell-shaft, Sergey saw a high moon, while below dark shapes emerged before him amid the dark.

---

119 "Genosse" is the German version of *tovarishch*/comrade, very much in use among German Communists at the time (and since).

CHAPTER TWENTY

A smidgen, a smudge, on the eleventh track . . .

Finally, Sergey convulsively kicked his foot out, wailing, "Ahhh-ahhh!"

His fingers spread wide and let go of the rope, and he fell face-down onto the soft, still warm and hairy corpse.

"What is this nonsense in my head, anyway? Evidently the maraschino really does have serious consequences."

Sergey got out a cigarette and nearly burned his fingers with the match, though he did manage to read what was written on the matchbox: *New Minsk, Damian Bedni Factory*.[120]

Oh, what a tender and sensitive soul, but such a dawdler—a lazybones, a broad, an idiot—plus all these fainting spells!

Sergey heard living human voices pleasant to his ears. Above he saw an early dawn sky, already growing pale: Cassiopeia, Ursus Major and Minor, the North Star—that's where Peterhof is. Lower down he saw a big star standing on the earth: a miner's lamp with a factory logo, a bat on the glass—*Fledermaus*—a Viennese operetta.

So at least I'm alive, thought Sergey. *How good it is.* Strauss the Father, Strauss the Son, and Strauss the Holy Ghost; that is, they're both Johanns; dance halls where you can splash your beer right into the blue Danube. The fast waltz "Du und du" resounded. He moved his hand, imitating the man who'd conducted the Philharmonic last winter. When that fascinating foreign back had pranced, the tails of its coat had been held together with a black ribbon to keep them from flying off in different directions. The audience shuffled their feet or shrugged shoulders; an elderly *frische Blutpolka*—a little chunk of Europe—leapt across the heads of the Soviet office workers, and the lady next to him whispered, 'You know, it works just as well as a mineral-water bath.'"

---

120 The matches are labeled in Belarusian, with the name of the town and factory of production. Demian (here, Damian) Bednyi was a tendentious Soviet poet very popular in the 1920s.

Sergey pronounced quite clearly, "*Du und du.*"

"Dummy, dim-dim, dolt," friendly voices yelled above him. The mining lamp illuminated homemade silk pumps, stamping in place, goatskin boots, slippers, callused bare feet. Leocadia slapped him across the nose with her scarf, the co-op operator wagged a finger at him.

"Don't shame us old students, get up. Why are you kissing this earth here—it's not like it's Leo Tolstoy's grave. But your whole hand's all bloody. Did you knock someone off or something?"

"Knocked on a window," answered Sergey. "A window, who do you think? No, I have nothing to do with any of this. Let him go on sleeping peacefully in the hayloft."

"You just took me away from my work," cursed the mining boss. "I thought there was a fire somewhere."

"Thanks be to the Lord, and you can bite your tongue," the kulak would say, and start thanking Sergey for finding the colt.

"Now you can be a witness that they aren't covering their bell-shafts and all our livestock is falling in there, to our detriment."

"You oughta make 'em compensate you, Syssoyich."

"Oh, I'll make 'em compensate for sure. No less than twenty rubles. That was a real fine colt: soft, a light chestnut. And if Fyodor Fyodorovich starts saying it was the same one Queenie ate the leg off of, well, that's a pack of lies: he broke that leg when he fell into the bell-shaft."

The kulak would reach a friendly fist out to Sergey and help him up from the ground. The alarm bell started ringing: the old bell tower would bend beneath the weight of the frantic drone. Dunya, the other Dunya, Fenya, and Domasha would take Sergey by the arms, and the whole cheerful, bouncing company would run off to where the fire was. The grain was burning, still unthreshed. People in the crowd were talking about arson for the sake of revenge, since the peasants were struggling against the kulaks. The owner of the grain stood fidgeting with a bucket of water; no one else was doing anything. The low-lying blaze cast a rosy blush on all the faces. The old ladies huddled closer to the flames, warming their cold bones for free. The boom of the alarm bell drowned out all the voices; only snippets of nearby conversations would make their way to Sergey.

The priest, Vasily Germanovich, having made his staid arrival on the scene, would be disappointed: he had thought a house was burning and that brave souls were leaping into the flames, hoping to save icons and winter clothing, and that someone would definitely get burnt up or suffocated in the process. He would receive compensation for the funeral services, and get to eat at the wake, concealing his hiccups with sighs. At the last one in Oslonovka they'd had a great time burying an old man: they drank and drank, then started dancing, and then Vasily Germanovich had picked up a bucket full of water with his teeth.

Leocadia, in a white dress tinged pink from the fire, stood next to the priest. "Father, when you have a soul as exhausted as mine, you so thirst for stronk new impressions."

"Yes, it's terrible, just terrible," the priest would answer. "It all comes from our sins."

"Was he really such a sinner? How interesting—do tell!"

"The donkey of Siloam was no guiltier than any other, and the tower fell on her and crushed her beneath itself."[121]

Leocadia would stare straight into the burning sheaves: the ones at the top of the haycock were burning freely, and in the heart of the fire, the ears were gleaming as they had only recently out in the fields under the noontime sun. The lower sheaves were turning red, and the indecisive flame attempted to lick at them. Leocadia was inspired to begin a theological dispute with the priest. "So how is this other think a sin too?"

"Depends on the circumstances: how, when and who."

"Yes, that makes sense. There's a lot of variation there. Don't you think, Father, that in ancient times I would obviously have been Nero?"

---

121 The priest demonstrates his dubious command of Scripture by conflating two different biblical legends: the donkey of Balaam, who resists her owner's desire to act on his greed (Numbers 22:27–28) and the tower of Siloam, which fell and crushed eighteen apparent innocents (Luke 13:1–5).

CHAPTER TWENTY-TWO

"What do you think about Rome, Father?"

Dunya, the other Dunya, Fenya, and Domasha gazed at Leocadia enviously.

"Well, Madam, your name really does seem Roman Catholic."

"I should think so!" Leocadia would shrug and strut off dashingly. But since she was wearing white, someone's black sleeves noticeably formed a dark cross around her waist.

"What's on your mind, Essess?" Lamere asked. "Are you already sick of Mirandino?"

"No, it's nothing," answered Sergey.

"I like it here. Or is it just because I came here from Moscow? Look: poplars, children, dust on the road, Fingal under the balcony. Why do you think he's just been lying around all day today? None of those, you know: trams, orchestras, directors."

"No sugar either; and who wants to drink tea without it?" said Fyodor, walking up.

"Ah, we've already risen! And on the wrong side of the bed, it seems?"

"Faiginyu, leave my bedside alone. Sergey, come give me a bath."

Fyodor really did look sleepy, disheveled and lackluster, rubbing at his eyes with childish fists.

Sergey poured water into Fyodor's outstretched palms, and the latter's face brightened instantly, covered in a watery lacquer.

"You're really feeling down-spirited, Fyodor?"

"For the last time, there's no such thing as spirits. Give me the towel."

Back on the balcony, moving his glass of tea aside, Fyodor turned his attention to the cheese pastries prepared by Grandma. He peeled back the top layer of dough and extracted a fly baked into the cheese filling. After three pastries his face cleared completely, like the visage of an icon of the Assumption.

"Well, Faiginyu, Seryozhka, things are coming to a head: I say to you truly that, whilst, forwith, indeed—tomorrow when we drink tea it will be with sugar."

"Don't tell me they're doling it out!" exclaimed Grandma. "All this time we've been living here and haven't seen a speck."

"Since when did you start playing prophet, Fedya? Especially considering you got up all gloomy and jaundiced."

"I'm upset, Faiginyu, and for good reason. Plus Seryozhka's leaving. The sweet tea will pass him by. Come on, stay for another day at least."

"No, Fyodor, there's no way, you know I can't stay. But if your prophecy comes true, then may the sugar sweeten for you the bitterness of parting."

"*Who are you leaving us for, o Father of ours?*"[122] Lamere sang out, getting up from the table.

Fingal's aggravated growling emanated from beneath the planks of the balcony, which were creaking beneath the dancers.

"He's displeased," said Sergey. "He's a local boy. He'd evidently be much happier with *Ay-da, troika, fluffy snow! A pair is rushing . . .*"[123]

"In trio," added Lamere.

But now the moans coming from under the balcony had changed. Fyodor couldn't wait, lay down on the ground, and crawled under the balcony.

"Scandalous, scandalous!" Fyodor's boots, still visible from the balcony, danced irrepressibly. Finally, brushing the dirt and chicken feathers from his elbows, Fyodor crawled back out, bright red in the face.

"Who would have thought. Bravo, Fingal," Fyodor whispered something in Lamere's ear. The word "six" was audible.

"Then give them some milk right away." Sergey guessed the secret.

"Ah, you foreigner! They don't know how to drink from a saucer yet. Fingal will feed them himself. But we can certainly give him some milk."

The landlady, informed of the event, noted curtly that they ought to call Motenka as soon as possible. Sergey begged her to invite somebody, anybody, just not Motenka. The landlady indicated that the procedure was not a lengthy one, of course, but that she would like to give Motenka the pleasure, since he sometimes carried out business for her in Tula. Finally, Isa Makarovna herself crawled under the balcony. Through one of the cracks in the floor they could partly observe her battle with Fingal: the landlady's heaving meaty spine, a sharp-clawed canine paw, growling and shrieks of "hush!"

---

122 The prologue from Mussorgsky's opera *Boris Godunov*.
123 A late nineteenth-century romance attributed to Mikhail Steinberg.

Finally, hauling a full sack, the landlady made her way to the bucket that Sergey had recently scooped water from for Fyodor's bath. Without taking anything out of the sack, she squashed it some, thrust it entirely into the bucket and took off for the well. Sergey recalled the words Fyodor had pronounced while bathing.

"So," he said. "Queenie's smarter than Fingal and that's why she chose the tumbledown cottage."

"Go on, Fedya, go take a walk with Sergey—he's leaving tomorrow, after all. I'll take care of poor Fingal. It's a maternal thing."

Fyodor, wearing a Russian peasant shirt, walked through the fields, which today were utterly spacious. Yesterday's golden strip had disappeared. They started smoking and singing, first operas—Lamere's influence—but the singing didn't go well.

"To hell with cigarettes!" cried Fyodor. "Let's just be quiet."

The gently sloping ravine looked spiky from the rye, which had been trimmed but not yet shaved. The grove where they'd met the girls two days ago stood quiet, not knowing what to do with itself on a Sunday.

They sat down on a bumpy hummock. Fyodor began to explain boring. "They screw a boring spoon onto the end of one of the rod links, Seryozhka, and an eye onto the other end, and they put the handle into the loop. Everything is so simple for this mining boss: a little vodka and some girls, and his Sunday flies by in a jiffy. He's the same age as you. Saucy pale blue eyes. He's probably cooling off now. What do you think, is it good to be like him? Remember the girls in the grove that time?"

"I remember them in the grove and on the village street and yesterday at the priest's wife's. The only thing I still don't understand is why, when I first got here, they told me they have tons of Stratelates?"

"Oh, that's silly—it's a song the mining guys made up. Forget about it."

Laughing out loud, Fyodor leapt down from the hummock. Wallowing about in the grass and kicking his legs up in the air, he yodeled, "*Oh, Saturday, a cloudy day, can't go work out in the fields, can't go harrowing, can't go sowing, can't go strolling in the park.*"[124]

He's doing pretty well—I have to try too, thought Sergey. He flipped backward and tried to do some loop-de-loops, but he was no match for Fyodor. However, both decided that it wasn't bad to be fifteen again.

---

124 Folk song ("On Saturday, a Cloudy Day").

Laughter came pealing out from the bushes: the other Fyodor was sitting there with his accordion and Maryanka. She began dancing—barefoot, in her raspberry-colored skirt—to the songs of both Fyodors and Sergey. Finally, worn out, she got shy and sat down a ways off from her fiancé, nibbling on a blade of grass. Sergey and Fyodor bid them farewell, kissed Maryanka's hand, and winked at the other Fyodor. The orchestra—which consisted of tongue clicks, lips pursed for a whistle (with two fingers stuck in, to lend the whistle a touch of the pirate), and the bronze clapping of palms—went along on the ploughed black earth.

A plowman along the way, working despite the Sunday, watched a while, took off his hat, and pronounced, "God help them."

But the orchestra had no time to respond to his greeting. The bronze trumpets were assiduously sucking in hot air, preparing for three deafening and conclusive chords.

"Hold up," said Fyodor. "Let's go check on the foreman while we're at it: My Innocence sometimes forgets to cover the bell-shafts, and all kinds of trash can fall in."

A little threshing floor had been stamped out in the middle of the field of grain. According to Fyodor, the miners called this brown sand "tobacco."

"It has phosphorites beneath it—hard, gleaming tumors."

"But what's under this cover? And what do you feel down there at the bottom of the bell-shaft?"

"This is 105, thirty meters deep. And here's the man himself. Well, everything all right?"

"If you weren't my boss, Fyodor Fyodorovich, I wouldn't be speaking to you right now, after what happened."

"What? So it's already happened? There they are, my tacks! They split right in half!"

"You know what I mean. It's not about the tacks. As soon as they read it, they all just lost it."

"But you know very well," Fyodor objected. "Why didn't you look at it yourself? It could have gone much worse. And see that the wife reverences her husband.[125] Don't be mad at me, My Innocence."

The foreman was still hesitating, but finally shook Fyodor's proffered hand.

---

125 Fyodor refers to the line in Ephesians 5:33.

"There was so much noise, so much squealing," he said. "I just ran away from them. But maybe you're right, Fyodor Fyodorovich, maybe it's better this way—if I'm lucky, this really might knock some sense into her. Goodbye for now. I'm off to inspect the other bell-shafts. Only, after everything that's happened, there's no way I can stay here. I'll ask to be transferred to a different district."

Fyodor watched the foreman walk off. Sergey began badgering him, wanting to know what was going on.

"This is a great mystery," answered Fyodor.[126]

"Just give me a hint. I'll guess."

"No, I really can't. Knock yourself out."

"All right, I'll do the knocking out loud. Listen: we just encountered Leocadia's husband. He's a foreman, and you're a red Soviet engineer. The village here is obviously overrun with kulaks. Thus you're dead, Fyodor."

"But the facts contradict this conclusion: I'm alive and kicking."

"Yes, you've got some pretty nice muscles, but the other Fyodor's are better. Fine then, it's something else. You secretly got married to someone, right? That's why you kept talking about the girls in the grove. You're going to kidnap Leocadia tomorrow? She'll get some sense knocked into her. That's why her husband's here. He approves, obviously."

"Close, but not quite right. Of course, that's what I'm going to do first thing tomorrow. Don't leave—you can see for yourself."

"There's no way, Fyodor—I'm due for a serious scolding as it is. But I can see it all even now. A closed carriage clatters up to Leocadia's house; you whistle thrice, as agreed. Leocadia, wearing a hooded cape, shimmies down a rope that she's fashioned out of a sheet and attached to the windowsill with tacks. When she gets down, Leocadia starts dancing, but pricks her bare sole on one of the tacks that's fallen down, and squeals. The carriage doors slam shut, the coachman's assistant whips up the horses headlong; but at the bridge, masked fooools and koolaks surround the carriage with their clubs, pitchforks, and truncheons. 'Death or your wallet!' We don't have any wallets, so it's got to be death. The carriage is overturned; Leocadia drowns in the river and becomes a green nymph entwined with algae and holding a mirror. Everyone runs to see the drowned soul, and when they see the water—rusty as tea—they wail; the girls chant: *I suffered—oh I suffered so, I*

126 Ephesians 5:32.

plopped from bridge to river below.[127] Meanwhile, Fyodor, you go sailing up out of the charabanc."

"Now this is really starting to sound true," said Fyodor. "And when we get home now, it'll turn out that the kulaks have reestablished the old regime. We'd have to read French novels with Susi, go to mass every day, and then we'll both quickly be arrested, deprived of all our rights and property, which of course we don't have, and exiled to Siberia."

"No, actually, Fyodor, you know what else it could be? The mining boss snuck into Helen's lean-to. Though, you know, I don't mind. He has such saucy pale blue eyes."

"Well, Grisha Ermolov wouldn't let him lay a hand on her. Let's hurry on home. I'm hungry. But here's Faiginyu coming to meet us. And you're total trash, by the way."

Lamere was coming toward them alone, her arms crossed behind her.

---

127 *Chastushka*, a folk rhyme.

CHAPTER TWENTY-FIVE

"Come and drink some milk. And we've received some letters, Fedya: one's from Moscow, the other's local, no stamps—Domasha brought it over."

The sides of their glasses whitened. Fyodor fished out the milk scum with a finger and flung it into Ossian's accommodating maw. The dog licked his lips in confusion: this communion seemed sweet, but so fleeting, as if it had never been.

Fyodor inspected the envelopes. One of the letters was fat, the other thin.

Maybe the answer's in the letters, thought Sergey. He pressed Fyodor to open them.

"Don't be in such a rush, Seryozhka. We should have a rest after our stroll. Go get a blanket and some pillows. I'll take Faiginyu. We can go into the orchard, under the apple trees."

They got settled on a sloping knoll. The pillow turned out to be grayer than the freshly limed apple tree trunk it was leaned against. At Sergey's insistence, the fat envelope was opened first, though Fyodor noted, "So the post from Moscow must have already arrived. I wonder what that means for your namesake. All right, Sergey, read me what they write from Moscow."

"It's probably from some maiden?"

"Well, it docs happen from time to time, what do you expect.

Hiya, Fyodor my friend! I send you ginormous greetings and wish you great success in your work. I still haven't settled into the academic soup pot after vacation, but the temperature has tripled and the pressure, I think, gone up by about a factor of five. They say it's good for you. What can I say, given our diet: H_2O plus cabbage. Well, what will be, will be! If I can't take the pressure and start to get burned by the academic soup, it won't be my fault, but that of my health. Right now I feel like a great ship must feel after a victory against the elemental whirlwinds. So, now I'll describe my trip to Moscow *from a certain station well known to you. I got in fine. I was in the train for 5 hours. As soon as I got into my train car, a string orchestra was already thundering away, warbling in a minor key. It was all our students. There were girl students from the pedagogical institute too; one of them was slicing at my eyes with her gazes, as if with a bright ray of sunlight, and I had to look away. I immediately became someone else. My face's cheerful grimace became serious. Phrases came out of me without completing themselves, and in another moment I had already been introduced to her. This was the exquisite Nina, a southern girl, after which I dubbed her "Accidental Joy." The ride was so much fun that the hours seemed but minutes. Accidental raised my spirits, and I was so enchanted that I laid out my entire repertoire to the strains of tender strings. But the enraged steel steed, paying no attention to anything, cut through the dry, burning wind; it hurried to deliver us to our destination. The gusty wind, making way for the proud trotter, sped noisily past the windows and greeted the passengers with its shriek. The springs, like wings floating in the air, strove to rock our cradle quietly and smoothly, in order to observe the harmony of life's actors. The strings crooned the "Hills of Manchuria" waltz;[128] their sobbing, like hypnosis, pulled the ardent, responsive youth under their influence. But then our trotter whinnied, seeing the vigilant eyes of an oncoming train, and for an instant this meeting distracted everyone from the stringed magnet.*

Breathing heavily, the hardy steppe dweller ran along the windows of the cars and, like a steam hammer heavily banging its iron feet, heaved its burden along in melodious covered wagons. Finally, the last one dove under, its ungreased axle gnashing. And all was quiet again, the thundering orchestra released an unwanted sound, and for the second time we were under the sway of the sobbing strings. Oh, why do these sounds exist? . . . Why do they, like mustard gas, pull us under their sway? Why must the heart be tortured? Quit sobbing already, o cursed strings! What is this meeting for? Enough rubbing salt into this wound in my breast! But the strings refused to fall silent and their weeping but intensified the feelings of the weak creature. She began singing with me yet again. Her exquisite pearls were once again fixed on me; they were aflame and burned my heart with their elixir. "Fyodor," she declared upon finishing. "Sing another one or read something out loud while the strings are still playing 'Sadness,' —it's my favorite waltz, after all!"[129]

---

128 Music by Ilya Shatrov, bandmaster for a regiment that fought in the 1904–5 Russo-Japanese War.

129 Music by Nikolai Bakaleinikov.

I couldn't refuse and began declaiming "Woman"[130] *... Why? For what purpose? To what end? ... I don't know ... My intellect is to blame; at this moment it was under the influence of emotion, which happens with me rather often. Yes, there are such minutes in life that make you agree to go on existing for hours, just in order to relive those moments again! The strings trembled, and we, weak creatures, unwittingly imitated them; and the iron steed went on dashing, slicing through the burning wind, the wheels clacking, our hearts beating and the heartbeats, like Morse code, conveying ever more emotions. Gazing at her, I kept recalling the summer, when I was lightheartedly doing my apprentice work in the magical village of Mirandino, where I also unexpectedly met ardent gazes and long waving braids. They resemble each other. Now that's a magical spot. Summer. July. Evening coming on. And the sun, retreating beyond the horizon, strives with its vivid purple rays to seek out the fleeing clouds, to embrace them passionately and caress them tearfully for the time they have left together. The forest, without gesticulation, doesn't breathe ... as if dead. Only the pairs and small groups arriving there indicate that everything is alive and wishes to go on living. It is a pretty, brave, and sturdy pine wood, witness to all its guests. And then there's the calm river Upa, with its precipitous sandbanks, along which a lavishly decorated gondola scuttles, full of cheery company. But wherefore all this cheer? ... Wherefore this boisterousness? ... To what end these strains of the accordion? ... It's a shame that this company doesn't understand that its good cheer destroys the peace of the mirror-like river and the reposing pine wood. Wherefore this crowd? ... Why are her braids lying on my breast? ... Wherefore these caresses, false words? A game of gazes? Oh, Leocadia. But it is better, my dear Fyodor, not to name names. Finally, the hillside sets are illuminated by the sorceress moon! My partner is enchanted! Her eyes are glued to the stars diving among the floating cliffs; the picture is made complete by my departure. I thought I would never see her again, but now on my way to the north I have met just the same eyes and hair, as if it were she; and she is sitting by my side just as before, and her hair hangs down on my breast. She's already shoving me in the side.*

---

130 Poem by the Symbolist poet Valery Briusov.

CHAPTER TWENTY-EIGHT

"Drink up your tea already, what are you daydreaming about? We're almost there!" She didn't even have time to finish speaking when the door opened and a bespectacled conductor bellowed: "We are now approaching the final stop; gather your belongings; you were nice enough passengers, but what can you do?" The strains of the strings seemed to take fright at the husky bass, stopped short, and sent their final sob echoing through the car. The individuals who had been under the sway of the strings did not start gathering their belongings immediately and with a certain peculiar skill strove to catch hold of this final singing echo!

Oh, Fedka my chum, you understand me without words—you know the feelings of young people yourself. Dunya wrote me a telegraph and told me you'd started pursuing the priest's wife; I wish you luck; of course, there's no arguing over taste. How lucky you are that you've stayed in Mirandino; but don't you go sniffing around my Dunya (not that Dunya, the other one), or else we'll have to settle up later.

I remain hopeful regarding your nobility your tenderly loving alumnus of the Moscow Polytechnical Institute.

Fyodor balled up the pages and tossed them away.

"See, now you too are leaving for your Peterhof, Seryozhka, and Faiginyu's off to Moscow. You had better be careful, Faiginyu: next thing you know you'll meet a little sailor, all neat and clean. Nowadays you'd never hear, 'Hey there, whiskers, where d'ya think you're going, these are decent folk here.' Everybody's clean-shaven nowadays. Only out here in the sticks people still—but the young ones are shaving, so look sharp, Faiginyu, take care."

"Look sharp yourself, Fyodor. I for one will remember these sticks fondly. Sometimes when you're singing onstage, you suddenly remember something completely inappropriate. That is, of course you're thinking, now I have to get to that 're,' and then get up to 'si,' but at the same time for some reason something else pops up like, well, like these apples hanging above us, or this shimmering air. You can't know it now, but then in the winter sometime it turns out that you committed it all to memory."

"Just like Fil d'Écosse remembers everything: the sunsets, the brook, the pine forest. Are you going to write me letters like that, Seryozhenka?"

"I'll say to you what you said to me back in Peterhof: perhaps. You know, Fyodor, writing letters doesn't necessarily mean putting them in the mail. I love waiting for the reply to an unsent letter. The letter is completely ready to go; it even has a stamp (featuring a worker with an energetic face against an industrial background). I run my tongue along the triangular fold of the envelope, tasting the glue, and remember that it's not hygienic. All kinds of illnesses commence: lupus, tongue cancer, aortic aneurysm. Finally, the letter is sealed and dropped into the box—on your desk. I wait for the reply, and the replies come in droves, every day. I am pelted with joyous, horrible, and passionate epistles. After all, I could have written my unsent letter to anyone. Finally, after about a month, sometimes a little earlier, when all the replies have been inspected and experienced, I remember my letter and send it. The reply—if there is one—is no longer of any import; I got more interesting ones. So I don't always read the letters I receive."

"So that's how it is," said Fyodor. "I'll have to bear that in mind. I sure wrote to you, out of foolishness, I suppose."

"And bear it out in practice, too," added Lamere. "But Essess, can you really do that with your business correspondence as well? Now I can see why you never made a career for yourself and just stayed a girl typist forever. Careful now—you might end up an old maid. You and I are the same age, but I have a son and you don't. But I can see from Fil d'Écosse's letter that around here the romances run thick and fast—I had no idea. For some reason we're the only ones things aren't working out for."

"Things are working out beautifully," Sergey objected fervently. "Let's do the math: I'm Fil d'Écosse's successor, there's my affair with Leocadia—that's one. Fyodor has his affair with the priest's wife Sara—two. He has an itch for all things ecclesiastical. Grandma and the church elder (note the similarity in their names)—three. The very same Fyodor and one of the thermometers—four. That was before I got here. Finally, we have your affair with the co-op operator—that makes five."

Lamere was playing with a twig. At these words, she placed it on the blanket, its sharp end toward Sergey. "I'm thinking about a sixth."

"And I'm thinking about a seventh," said Sergey.

"What seventh?"

"Well, you know—our romance, Lamere. Yesterday we took a stroll in the moonlight—by village standards that's more than enough. And then there's the Adored . . ."

Lamere picked up the twig again. "Well, Fedya, what do you say."

"I, Faiginyu, in your presence do solemnly swear that I shall most piously fulfill the request of Fil d'Écosse."

"That poor Dunya." Lamere sighed. "And she's really not bad-looking: something melancholy in the face, her black bangs. Which hair color do you champion, Sergey?

"Leocadia is so flaxen-haired, it's just luxurious. You know, Fyodor has some kind of secret going with her husband."

"Now it's not a secret anymore; have a look." Fyodor dug into his pocket. "Damn, that's not it." Fyodor finally opened up the second letter. Inside was a quarter-sheet of paper, partially torn and with little holes at the corners, evidently from tacks. A few lines were written in large block letters, while others in between them had been scrawled in with a hasty pencil: *Citizens of the village of Mirandino! You are a scoundrel and a lowlife! Today on Sunday To insult a woman so deeply! Come one and all at one o'clock. Just you wait, I won't let you get away with this! To Leocadia's to drink. There's no reason to sign—she tea with sugar who shall not be named, you viper. Admission free.*

"Fedya, do you think," said Lamere after some thought, "that you're right? After all, she really is a woman. I can imagine how devastated she is."

"Faiginyu, it makes no difference whatsoever who's devastated—a woman or not a woman—we have equal rights now."

Lamere embraced her son and rumpled his golden curls. "Oh, my grandiose Fyodor, everything you do is right."

"It wasn't just me, the other Fyodor helped out."

"So both Fyodors are birds of a feather. But both Sergeys . . . But Fedya, just look at Essess's expression."

Sergey was straining himself to the limit in order to understand, wrinkling his brow and wiping it with his handkerchief.

"Another man down, that is, a woman. But that's it for me. Enough."

"What are you thinking about, Essess?" asked Lamere.

"I'm thinking about how to say granulated sugar in German."

"Well, did you think of it?"

"Faiginyu, don't you think"—Fyodor laughed—"that there's something poetic about Sergey's face: these droplets of sweat on his brow, like Dunya? And then there's his resemblance to the co-op operator. They share more than just a name."

Fyodor started whipping both Sergey and Lamere with a branch.

"What did *I* do?" Lamere fended him off.

"Oh, you've done plenty too, Faiginyu. You're just as much of a fabricator as Sergey."

"Pardon me, my son, but I don't write poetry. Speaking of: Essess, read us some poems."

Since Sergey didn't remember anything by heart, he had to go off to the hay barn to all of his goods and chattels.

Taking advantage of Sergey's absence, Lamere turned to Fyodor. "Well, Fyodor, how are things?"

"Things? Fine, Faiginyu, thanks. Work is piddling along."

"Oh, ye great silent one of the Russian lands. While your Sergey babbles on and on without a break."

"Seryozhka? He's pretty nice, it's true, but a terrible blockhead. What do you think, Faiginyu mine?"

"You know, Fyodor, he's spent far too much time with this Iceland of his, you can tell right away."

"So what kind of dresses will you have made when you get back to Moscow? A bit longer, right?"

"All different kinds, but we're not talking about dresses right now. You should bear in mind anyway that Sergey is some kind of mix of Margaret and, oh, what's his name?"

"No, it's much simpler—he's more like her old aunt Marthe. Oh, right, I have to go do some sketches."

"I'm not letting you go anywhere, there's absolutely no need. So the two of you spent time reading together in Peterhof?"

"Well, yes. You can feel the West there. I came to him, and we started reading about that Margaret. The binding was all leather—nice yellow leather; they do publish nice books abroad. But tell me, Faiginyu, what's the main street in London called?"

"I don't remember, maybe Picadilly. So those were some fine spring days, Fyodor? Mind you, they won't be repeated. Everything passes in life."

"And what's the main street in Berlin?"

CHAPTER TWENTY-NINE

"Is that when you had jaundice, Fyodor?"

"Well, yes—and what about Paris? And anyway, what do you think, Faiginyu—is he a blockhead or not? Everyone in the village says he is."

"In part, to be sure," answered Lamere.

"Back then, when we first met, I asked around our mutual friends. They shook their heads and said it straight: 'Sergey Sergeyevich? He's a little soft in the head.'"

Mother and son were floundering, helplessly sliding down the hillock. Lamere finally shoved Fyodor away. "It's too hot. Refresh me with apples,[131] for I am spent."

"From love?" inquired Sergey, having just returned.

"From the heat, though that's practically the same thing."

Without getting up, Fyodor reached for some apples, which were all around, lying in great abundance beneath the trees.

"I'm spent too, Seryozhka."

"For the same reason?"

"No, I could care less about all that poetry. It's these flies. Hard to believe there are so many of them, even in the orchard. The wind is probably useless against them?"

Fyodor propped himself up on an elbow and began shaking the apple tree. The branches loosed their burden. Lamere and Sergey leapt to the side. Fyodor addressed them.

"Hey Newtons, discover some laws already. This isn't helping with the flies."

"In Peterhof," said Sergey, "they drive away the mosquitoes by smoking."

"Right, let's have a smoke then—we won't start any fires here. How are things back at our place, anyway?"

"Fine," answered Sergey. "My barrel's intact."

---

131 Lamere quotes from Song of Songs 2:5.

"But there's no livestock?"

"No, because we're here right now."

"I was talking about the dogs."

Sergey should have said that the vetch had been harvested, that the fields had grown more spacious and the hayloft more cramped. The light was still falling in thin stripes through the thatched willow walls, but inside things were no longer as yellow as before: the green of the vetch had been added to the straw and grain. A crumpled newspaper, dropped by a worker, lay pinned to the earth by someone's heel.

"Oh, we should go swimming! Like how they sing in the village: *How fine to stay down by the pond, only by the pond can we be found*"—Lamere fanned herself with a handkerchief.[132] "If it's this hot under the apple trees, what can it be like right now out in the fields? Yesterday when I was singing at noon beneath a dark sky, my nose got sunburned and the skin is peeling, I put cold cream on it last night before bed. I could sleep now, I'm exhausted somehow. Come on, Sergey, read us your poems already!"

Presently Lamere muttered, yawning, "Well, that's it for one of us. He's got to catch up on a whole week of sleep. Look how he collapsed. Arms akimbo. Go on, keep reading, don't stop. You have a different audience today from yesterday. Test your work on this one now."

Sergey, sitting by the sleeping Fyodor, swatted at the flies and thought. *If my poems were printed on rat-poison-infused gray paper, every poem would be accompanied by a stamp: "OSOAVIAKhIM. The fight against vermin."*[133] *My poems would be put on plates and covered in water with a little sugar sprinkled on top . . . granulated sugar . . . And this would mean death to the flies; they would all swarm in and die. Their corpses would pile up around the room. Grandma would sweep them out, and the chickens would peck at their arsenic-filled corpses and die too. They're sold for our dinners at six rubles apiece. We'll eat them, and there'll be two more corpses. Now I'll end up like that too. A fine languor, if only I could stretch out more comfortably. My legs are stuck to the sticky paper. Some of the flies have lifted their front legs and are desperately waving them around, which only gets their hind legs more bogged down. No one pays any attention to their waving.*

---

132 Lamere quotes another *chastushka*, but replaces the traditional verb "to suffer" with "to stay."

133 OSOAVIAKhIM, short for the Society for the Promotion of Defense and Aviation and Chemical Construction, was a revolutionary-war-era volunteer defense brigade that, by the late 1920s, had become a sociopolitical organization with ties to sports.

"Citizen, let's have another glass here. Citizen, I believe I'm speaking to you, but I'm getting no response."

"My dearly beloved other half is at the dacha; you sell your wares all day long, then come home to a paltry dinner: the cabbage soup is watery, and your bed isn't made."

"What can I say, Osip Prokofich—that's why you get married in church."

"I'm sorry, Osip Prokofich. I didn't recognize you. What can I get you?"

"See if you can rustle us up an omelet, and a bottle of . . ."

The big shots on their way from Moscow to Sochi and Kislovodsk gobbled down Tula gingerbreads and ham sandwiches and burned their mouths with coffee. The waiters stood behind them, mentally noting how much each of them ate. One of the waiters thought to himself, *That was a good session of the State Duma. Zamyslovsky spoke, and the café was operating. But that's all over now. Only the ham is still here.*[134]

Silver coins jangled along with a clang on the platform, and the whole vision of the express train disappeared in a cloud of steam. Then Sergey too was served a glass of hot tea. He decided to make like the big shots and ordered gingerbread as well. He had traveled through Tula before, but it had always been at night, around two a.m., and Tula had always meant streetlamps and the sleepy café-car operator, grudgingly selling stale gingerbreads. But now, around sunset, the gingerbread was fresh and filled with pinkish jam, and the posters around the train station were freshly turning pink. Meanwhile, the café car was filling up with Tulans unafraid of missing any trains. Looking from side to side, Sergey thought, *But I really am an idiot! . . . I slept through nearly the whole day. What about my observations, what about the peasants' way of life? For shame!*

Sergey leapt up. The poems that had recently fallen from his hands were scattered atop the bodies of Fyodor and Lamere.

One of the pages was sticking out of the tender mouth of a calf who'd wandered up during the collective slumber. The sun was clearly waning, and the suffocating heat had already passed.

Darting around, Sergey stepped on the sleeping Fyodor's foot and automatically apologized. But Fyodor half-opened his eyes. "It's fine, Seryozhka, no problem. I like getting up early."

---

134 Georgy Georgyevich Zamyslovsky was a conservative (monarchist, nationalist) Russian politician, who would have seen his last appearance in the Duma before October 1917.

Lamere woke up too and said, "I was wonderfully impressed by your poems. But now we should take a little stroll before dinner. We have to shake off this sleep. Let's go over there. I think you'll take me to Helen."

"Take you to Helen? I wasn't planning to, but if you want, then by all means—Fyodor and I will take you there together."

Hearing his mother say his name, Fyodor was first taken aback, then threw himself on her with kisses, singing his "Hymn of Motherhood": *Oh my little flapper-jack, my Faiginyu, my favorite! . . .*

"Enough, Fyodor." Lamere fended him off, imitating Leocadia's intonations. "'Ah, leave me, you madman, you're disgustink, disgustink!'"

Sergey took Lamere and Fyodor by the arms and led them off, making conversation along the way.

"In the Caucasus, for example, in Svanetia, people are always finding ancient coins. Look at this gold tooth of mine." Sergey lifted his upper lip. "It has a crown from the age of Vespasian. They really have great dentists in Tiflis."[135]

"Come on, Essess, enough with the golden words—just take us straight to Helen."

"I haven't strayed a foot from the straight path, but let me finish . . . A young lady I know bought three silver Roman coins for thirty kopecks at the Tiflis bazaar. When she showed them to her fiancé, he explained that with these coins you could have two good dinners in ancient Rome, while for thirty kopecks you'd be lucky to find a plate of Tiflis's worst *chakhokhbili*."[136]

"I suppose Vespasian's money is as worthless as Tsar Nicholas's nowadays," noted Fyodor.

"In Svanetia," continued Sergey, "in a mountain chapel, they discovered a gilt-covered silver icon of the crucifixion. As usual, it had the sun and the moon to either side, but do you know how they were made? The sun was a head wrought in coin, while the moon wore a high wreath."

"Enough already about the Caucasus." Lamere was incensed.

"There's never enough Caucasus, especially since we are entering it as we speak. This apple orchard is large—almost forty-five acres—and divided into parts: Burndown—there was a fire here once; Kennel—named after the dog run that used to be here; and finally, the Caucasus—the homeland of

---

135 Svanetia is a region of what is now Georgia; Tiflis is the old name for the capital city, now Tbilisi.

136 Georgian meat stew.

your Georgian ancestors, Citizens Stratelates. Look at these ruts and pot-holes and pits—this is where the best apple trees grow."

"Farewell, grandmas, farewell, girls—I'm leaving, leaving you for the ill-starred Caucasus!" Fyodor bellowed.[137]

Lamere stumbled over a branch. Sergey was leading both of them along. The gardener they met along the path served as further proof that they had indeed reached the borders of the Caucasus, since he was Circassian. He had been hired to guard the estate by the old landowner, in the hopes that not knowing Russian would protect him from the influence of the local peasants and make him a loyal watchman. Now he was elderly, but had retained his narrow nose and even narrower waist. He was sitting beneath an apple tree weaving a basket, singing something with lots of "ch," "kh" and "rrr" sounds.

"What are you singing?" asked Lamere.

"These are the words of the song," answered the Circassian: "*Why, God, do you give me bad? I want the good!*"

"The first stirrings of antireligious feeling," remarked Fyodor and was on the verge of singing the funeral march, but Sergey dragged him on.

"Don't waste time, there are far more interesting things ahead. This Circassian—his name is Servir—he's completely ordinary."

Lamere, dragged along by Sergey, still managed to ask him a question as they ran.

"Well, yes," answered Sergey. "At that time there were still swans in the Thames; before they went off to play Juliet or Rosalind, young actors would swim under the bridge and, diving down, open their eyes and see the green water and through it, the blurred Globe Theater. Afterward, getting dressed on the banks, they would repeat to each other: *Thou art all my art.*"

"English lessons—that's a good idea," exclaimed Lamere, gasping at the sight of the glade before them.

The view really was fine: a fresh meadow with the best apple trees clustered around it. Ruddy gardeners lay resting on the greensward. There were Vasya Muskoboilov, Petya Petrov, and Grisha Ermolov, the last in his felt hat. The opening of the lean-to revealed Helen's plump knees—it appeared she was really feeling the heat and wearing light attire. In short order, they heard her heavenly voice filling the clear field.

---

137 Folksong "On Saturday, a Cloudy Day."

"What magnificent technique," whispered Lamere. "What a cantilena, what high notes."

"Yes, those are very high notes," confirmed Sergey.

"Which one of us should sing?" Lamere, Fyodor, and Sergey conferred, embarrassed. "Sergey can't sing at all, and Fyodor just yells."

"It'll have to be you." They turned to Lamere.

"So be it," she agreed. "Although it's much scarier to perform in front of Helen than at a concert. It can't hurt to try, though; I'll do the Kostroma song."[138]

Lamere sat down on a stump and began.

"Something more cheerful!" An imperious order bellowed from the lean-to.

"Even more cheerful!" The lean-to exclaimed shortly thereafter.

Lamere had long since leapt up from the stump. Her elbows and shoulders moved in time with the song, her face was ablaze and the corners of her mouth twitching. Only now did Sergey fully understand what an amazing performer was hidden inside her. Glancing around, he noted that all of the gardeners really had joined hands and formed a human ring, golden at this hour. Fyodor was squat-dancing in the middle. Helen's feet, visible through the crack in the lean-to, were tapping regularly in harmony with the goings-on. Then there was nothing left for Sergey to do but clap his hands, which he began doing assiduously. The shaken apples fell from their branches.

Finally everyone got worn out. Helen invited Lamere into her lean-to. The gardeners meanwhile gathered up the fallen apples and divided them into piles by sort.

When they set out on the return journey, Lamere took Fyodor and Sergey by the arms and led them. Everyone had stocked up on apples before leaving: russets and Rome beauties and arcades. The arcades turned out to be the sweetest of all.

"So what did Helen tell you?" Sergey asked Lamere.

"A lot, but my thoughts are all scattered right now. I remember her informing me that expertly flavored eels are her sustenance. Then she praised these Arcade apples. Then she said something else that I don't feel I can repeat."

---

138 Lamere sings a folk song connected with the pre-Christian Slavic deity of spring and summertime, Kostroma. Rites associated with Kostroma often involved participants dancing a ring dance.

"No, Faiginyu, you have to say it," insisted Fyodor, "or else we'll have to resort to disciplinary methods."

"All right. Helen said that I am a very intelligent woman and an intelligent mother. That's it. Well, and in conclusion she kissed me on the forehead, right here."

Lamere pointed to her forehead, partially covered by a yellow scarf from above and encircled by blond tresses. Sergey and Fyodor detected the aroma of the recent osculation.

"Isn't Helen beautiful?" asked Fyodor.

"It was dark in the lean-to, and I couldn't really see her, but I suppose she really is very pretty."

"I told you," confirmed Sergey, and, turning to Fyodor, added, "See, Fedenka, this Caucasus you were planning to leave for isn't nearly as wretched as Peterhof."

"Yes," said Lamere. "I never liked resort areas: canvas drapes, tennis courts, bicycles . . . In that kind of environment, I don't look anything like a housewife or a mother. Fyodor was very small then. An acquaintance of ours showed up uninvited in Podsolnechnaya, where we were staying at our dacha. He didn't have our address, and he didn't know my last name, but he could give a good physical description of me. He started asking around door-to-door, and everyone told him right away: 'Oh, that young lady with the little boy, the one who doesn't look like a mother at all.' On the day this acquaintance found us, we ate the apricot torte he'd brought, which, to be honest, had gotten a little crushed along the way. But look: Georgie Gusynkin is guzzling apples again. Careful, Georgie—it's going to be the same thing all over again."

"I'm not going up there," implored Fyodor, looking up at the balcony. "God damn! Someone's visiting again. This is what I call reviewing old material."

"Oh," exclaimed Sergey. "If only we could turn everything back by three days. How wisely we would live them! No co-ops, none of this nonsense."

CHAPTER THIRTY

"I would head for the village first thing, make a study of peasant and worker life, the regional geology, et cetera."

Sergey absentmindedly took a step toward the house. Fyodor shouted admonitions after him. "Yes, Seryozhka, everything is happening very fast. Seventy years ago we still had serfdom, and before that there were various Sillurian and Devonian formations. Now Europe is losing its advantage: lickety-split. Who can say what's going to happen fifty years from now?"

"Well, let's go together, Fyodor." Sergey pointed to the balcony. "Let's start over from the beginning. Life in the country is monotonous, after all."

"No, let him that is able to receive do so, but I'm gone."[139]

Sergey trudged on alone toward the balcony.

But only the Spawn was sitting there next to Grandma. The table was criss-crossed by rows of playing cards with blackish and reddish figures. The Spawn's unbending hand trembled above the cards and moved them from one row into the next. Then the dry rattle of bones brushing the table could be heard. Grandma followed the Spawn's movements with interest and engaged her in conversation.

"How come you didn't come by yesterday, Spawn? We had cold soup for dinner."

"I was scared of your madam."

"I'm not a scary madam," said Lamere, greeting her.

"Who knows if you're scary or not? Today you're definitely not scary, but yesterday—there's no saying. And I already mostly forgot what happened yesterday anyway. I think it was summer, but maybe it wasn't. I've forgotten everything: I can't remember when they burned down our estate,

---

139 Fyodor quotes from Matthew 19:12: "For there are some eunuchs, which were so born from *their* mother's womb: and there are some eunuchs, which were made eunuchs of men: and there be eunuchs, which have made themselves eunuchs for the kingdom of heaven's sake. He that is able to receive *it*, let him receive *it*."

or when Papa died—it's either from the champagne or the starvation. Little Lida Vorontsova—see, I've forgotten her too. Hurrah, hurrah, hurrah, I get my wish: four Kings," the Spawn declared in a most indifferent tone.

"All four?" exclaimed Sergey. "Now that's what I call excessive monarchy."

Meanwhile, the Spawn was stealthily stroking the Queen of Hearts with great affection; she lay between two Jacks.

Grandma fussed. "May God grant your wish. But how will we dine today, like nobility or like us? Here, take the cards."

"I'm a noblewoman," answered the Spawn, "we were written into the Velvet Book."[140]

Grandma understood and put on a tablecloth sewn from two sheets.

"You'll have to forgive us, Spawn: we're having wheat porridge for dinner today. All sorts of rumors are flying because of these folks. They say that Fyodor's fantastically rich Muscovite so-called mother came to visit; that she sings shameless songs naked onstage and, of course, rakes in a thousand rubles a month. So naturally they wanted seven rubles for the chicken today."

A tureen with cabbage soup appeared at the same moment as the priest's wife and a little lady with a cigarette. She actually hadn't lit up yet, but her cocked elbow and the dandy-like arch of her fingers and lips meant that even without a cigarette she was a little lady with a cigarette. Sergey dragged some chairs out of Fyodor's room. The balcony was full of twittering, movement, and kisses. The priest's wife was explaining.

"She won't give birth for another two hours at least."

"We had a birth here this morning too," said Lamere.

The priest's wife inspected everyone suspiciously—Lamere, the Spawn, Grandma, Sergey—and continued. "I've dropped in quite by accident; we were just wondering where we could have dinner, and Fyodor Fyodorovich's boss always says the dinners here are pretty good. Usually I don't go six miles away for a birth, but after yesterday's party I decided to go for it. But where's the life of the party?"

"I'm right here," Sergey answered.

"I'm not talking about you, hush up. Even Leocadia's not enough for you, you awful man. But where's our Fyodor? I know, after all, I heard the whole story: makes you feel bad just looking at Leocadia; she's beside

---

140 A genealogy of Russian noble families first published in the late seventeenth century.

herself, tearing and raging, tearing up prospecting magazines and raging, raging. Oh, Fyodor Fyodorovich is such a child, he still doesn't know how to hide his feelings!"

The priest's wife tore off chunks of bread and tossed them into her soup plate. Black crumbs floated like cockroaches amid the cabbage. The little lady with the cigarette was carefully spooning up the liquid, moving the solids away with her pinky. Lamere didn't say a word. Grandma was staring into the tureen, calculating in her head whether there would be soup left for Fyodor.

"But where is he? Where is my Fyodor Fyodorovich?"

"He's at work," Lamere said drily. "And he won't be back till late in the evening."

The priest's wife stretched out a hand and started counting something on her fingers.

"Today is Sunday," she said triumphantly. "There's no work today. It's just us medical workers get worked to the death: these birthing mothers know no restraint. Yes, today is clearly Sunday: on weekdays Fyodor Fyodorovich's boss comes to have dinner with you after work, and today he's not here."

Grandma sighed. Lamere exchanged glances with Sergey.

"Well," he said, "it's true, no one has work today, but Fyodor is a fanatic, he went out to work in the fields by himself."

"What's his problem?" the priest's wife exploded. "I guess that's real passion: first he insults Leocadia because of me, then he goes off wandering the fields by himself, not eating or drinking. Romeo! He could use some bromide: one teaspoon per glass of water."

"Would you like some more porridge?" Sergey offered the little lady with the cigarette.

"I never eat anything," she answered, sucking in.

"Me neither. That is, I sometimes make exceptions. For instance, this is the menu of my daily dinner in Peterhof; as you surely know, I live in the palace there."

"Maraschino too!" The priest's wife brightened up. "So you left Peterhof for here? I would dump all of my patients in an instant if it meant I could have a dinner like that just once. My god, the roe cheeks! But who's that I see coming down the path? So gloomy! Fyodor Fyodorovich, whatever is the matter?"

The priest's wife tried to jump up, but Sergey held her back, seizing her voluminous waist.

"Shhh, don't call out, it's not him—it's his shade, you see. Ghosts are dangerous, you know."

"Well, then let's hide and see what this pleasant shade does."

It got quiet. The Spawn had dropped her spoon of wheat porridge and slept, giving out faint whistling sounds. A lump of porridge stuck to her cheek was thickly clustered with flies.

Fyodor's shade was meanwhile strolling along the path, moving in and out of patches of shade and sun and clearly believing itself invisible to the people on the balcony. Turning to face one of the apple-tree trunks, the shade remained in this position for a time. Branches hung thickly above it, weighed down with ripe fruit.

Noticing this pose, the priest's wife uttered, "Well, I don't care what you say, I can see for myself that's no shade. And there's no such thing as ghosts anyway. Hey, Fyodor Fyodorovich! Come on over, I've been waiting for you for ages."

"Careful," whispered Sergey. "You really shouldn't invite it over; you don't understand the nature of ghosts. How can it come over here anyway? These are great mysteries. Do you know what we're standing on right now? Until just recently, the space beneath us was home to six infants all covered in Fingal's slobber. Can't you feel how spooky that is?"

"Like I care! You're the shade." The priest's wife seethed at Sergey.

"Is this horsemeat?" she wondered out loud, fishing a fatty reddish chunk out of the soup.

Grandma pursed her lips. Only Sergey was glad: he was still in Tula, and now he would shower this friendly neighbor of his with tender words. But the balcony steps creaked. Lamere and Sergey hurried to seat the new arrival and to introduce him to the ladies. The priest's wife was displeased.

"This isn't Fyodor Fyodorovich, I can see: he was wearing a white shirt, and this one is dark blue; he's thinner and this guy is thicker."

"It's from manual labor, I turn the winch," said the new arrival. "Here, feel my muscles."

The priest's wife groped the guy's shoulder.

"What's your name? Are you Fyodor Fyodorovich?"

"Yes, I'm Fyodor Fyodorovich, but you can call me Fedya."

"Impossible: he doesn't look anything like you; I didn't do the foxtrot with you yesterday."

"No, that wasn't me."

"Of course it wasn't him. Don't tell us you can't see that he's a simple workingman." The little lady with the cigarette wrinkled her brow.

"Fyodor wasn't at the party yesterday," Sergey began explaining. Lamere confirmed this. The priest's wife stared at the little lady with the cigarette.

"Well, all right, maybe I've been madly blinded, but I saw the light last night: Leocadia taught me everything I need to know. And just imagine my good luck: this afternoon I was told that her star has already fallen, and it's an open playing field. I understand, Sergey Sergeyevich, you're suffering, perhaps your head is all a-muddle, but tell me anyway: you were there yesterday, you saw Fyodor?"

"Yes, from a distance, dimly, through clouds of tobacco smoke—I was sitting at the other end of the table, after all. But I don't count. There is no Fyodor. I dug him up and divided him into various layers: the geology of the Tula district."

"Pack of lies! True, I didn't see much of him either, but believe me, I could feel him, when we were dancing the foxtrot—yes, I felt him," the priest's wife drawled.

"That was just a mirage—yesterday's maraschino is entirely to blame. For instance, at one point it seemed to me that the priest's wife was there, but she wasn't, was she?"

"Right, she had left the house early that morning; but I don't understand. Of course, we could have hallucinated the priest's wife, she's connected to spiritual matters; but for me—a medical worker well accustomed to working with pure alcohol—if you think that I would lose my head so completely from a little maraschino, well, you can spit in my eye. There's something else going on here. What, he dyes his hair a different color every day? Believe me, I know that the guy yesterday was fairer than this one. And his head's a different size."

The priest's wife, bending the other Fyodor's head toward her, spread out her fingers and quickly measured the circumference of his head.

"Five spans, and I have a good eye; so that's forty-six or forty-seven centimeters, but yesterday's Fyodor needs a hat sized at least fifty-two."

The gathered company divided into two camps: the priest's wife exchanged glances with the little lady, and they both hurriedly ate the last of the baked apples; Lamere was looking after the other Fyodor in motherly fashion, putting more porridge onto his plate while making signs with her hands. The boy chewed fast and was evidently having a fine time; he tried to engage his neighbor in conversation.

"So a guy comes home from Tula, goes into his house and says: 'How come I'm here in the house and my horse is outside?' and brings the horse inside. His wife jumps back but then keeps her mouth shut, and he shakes some oats out on the table and keeps repeating, 'Eat up, auntie, eat as much as you want.' Y'know, my Maryanka makes porridge even tastier than this."

The little lady with the cigarette cringed and, finally, stopped eating. Sergey was absentmindedly spinning an apple stem and thinking about how horses pick up grain with their black soft lips; then he looked at Grandma. Even she had gotten tanner in the past three days, and her wrinkled face was quivering like a brown overripe apple on the branch.

"There are rumors that you're Fyodor's mother," blurted out the priest's wife, grinning thinly. "If that's true, then it's your turn to talk."

Lamere blushed very slightly and instead of placing the next spoonful of porridge onto the boy's plate, she took his head in her gentle, slightly trembling hands, paused for a moment, then decisively kissed him on the forehead. The boy choked on his porridge and cast his eyes down: in the course of the dinner two different women had already touched his head.

"And I once gave birth to Fyodor in agony," Lamere stage-whispered. Still holding the boy's head, she suddenly frowned and exclaimed, "Helen's one thing, but I can say it too. Yes, I am an intelligent mother. We'll see."

Wrenching wails began to carry over from the direction of the village.

"*I been suffering all night, suffered out a daughter right,*"[141] guffawed the other Fyodor.

The little lady with the cigarette leapt up and began hurrying the priest's wife. "Come on, we can't be late. I have to know what you've got at stake."

The wails were growing fainter.

"Such a lack of culture, such a lack of restraint. We are so far behind the West," the little lady continued.

"I'll say," Sergey cut in. "I read that in France, for example, the marquise asks the viscountess: '*Et vos couches*?'—'*Ah, un coup d'éventail.*'"[142]

But, having said this, Sergey felt something stir beneath his heart, something still formless, resembling a worm, a green frog, or a crushed kitten dragging its paralyzed little paws.

---

141 Folk saying (*chastushka*).
142 Sergey refers to a famous poem by Sully-Prudhomme, "The Broken Vase," which uses the conceit of a vase cracked by a blow from a fan (*un coup d'éventail*) to talk about a broken heart.

He knew that he would later have to cut the umbilical cord connecting him and this unusual infant.

The little lady with the cigarette gave him a knowing look and hissed between clenched teeth. "Vulgar. You city types came barging in, and you don't even know how to treat your guests properly; you sat me next to a worker."

Both of the guests disappeared without saying goodbye. Sergey watched them go and thought. *The baby has probably already come into view, headfirst, nimbly tearing apart his mother's womb. Blood spurts forth, and the birthing dregs come tumbling out. Finally, there's a scrunched-up little zoological corpus lying there in an untidy puddle. The scissors clank in the hands of one of the Fates, the steel cuts through the umbilical cord, the infant begins to live on its own. In twenty years it'll be a big healthy guy. He'll harvest rye in the golden afternoons and daydream in the evenings; this will result in another infant, and more rye, more afternoons, more sun. But science is moving forward: women will start giving birth under hypnosis. The mother will be convinced that she is not giving birth but rather participating in a women-activists' group meeting and helping write a proposal for a resolution. Zap! No pain at all, and the baby's already here—but not on God's green earth, that expression will already be considered a kind of legend—on the godless green earth. Class won't exist anymore, so the infant will grow up neither proletariat nor bourgeois, but just a youth; and in the sunny afternoons he will harvest rye, wiping away youthful sweat with his shirtsleeve.*

The Spawn woke up from the silence and immediately spread the cards across the table, which had already been cleared of foodstuffs.

"A wedding, a wedding, a happy ending," it said listlessly.

"Who were you reading for?"

"Nobody. Maybe for myself, how would you know, you rascal? We'll marry off whoever needs to get married. Just now I had a dream that Father Alexander was marrying me to the Queen of Hearts. All the Jacks got very depressed, because I've got one up on all of them. And I had the King standing behind me, cause I'm not just any ordinary soul off the street."

"Well, I'm against domestic life," Sergey objected. "What use are all these congratulations, weddings, relatives, pancakes? I'd do it simpler: the fiancée and two witnesses. Or maybe just one witness. In the end, you can do without the fiancée too."

"Yeah, anyway, fortunetelling is stupid," cut in the other Fyodor. "But I'll tell you what's true: I'm going to marry Maryanka tomorrow. We arranged everything already. We're going to the registry, of course, none of that wedding business."

Everyone started congratulating him, even the Spawn whispered, "Go ahead and get married, if you can't get that bee out of your bonnet."

"Let me add my congratulations," said Fyodor, coming up. "I'll baptize your children. Remember that the baptism is a great mystery, during which the one being baptized, in the course of three full immersions, loses exactly as much weight as the weight of the liquid he supplants."

Grandma made a shooing gesture and left the balcony. The Spawn began getting up from her stool. Both Fyodors and Sergey wanted to help her, but she pushed all three of them away fastidiously, spat on the floor, and plodded off after Grandma. Things on the balcony got loud and cheerful.

"So what, Seryozhka, we go back to the beginning, start reviewing old material? Time for me to tell jokes again?"

"Do tell us, tell us, I'm mad for high-society stuff." Sergey was imitating somebody, fluttering an imaginary fan.

"Once upon a time a teacher of the law had a bit to drink and said, *Hey noble lads, get up*," Fyodor began.

"Hang on, Fyodor Fyodorovich, I came to see you on business, after all," said the other Fyodor. "We're having an assembly at seven. I know it's a Sunday; we did it on purpose: to distract the boys from their usual drinking and carousing. You have to be there. Our agenda includes skipping work, taking out third loans, the local co-op, and other matters—they're going to discuss you and me both, whether we did good by them or not. Well, you'll have to take a look at it yourself. Soon as the mail from Moscow came in today, sometime after dinner, the co-op operator disappeared. Somebody saw him this morning, sitting in the Awakening teahouse, looking at some papers and drinking lemon soda: 'I gave my word,' he said, 'that I will touch nary a drop more, as a man fighting the good fight.' So, get ready, Fyodor Fyodorovich. I'll go get the horses saddled."

Fyodor started wolfing down his dinner.

"It's all over, Fyodor," said Sergey. "The sun will rise one more time, and I'll be gone. We do still have the evening and the whole night ahead of us; perhaps it will bear some fruit. I'm afraid you'll be convicted at this assembly. Why has the co-op operator disappeared? Why is Leocadia's house so silent? Why is there a baby being born, and to whom? I need to figure all of this out, since I am leaving in the morning, alas."

"You're leaving, and of course you're going to forget all about our modest little existence. Back home, before you know it, some little romance is going to pop up and that'll be it . . . And I will be so bored here without you."

"But you said yourself, Fyodor: *why dya need a ram when ya got a Sam—lotsa fun.* But I don't even have a Sam."

Sergey didn't notice that Lamere had flushed and was biting her lip.

"As for me, I am positive that Essess will long remember his adventures here. If not us, then at least the flies—it's truly rare to see them in such numbers."

"You forgot about Leocadia, Lamere. Oh, Innokentievna, to slay a poor human heart with such ferocity!"

"So immortalize her in your deathless verse."

"It's hard: I can't for the life of me find the rhymes. All I've got is 'Leocadia/the radio.' Or compounds: 'crowded jaw,' 'petit bourgeois.' But that's not poetic, and one can hardly talk about Leocadia in cursed prose!"

"Really, Seryozhenka, you should write a novel about our life here; Faiginyu and I can help."

"Well, then help me, Fedenka. First of all—alas—I failed to acquaint myself with domestic life in the village. If I had only spent five weeks here, or at least if I hadn't slept through most of the day today . . ."

"Just make it up—that's what storytellers are supposed to do."

"Then there's the very serious problem of inventing a plot."

"Oh, right. But wait, let's think about literary history. The wrath of Achilles—that's the plot of the Iliad; then Tatyana's love . . . We didn't have any wrath here, so I guess it has to be . . ."[143]

"Hush, Fedya," noted Lamere.

"Why? The mutual love of both Sergey Sergeyeviches and Leocadia is a great plot. You both came here, she was standing at the gate in her white dress, you both wanted to marry her, but she's already married and thus goes off with her husband to a monastery."

"I think it's rather uncouth to base it on real people." Lamere was indignant. "They might recognize themselves."

"Well, Seryozha can change the plot. Maybe it's Leocadia who comes here, and he and Sergey Sergeyevich are standing at the gate in white dresses, but she's already married, so both Seryozhas immediately leave for the monastery."

---

143 Tatyana (Larina) is the female protagonist in Pushkin's *Eugene Onegin.*

"Fedenka, what's with you and monasteries today?"

"Please don't inhibit the child's individuality. In ten or twenty years religion will have completely disappeared, and we won't need any more propaganda. But novels always have an epilogue: ten years later—who got married to whom, who had what kind of kids."

"You're obviously going to marry the priest's wife, Fyodor, and you'll have to dance foxtrots with her first thing every morning."

"No way, Seryozhka, no priest's wives—phew, I shouldn't even say it out loud—there won't be any left then. But in twenty years I'll have a great big belly. I'll be a terribly solid engineer; I'll come visit you in Peterhof and rent the finest room they have. Grandma will already be over a hundred. I'll show her off in circuses for money, damn her eyes; and our mama here will still be a lady in the prime of life, and we'll marry her off to . . ."

"Hang on, Fedya," Lamere cut in. "Let's be serious. There always has to be some kind of sumptuous woman in the spotlight. Helen is out of the question, of course. So let it be Leocadia, I concur. But endow her with every possible perfection: young, beautiful, attractive, a brilliant public figure, committed to building a new world. In describing her appearance, stick with the 1903 *Knowledge* almanac.[144] But make sure the protagonist has some flaws: under Leocadia's influence, he'll rid himself of them."

"All right, I'll try that out. What about the secondary characters?"

"They're always easy to find. Take any of the real-life examples: the co-op operator can tempt Leocadia with sugar, but she remains steadfast. Or she can take the sugar, but then distribute it equally among all the villagers. Domasha can be an ideal village schoolteacher and hand out handkerchiefs to all the little kids."

"And Fyodor is the ideal engineer?"

"Why not? But bring in a couple of negative types: the local priest, the local kulak. Don't forget that everything is happening in the immediate vicinity of Yasnaya Polyana. All of your characters should be reading

---

144 Lamere refers to a St. Petersburg publishing house, Knowledge (Znanie), founded just before the turn of the century and promoting an antimodernist, Marxist, and critical strain of literature. Maxim Gorky, subsequently the father of Soviet Socialist Realism, took over Znanie in 1900 and the materials published in the publisher's annual almanacs held to the socially critical and morally didactic tradition of mid-nineteenth-century Russian literature. In her advice to Sergey, Lamere parrots the general requirements of Socialist Realism, which would become official (required) Soviet aesthetic policy just about a year after this novel was published.

Tolstoy, but the negative ones should be reading his religious nonsense. The positive ones can read the literary works appended to *Little Flame*."[145]

"Can I do you and Fyodor?"

Fyodor leapt up and started prancing along the rickety boards of the balcony:

"Atta boy, Seryozhka, damn your eyes—now he wants to 'usage' us too!"

"I can see it now, Fedya—he does have a touch of the demonic. He 'sucked us dry like a lemon,' and now he's leaving." Lamere laughed.

"Don't worry," Sergey assured them. "I'll only use a couple of your features, dramatically altered; I'll only depict that which never was, I swear. For instance, I'll make Fyodor an ideal opera singer passing through Yasnaya Polyana on tour. I'll give him a magnificent tenor, he'll be a veritable *angel crying out*;[146] and I'll make you . . ."

"Just not Leocadia, she's supposed to be a positive character, right?" Lamere exclaimed.

"No, no, of course not! I'll make you . . . who? Want to be the Beautiful Helen?"

"*Merci*, that won't be necessary."

Fyodor jumped on top of Sergey and grabbed him by the forelock.

"Only mind you read your story to us first, so we can *make significant changes*. You promise?"

"Fine."

Then Fyodor stroked Sergey's hair and said, "And if you want to be as charming as always, Seryozhenka, it would be even better if you made the whole thing into a historical novel. You can leave in the mines, but make it all happen under Ivan the Terrible—after all, they were mining this area back then, too. It'll be great and no one will get offended. Want an apple?"

"The horses are ready," the other Fyodor walked up.

"What, there's only two?" Sergey was incensed. "What about me?"

"You don't even know how to ride horseback."

"No, Fyodor, I absolutely have to be at this assembly; otherwise I won't find out about anything. Also, Fyodor, so that I don't forget: what will become of Helen after I leave?"

---

145 *Little Flame* (Ogonek) is a monthly illustrated journal founded in 1899 and issued throughout the Soviet and post-Soviet period.

146 Part of a Russian Orthodox prayer to be sung in the period between Easter and the Assumption.

"No, Sergey, I can't take you with me. You'll start in with your Fenimore Cooper antics again. You're only fit for domestic use. Seriously, Seryozhka, it's not that hard to understand: this is a work meeting, and you don't work with us. As far as Helen is concerned, something will happen, but it's impossible to know what ahead of time. I'll try to get back as soon as I can. These are good steeds. Hear them snorting and chomping at the bit?"

"Fine, Fyodor. Just make sure this doesn't turn into some kind of a Kulikovo Field—that's your specialty, too."

"Don't worry, that won't happen. Bye, then."

The horses curved their firm necks; both Fyodors dug heels into their supple sides and galloped off. Sergey watched after them, trying to imagine how their journey would go.

The doors of the hayloft stood uneasily open. Inside it was dark and sweet with vetch. Sergey slouched around the yard. Finally, he sat down on the balcony steps and started scratching at the vague earth with a twig, sketching out his future story. He suddenly saw it in its shining entirety, like the golden band of light that he had walked in for an instant yesterday with Fyodor—he saw it as it could never be in reality, like how these three days spent in Mirandino had not actually been that which they could have been. And Sergey cheered up: he started reckoning what he could piece together out of it all. As tailors say, there wasn't much cloth. If he used up this piece for sleeves, where would the back panels come from? And then there are the pants. Well, here goes. Sergey pinned down the pattern with tacks and started cutting at random.

First came Fyodor's childhood and youth—spent in Petersburg corners, the back alleys around the Haymarket. Some heavy borrowing could go on here—from whom?[147] Or, better not to borrow, but to push back against him, so that what results is completely unrecognizable. Sergey knew the pleasures of reading foreign historical novels when riding the tram: when Kirillov talks about God, how nice to see the wide gray pantaloons popular in the 1870s; to imagine Ivan Karamazov in a suitcoat with ribbon-edged lapels; one of the gorgeous infernal women in a lush skirt with a frou-frou flounce and all the appropriate padding. Paralytic mamas and intelligent children borrowed from foreign children's books, Russian people—Smiths, Lamberts, Nellies, Millers, Herzenstubes, and the old-fashioned foreign Russia tailored

---

147 The answer to this disingenuous question is given in the following paragraph's multiple references to Dostoyevsky.

in London and Paris. Fyodor grows up, the revolution happens. At this point Sergey decided to throw in some astonishing scenes—fanfares and pathos. Fyodor's wonderful voice is revealed. Given his humble origins, he is sent to the conservatory utterly gratis. The conservatory would be described in exacting detail; not even the little house on the street next to it would be forgotten.

I'll have to meet some conservatory students and ask them about everything, thought Sergey. *And I'll have to find out how they teach singing, all those diaphragms and masks, messa di voce, et cetera.*

But since Fyodor's voice was truly exceptional, he was sent to Italy for further refinement. Oh, at this point all kinds of wonderful things come into play. The Italian sun, wonders of art, we can bring in some ancient Rome—all this after the Petersburg corners.

Fyodor's romance with Annunciata is staged in the Roman Coliseum. She is all fire, all ecstasy. Leocadia will be Annunciata.

There the people's singer betrays the revolution and remains abroad, going visiting with a jar of black caviar in his pocket; he eats out of it with a teaspoon while complaining about his confiscated properties. But Fyodor Stratelates faithfully serves the people's cause.

By pure chance, he finds himself performing at Yasnaya Polyana. A fiery beauty brought over from Toulouse stands by his side. This is Leocadia. Everyone admires the splendid pair. But the local kulaks, led by the priest, never rest. While Fyodor sleeps, they sneak up and slice through his vocal cords.

You might think it was all over. But no: Fyodor, muted, begins dancing. He performs a pathetic symphony. No, that won't work. It has to be something else (look up other kinds of symphonies in the music dictionary). The kulaks break his legs with clubs. Then Leocadia stabs herself on his grave, and the kulaks go to trial.

Only, what about Signora Stratelates, what do I do with her? Luckily, I still have one more night here. Don't forget to ask Fyodor about the signora during our nighttime conversations.

Sergey did some mental calculations: if this line goes this way, then that one goes the other way. Right. But then they intersect here. No, that doesn't work. This line should slant down and create a new plane. And I bend it here like this. Fyodor should really be turned into a woman. And then he can be Signora Stratelates. And Leocadia can be a man, an Italian with the last name Leocado.

Instead of Yasnaya Polyana, Signora Stratelates should sing in Italy, in Trebisonda (check the geography textbook for other Italian city names). Then it'll be easy to bring in the kulaks—they can be Fascists. The local priest can be the pope. Leocado started out as a socialist-fascist in Toulouse, but under the signora's influence changed for the better: she comes to Tula and works for free in the music technical school, teaching *bel canto* to the Tulans. Oh, damn, but my Signora Stratelates is Italian too, how do I motivate her coming to Tula? Unless I make it so they're pursued by Fate. But no, fate won't work. So then they're pursued by the police, and they . . .

"What's wrong, Essess, you're bored? This is your last night in Mirandino, after all."

"Not in the slightest. I'm busy. What about you, Lamere?"

"I'm not the slightest either. Let's go meet him."

A candle had been lit on the balcony. The stupid moths had forgotten about what happened yesterday and were flocking to the flame again. Lamere's face was obviously smiling.

The moon was shining somewhere off to the side, hesitating to rise up to the peak of the vault. One half of Lamere was flooded with violet-colored light, the other merging with the black field. Sergey gazed at the long shadows of his shifting legs. They made a dark network: the longitudinal ruts of the road criss-crossed by these shadows. The lines were sketched in by the walkers: as Lamere and Sergey approached, a grid fleetingly covered the dim fields.

"A man is always a mathematician." Lamere sighed. "Somehow I don't even feel like singing."

For some reason they were walking rather quickly, as if they weren't just strolling but on some kind of mission. They were listening intently to catch the stamping and snorting of Fyodor's horse. The moon went down silently, and the grid was replaced by darkness. Lamere suddenly darted to the side of the road: probably she thought she'd seen a horseman.

"Get down, Sergey," she said.

"Are they shooting already?"

"You're not on the front here. Put your ear to the ground. Is he coming? Well?"

"I didn't hear anything. Just got a bunch of dust in my ear and maybe a grasshopper too. What an absurd night," Sergey said, still lying on the ground. "Right now everyone in Mirandino is probably already drifting off: the newborn child, the priest's wife, the girls, the Adored, and the earth goes on turning. When it turns just enough, everyone will get up and start doing their ordinary activities. If only it would turn just a little slower; this is my last night in Mirandino, and we're wandering around like lost souls and not at all like angels. I hate all these sunrises and mornings."

"Well then, 'enough, get up, I have to tell you the whole truth.'[148] One time this very temperamental songstress was touring with us. She would sing Tatyana's lines '*Today it's my turn*' with an infernal smirk, rubbing her hands together. Everyone would start feeling terribly sorry for Eugene: any minute now, she's going to knock him off."

"Don't talk that way, Lamere. Anything is possible. Why isn't he back yet?"

Lamere and Sergey stood surrounded by darkness. They flared their nostrils, sucking in the night air, in which they could distinguish the smell of straw on the newly mown fields, manure on the road, and the dark that had fallen from the sky.

They decided to head back toward Mirandino. Lamere had long since draped herself on Sergey's arm; some hollows in the road forced them to go uphill, then down, when suddenly they heard a cry.

"Hey, off to the bazaar, are you?"

The newcomer stopped and inquired whether they too were on their way to Tula, but when he noticed that Lamere was arm in arm with Sergey, just whistled.

"Are we going the right away to get to Mirandino?"

"Yep, just keep straight, then turn right. So you're from Mirandino? Of course, I've heard all about you. Today at dinnertime there was shrieking and wailing. The girls were all pressing in. 'We've come over,' they said, 'to have tea with you. You drank up all our sugar and poached all of our fellows.' And she was yelling, 'I know who's behind all this. He's a viper, he's a stratelates.' And they just started brawling. The guys and even some of the old codgers—the more modest ones—had to drag them apart by force. Poor thing. Why'd you all have to do her like that? Maybe you're no purer than her anyway. You think if you keep a ways off from the village no one'll find out? Big-city techniques. Riding with no shocks for four miles all around!"

---

148 Lamere quotes the well-known opening lines to Tatyana's reply to the smitten Onegin at the end of Pushkin's *Eugene Onegin* (an opera arranged by Tchaikovsky, to which Lamere presently refers). Earlier in the novel, the younger Tatyana was coldly rejected by Onegin, and she refers to this rejection when she says, "Now it's my turn."

Sergey shuddered and noticed something rounded behind the man's back. Abandoning Lamere's arm, he walked up close to the cart. It smelled like hand soap and rubber.

"So you're headed to Tula, to the bazaar? Sell a few tires, huh?" Sergey whispered into the guy's ear. "Sell me a box of matches; I forgot mine at home. Know why? This morning in the valley he was lying in a leather jacket and with three bullets in his chest. You see why I'm dying for a smoke."

They haggled down to ten kopecks, since the guy claimed that, as a nonsmoker, he was particularly attached to matches.

Doesn't smoke, doesn't drink, headed to Tula, Sergey pondered. *Gotcha.*

"Hey," Sergey whispered again. "Which bell pit is he in? Tell me. It's all over anyway. What difference does it make to you?"

"Gimme a ruble, and I'll tell you."

"I don't have a ruble. That ten kopecks was the last I had."

"Ask her."

"No, no, she can't know about this. She's his mother."

"Ho-ho, guess you've had quite a night already. Well, bye—I don't want to be late."

"Bye, but tell me which bell pit. I know who you are, anyway—Motenka . . ."

CHAPTER FORTY

"What? What do you want? You want one in the kisser?"

The smell of rubber grew even stronger. The galosh held by the guy came very close to Sergey's nose. Then Sergey felt a barefooted kick, and everything dropped out of sight.

Lamere indifferently allowed herself to be led further. Fatigue meant that Sergey was practically carrying her. Finally the twilight began to fade, the hated sunrise neared, and a sign appeared on the pole the tired walkers were leaning against: *Bell Pit no. 105.*

Sergey lifted the cover, lay down at the edge of the black hole, and began tossing in lit matches. Lamere collapsed onto a pile of sand.

"Such indifference, and his own mother!" thought Sergey.

The matches allowed him an instant's view of the clay inner walls of the pit, with ridges left over from drilling. But lower down there was evidently a draft, and the matches couldn't be kept from going out. The clumps of earth thrown in made a faint squelch as they smashed against the firm bottom of the pit.

"So he's not here. But there are 105 pits. We'll have to check them all. There isn't enough night left, and it's time for me to leave anyway. Oh, cursed public service. It's all right, don't lose hope." Sergey comforted the dozing and silent Lamere.

Finally, the road appeared, lined by fir trees; church to the left, outbuilding to the right, apple orchard and the sun rising above the hayloft. Lamere went into the house. She squeezed Sergey's hand tightly in farewell. "Farewell, bon voyage. I would accompany you, but I can barely stand. Don't be cross with me because of our stroll. You think I did it on purpose, of course."

Sergey seized his head and looked around. Dawn was clearly already breaking. Lamere stood before him, rosy, exhausted, but smiling.

"Farewell," muttered Sergey. "Have a nice time staying here with the corpse of your grandiose son. Though I think it's already run away from you. I only regret that instead of the rubber guy we didn't run into Fyodor's Adored Management: he would have been pleased by such a clever manipulation of . . . objects."

Lamere patted Sergey's cheek. "Now now, my little object, that's enough bile out of you. Everything is for the best in this, the best of all possible worlds. I share your regret: who knows, maybe the Adored would have offered me a spot as foreman—then I would be in charge of all the bell pits."

In utter despair, Sergey ran into the dark barn and threw himself with all his might onto the hay.

The person sleeping there groaned and opened his eyes.

"Ow, you crushed my leg. Where did you get to, Seryozhka? Where did you lure my Faiginyu? I was already thinking you two had secretly wed, run off, and were basically on the verge of destruction. Well, if they've been destroyed, so be it. Tears won't help. But no one remembered to put the kid to bed; the hayloft remembered you."

"Get up, Fyodor, you've slept long enough." Sergey was bustling around the hayloft, "Helen has probably already woken up in her lean-to. Be glad you're alive, o red engineer; be glad you're young and will still be young in a few years' time. Look: the dawn, the morning freshness, the poplars criss-crossing the pale sky."

"I'm sick of your criss-crosses. Why are you teasing me like a monkey? I want to keep sleeping."

While they were busy shoving hay into each others' mouths and bouncing around in the piles of sheets, blankets, and Fyodor's abandoned clothes, the nearby barrel that housed their toiletries could not withstand the upheaval, and its bottom caved in. Sergey's cufflinks and Gillette razor blade disappeared forever into the hay.

"Just as I thought," Grandma declared, having come in to wake Fyodor. "You couldn't go three days without getting into a fistfight. You should be ashamed, you're older." She began admonishing Sergey. Noticing Fyodor's torn shirt, she responded very straightforwardly, in the way one ordinarily responds to five-year-old grandsons.

Kicking away from her, Fyodor sent Sergey toppling backward and jumped, naked knees atop his chest.

"Do you admit defeat?"

"Are you happy?"

"Sure I'm happy," answered Fyodor, getting dressed. "But not because you're about to leave. Why did you wake me up? It would have been better not to wake up. I would have woken up, and you would already be gone, Seryozhka—as if you had never been here at all, as if I just dreamed of you in the hayloft. Sigh! But we have to get up and shed the moisture of our eyes."

Fyodor pinched his fingers together and shook imaginary tears from his eyes.

Sergey had already climbed into the cart and covered himself with the blue flannel, just as he had done three days previously on his way to see Fyodor. There had been the same morning chill, only the arrival had cost more than the departure: the driver had skinned Sergey for fifteen rubles, assuring him that Mirandino was more than twenty-five miles away and that there were no roads leading into the village. Sergey didn't know what to do: in his detailed letters, Fyodor had forgotten to inform him of the distance between Tula and Mirandino. Sergey had arrived in Tula toward evening, and he had nowhere to stay the night.

Jolted by the cart, Sergey had felt that his feet were going to sleep from the unaccustomed Chinese pose he'd been forced to adopt. Little houses with carved window frames flickered past. *Seventeenth-century*, Sergey remarked to himself.

The town outskirts finally ended and the evening spaces opened out: telegraph poles, a black-earthed country road, free unending air.

Yes, this is definitely Russia, and Sergey felt himself to be a foreigner from Paris, London, and Peterhof. *So this is it, the Krapivensky district, the land of Leo Tolstoy. My, this really explains all of his philosophy.*

Beside the brook the cart crossed paths with a division of body-building Komsomol kids. They were singing: *And through the fields of this green earth the tired masses rise.*[149]

They had just gone swimming, and their nakedness conveyed the river's coolness.

Then silence and twilight began. The nighttime dew fell onto Sergey, and he covered himself with the blue flannel blanket. The driver looked at the stars and didn't sing anything. From time to time he poked his whip skyward, evidently aiming for the Little Dipper.

At dawn, when it had been just as fresh as it was now, Sergey surfaced from beneath his blanket. A string of peasants was driving out to work in the fields. Noticing Sergey's nose sticking out from under the blue flannel,

---

149 The Komsomol kids sing "We Are Blacksmiths," a song from the 1905 revolution written by a fighter from the barricades, Filipp Shkulev.

they greeted him, doffing their caps. Sergey would never have expected such a gesture; embarrassed by the patriarchal order, he dove back down into his den, but from time to time curiosity had him turn back the corner of the blanket and gaze out at the Tretyakov Gallery appearing before him—the rooms with the Itinerants.[150] Finally, the driver stopped.

"This is Mirandino. Who are you visiting? You're not here for the girls, I'd guess?"

"Please be so kind as to tell me where Citizen Stratelates lives!"

Sad Sergey stuck his hand out from under the blanket to press Fyodor's fingers one last time.

"Remember, Fyodor, if you ever fall on hard times, I'll sell some of my stuff, like my jacket. And let me give you a piece of advice: steer clear of the kulaks."

"Don't worry," answered Fyodor, stowing Sergey's suitcase on the cart. "Soon I'll start collecting a salary of three hundred rubles and marry Leocadia. If you actually do sell your coat out of despair, I'll buy you a new one at the Tula clothes outlet. We'll take care of the kulaks and then, Seryozhka: forget all your nonsense and join us in building, at least a little bit. Do it—do it for me. Well, good-bye, Seryozhka, and don't forget . . ."

"Oh, Fedya, I'll never forget . . ."

". . . Don't forget to send me the flypaper."

Fyodor came up right against the cart, kissed Sergey, and pulled the blanket over his head. Beneath the blanket it was rather stuffy and smelled of hay bedding. Not a sound carried through from outside. Sergey opened his eyes wide in the under-blanket darkness, but he couldn't make anything out: Mirandino no longer existed.

Sergey mussed up the hay, made himself a comfortable burrow, and sneezed—a piece of hay had gone up his nose. Evening had evidently arrived, a dark warm evening in the hayloft, where smoking was forbidden. The tobacco failed to drown out the intolerable scent of the hay, which had suddenly begun heaving, shaking, knocking, and sticking into Sergey's face.

Something moved closer and pressed down on his right eye: the coachman had shifted his seat. Through closed lids Sergey first saw orange stripes, then a white and streaming full moon.

---

150 The Itinerants (*Peredvizhniki*) were an influential late nineteenth-century group of painters known for their realist portraits of "real," often rural Russian life.

For shame, thought Sergey. *I really can't just go straight to sleep; I have to try to cast a final glance back at Mirandino.*

Sergey turned back a corner of the blanket. They were already driving through unknown fields. Not a trace remained anywhere of the fruit orchard or Fyodor's wing of the house. A pinkish morning coolness was streaming forth, and the last stars were hurriedly departing from the sky. The coachman was dozing, drooped over the reins.

Ah, I can still see the Mirandino belfry! Of course Fyodor is there now, at the top. He climbed up by the rotten staircase; all the steps are covered in pale blue pigeon droppings. Fyodor bends over to avoid hitting his head and thinks that it is long since time to abolish all churches. An enormous bell hangs above him, a rope tied to its clapper. Engraved images of saints: the robust iron cheeks of Saint George, the Archangel Michael's copper forehead. Running along the bottom, written in old Slavic characters: *This much copper and this much silver donated by the merchant Vakhrameyev.*

A children's flock of smaller bells, less deep-voiced, hung higher up.

Fyodor sneezed from the morning chill and shielded his eyes with a hand, finding the burnt-down village and making out the slow-crawling cart on the distant road, with its blue blanket beneath which the departing Sergey had just almost fallen asleep.

Sergey began waving his handkerchief, but the belfry was rapidly disappearing below the earth. Evidently it was being let down into the bell pit "with wind," and meanwhile thinking of something unrelated and insignificant: the price of chickens, the work assembly, Sergey, and pealing out with all its bells: *The vegetable earth, silt, floor of red sand, sandstone, quartz, ore, ore, ore!* Finally, the belfry fell silent, having disappeared entirely.

Proof of the earth's sphericity, thought Sergey and looked around.

All around him there really were green distances beneath a spacious sky. Slow-moving herds grazed in the empty fields. The cart bounced along evenly. There was no risk that Sergey would be thrown off at full gallop; no one was whipping him, no one was roaring into the fresh air.

He covered himself up with the flannel blanket. There really was a full moon beneath it, as round as Sergey's face.

The moon rose above the fresh-mown fields. At first pale as a white apple, after rising up to the pitch of heaven, it swelled with golden juice and hung for long night hours, like an overripe apple ready to drop on the heads of passersby. Then it would drop softly to the ground, cracking on one side and dousing everything around with its fragrant juice.

Fyodor would tire from work and fall asleep at nine p.m. Lamere would also go to bed early for hygienic reasons. There would be a party on the village streets, accompanied by the sound of a harmonica and the booming jokes of the mining foremen. Sergey would start wandering alone some ways off. He would try to remember this cheerful nighttime light coming down from above; this air, so thick that one would like to lie down on it; this earth, warm beneath bare feet.

"Pretty nice drive with such a cheerful passenger," said the coachman, pulling the blanket off Sergey. "At first I couldn't figure who was playing those songs under the blanket—almost as good as a samovar."

Sergey jumped down off the cart, stretching out his stiff legs. Right before him stood the white, freshly renovated pedestals, familiar from all the pictures, that indicated the entrance to Yasnaya Polyana. Across the road from them, to the left, the two-story Yasnaya Polyana school was just as youthfully white. Kids riding bareback barreled straight down the village street, then turned right.

Entering the estate gates, Sergey learned a great deal: there was a bus stop here; milk could be acquired in the farmyard; and the Leo Tolstoy Museum was closed on this day of the week.

An older woman wearing only a morning shirtwaist, but nevertheless of most aristocratic bearing, approached Sergey.

This must be Bibikova, flickered in Sergey's head.[151] He bowed to Bibikova with great ceremony, noting the triple ring of folds on her sagging neck.

With tremendous, extremely well-bred, and discreet simplicity Bibikova uttered, "You want to see the grave, young man?"

"I'll say! But how do I find it?"

"Just go straight, then turn left—you'll see a sign on the tree there."

In the yellow deciduous forest Sergey indeed found the sign: *To the grave.*

Skipping, Sergey made his way down the path until he was finally stopped by a little low fence surrounding the grave and a bench next to it.

At this point Sergey began to feel the full responsibility of this minute: for better or worse, he was standing before the tomb of Leo Tolstoy.

---

151 The Bibikov family owned an estate nearby Yasnaya Polyana; Leo Tolstoy was particularly fond of Alexander Bibikov, with whom he went hunting. Egunov most likely had in mind Varvara Vasilievna Bibikova (1874–1971), a niece of Tolstoy's neighbor and an employee of the Tolstoy Museum at Yasnaya Polyana.

Unless I'm a fool, an asp, and a Judas, I'm supposed to feel something very special right now. Let's say I am already feeling sorrow. But what about the lofty emotions? I certainly have them inside me. I just have to listen hard.

Sergey sat down on the bench and put a hand to his heart.

Well, what are you waiting for? Get feeling, you unbearable moron. Sergey pinched himself in punishment.

Well, yes, I can feel—first of all, these rotting autumn leaves blanketing the ground, then the soft earth beneath my heels, the hard seat of this bench, and the fact that I haven't washed today. How nice it would be to brush my teeth right now and then drink some coffee. No, Leo Tolstoy was right: the bitterest disappointment is disappointment in one's own self. Fyodor, Fyodor . . . oh, I mean Leo Nikolaevich, please inspire me. Come on, it's no skin off your back.

But all was quiet. No one responded to Sergey's despairing meditations. The bench had initials carved into it: *A. A. G. M. S.*

Ah, so I'm not alone here—people came here before, that is, tourists. Fate itself sent me here that I might pass the experience along to posterity.

Sergey leapt up and, holding his notebook and pencil, began to observe with reverence the fence and the trees leaning over the grave. He was seized by a warm feeling of communion with humanity.

After this traversal, Sergey's notebook reflected: "Bolkhin, Borya Epifanov, 1925, A. Rezunov, Varya, Besnosov, Sazykin, Silabb, Sorokina, P. and N. Tomazov, 1928. 'But let us sing.' 'No whining!' 'The gusli brings me joy, and we will build the age.' Evstopalov, Bedov, Dusya, Kolya, Batuzov, Lukavshin, Cooperative School 58 per. 6/VI 1929, Lyusya, Lyuda Golovanov, Ekaterina, Pavlik, Zhenya, Shura, Musya, Volodya . . ."

A vague memory of the old regime—probably because some of the carvers exhibited a passion for the old orthography—visited Sergey in this instant.[152] The grammar-school church. Everyone crowding in front of the iconostasis. Only the backs of the boys' heads were visible, all of them carefully cropped. The one closest to the chalice and the golden deacon would say his name, and you would suddenly find out that this black head was Vladimir, that reddish one—Nikolai.

There wasn't a single disgusting or indecent inscription, though between the lines of the sign hanging on the fence with its appeal—*Citizens,*

---

152 There were reforms to Russian orthography in the early twentieth century and following the revolution that simpled spelling and expunged several letters.

please don't carve inscriptions, don't kill the trees that Leo Nikolaevich loved so dearly—someone had penciled in a half-erased poem: *You died, our teacher so dear/So by your grave so drear/We will recall you for years . . . kneeling.*

And on the back of the sign someone had written: "Urkagan, Yaroslavtsev, and friend Feisty were here."

Sergey suddenly felt someone's eyes watching him from the bushes. So he sat back down on the bench, holding his melancholy notebook. He outlined in pencil the poem he'd just copied down, and it seemed to him that he had written it himself.

Uncertain steps approached from behind.

Sergey's pose became even more sorrowful and heartfelt.

Finally, someone shook him by the shoulder.

Both of them said at the same time, "Sergey Sergeyevich, is that you?"

Then the co-op operator added, "You're leaving too, brother? Yes, we've been tossed to the four corners of the earth, like these yellow leaves from the trees. Remember, brother: *Gold, gold, the heart of the people's falling from the sky.*[153] Ugh, slippery autumn. They showed me the door, brother—I got fired. A document came in from Moscow. Just yesterday. It's too soon to rejoice; we'll get out of the underground one day. But what an insult!"

The co-op operator swung his guitar and smashed it against the trunk of a birch. Before it split, the resonant base of the guitar had time to let sound a last mournful chord from its sturdy strings. Instead of a guitar, the co-op operator was holding a griffin's staff, with veins and wires dangling from it.

"I lay here on Leo Tolstoy's grave all night long, soaking it with tears. Perhaps the daisies will grow better now. But listen, why are you so doleful too?"

"Oh." Sergey clutched at his head. "Oh, Leocadia! How merciless to break a poor man's heart so cruelly!"

The co-op operator squinted significantly. "So what? Is it really that broken?"

"You bet."

"All right, get up, brother. Let's examine you."

---

153 The co-op operator misquotes a line from Nikolay Nekrasov's famous 1876 poem "Old Russia."

The co-op operator tried to unbutton Sergey's shirt, but Sergey was embarrassed and wouldn't let him. Then the co-op operator put an ear to Sergey's right side.

"Can't hear a thing."

"What about now?"

"I hear something, but just barely. It's kind of ticking, like a watch."

"That's the mechanism. They say we're alike. Remember the broken vase?"

"Is that what you have written there in your notebook?"

"Yes . . . But Fyodor assures me that soon all of this will be gone: property will disappear and fences along with it. Let's carve ourselves in, Sergey Sergeyevich—after all, we're both Sergeys."

"Oh, Fyodor. Well, I wouldn't give it to the boy if it weren't for getting fired. But listen, I heard a voice last night; I was lying on Leo Nikolaevich's grave, thinking about the oppressed honor of women, seeing as I'm a chivalrous type. The dew was settling unhygienically on me from above, and to the side there was a basket with provisions. It was dark, damp, the treetops were a-rustling, you know . . ."

"I know, I know. I love all that stuff too: being close to nature, like in the hayloft."

"Oh, brother, what hayloft? Leo Nikolaevich had it right: the hayloft has to be within us. And the trees rustling—that was bad: I couldn't get to sleep. And suddenly, from far off, you know, from beyond the grave, Leo himself spoke up: 'Drink, Sergey, drink!'"

Sergey tore away from the co-op operator, who had already broken one bottle against the trunk of a nearby alder.

Bibikova and two guards were hastening toward the grave, but Sergey ran headlong through the wood toward the whitewashed pedestals at the gates of Yasnaya Polyana and there, beneath him, he finally felt culture— that is, the leather seat of the bus.

September 1929–March 1930

ANDREY EGUNOV— BIBLIOGRAPHY

(In Order of Publication)

Platon [Plato]. *Zakony* [Laws]. Translated by Andrei Egunov. Petrograd: n.p., 1923.

Akhil Tatii [Achilles Tatius]. *Levkippa i Klitofont* [Leucippe and Clitophon]. Translated by ABDEM (translation group). Leningrad: Gosizdat, 1925.

Nikolev, Andrei. *Po tu storonu Tuly: Sovetskaia pastoral'* [Beyond Tula: A Soviet pastoral]. Moscow/Leningrad: Izdatel'stvo pisatelei v Leningrade, 1931.

Geliodor [Heliodorus]. *Efiopika* [Aethiopica]. Introduction, editing, and notes by Andrei Egunov. Moscow/Leningrad: Academia, 1932.

Egunov, Andrei. "Lomonosov—perevodchik Gomera" [Lomonosov as Homer's translator]. In *Literaturnoe tvorchestvo M. V. Lomonosova: Issledovaniia i materialy* [M. V. Lomonosov's literary creativity: Studies and materials], edited by P. N. Berkov, I. Z. Serman, 197–218. Moscow/Leningrad: Izdatel'stvo AN SSSR, 1962.

Egunov, Andrey. "Tragediia Evripida 'Elena'" [*Helen*—A tragedy by Euripides]. In *Drevnii mir: Sbornik statei* [Ancient world: A collection of articles], edited by N. V. Piglevskaia, 501–2. Moscow/Leningrad: Izdatel'stvo vostochnoi literatury, 1962.

Egunov, Andrei. *Gomer v russkikh perevodakh XVIII–XIX vv.* [Homer in Russian translations of the eighteenth and nineteenth centuries]. Moscow/Leningrad: Nauka, 1964.

Posthumous publications

Platon [Plato]. *Fedr* [Phaedrus]. Translated by Andrei Egunov. Edited, with an introduction, by Iurii Shichalin. Moscow: Progress, 1989.

Nikolev, Andrei. "Stikhotvoreniia" [Poems]. Edited, with an introduction, by Gleb Morev. In *Nezamechennaia zemlia* [Unnoticed land] Moscow—St. Petersburg: n.p., 1991, 84–89.

Nikolev, Andrei. *Sobranie proizvedenii* [Collected works]. Edited by Gleb Morev and Valery Somsikov. *Wiener Slawistischer Almanach*, Sonderband 35 (1993).

Platon [Plato]. *Zakony* [Laws]. Translated by Andrei Egunov. Moscow: Mysl´, 1999.

Nikolev, Andrei. *Eliseiskie radosti* [Joys of Elysium]. Edited by Gleb Morev. Moscow: OGI, 2001.

Egunov, Andrei. *"Bespredmetnaia iunost'" Andreia Egunova: Tekst i kontekst* [Andrey Egunov's "Objectless Youth": Text and context]. Edited by Massimo Maurizio. Moscow: Izdatel´stvo Kulaginoi; Intrada, 2008.

Nikolev, Andrei. "Po tu storonu Tuly: Sovetskaia pastoral´"[Beyond Tula: A Soviet pastoral]. *Russkaia proza* (2011): A.